Barbara E. Zahn

The Wainwright Inheritance

The Wainwright Inheritance

by ELIZABETH CORBETT

Appleton-Century-Crofts, Inc. • New York

To
Michael W. Corbett

The Wainwright Inheritance

1.

AGNES REACHED FOR A THIRD POPOVER, AND TRIED NOT TO glance in Miriam's direction. Her stepdaughter, who was her junior only by the years that separate thirty-three from twenty-six, was still on her second slice of dry toast. Not satisfied with committing an error, Agnes began to stammer an apology. "I thought for Sunday breakfast . . ."

"It's your house," said Miriam coolly.

It was. It had been willed to Agnes. But it was also Miriam's childhood home, which she had left only for four years at a women's college and three trips to Europe. After Mr. Wainwright's death a year and a half ago, Miriam had continued to live with her stepmother. She had lived in Antioch all her life, and did a great deal of civic and club

1

work. The present arrangement had come about naturally enough.

The two women differed in appearance as much as they did in taste and temperament. Miriam was handsome, spare, always severely tailored. Agnes was softly pretty, though she weighed thirty pounds more than was allowed her by "the tables," those inventions of the Evil One. Her candid blue eyes invited confidence; her mouth was always ready to break into a smile which would display most distracting dimples. She had come to breakfast in a frilly housecoat which did nothing to minimize her girth. Like the popovers, it was a Sunday indulgence.

She had lost her appetite for that third popover. She would have forgone it if Miriam had not repeated, "It's your house."

All at once there came sweeping over Agnes a realization which she had long been trying to ignore. She had inherited not only Jerome Wainwright's house and half his money; she had also inherited his daughter. This was more, much more, than gentle Agnes Costen had ever bargained for.

What could be done about it was more than Agnes knew. Much, much more. The immediate problem was simple enough. Agnes helped herself to the popover of contention. She not only buttered it; she added a dollop of jam.

That was mere bravado. An instant later, Agnes wished she hadn't. But she choked down the last crumb, while Miriam studiously ignored her.

This was no proper Sunday mood. On the last Sunday in August, too, when they had been in such excellent harmony earlier in the season.

On a Saturday afternoon last June, Miriam had inquired, "Are you going to church tomorrow?"

2

"I expect to."

"You were very faithful last summer, Ladybird."

"I felt that I had to be. So many Protestants seem to think the Devil takes a vacation in summer."

"But not you, Ladybird!"

Yes, she had said it. Said it twice in less than two minutes. Agnes, who had scarcely noticed it at the time, now had to force herself to ignore those two slaps with the ridiculous nickname.

When Agnes was married, the question arose of what her stepdaughter was to call her. "Mother" would not do at all; and Mr. Wainwright did not think that Miriam should address her stepmother as "Agnes."

Miriam, in search of a suitable term of address, tried "Lady Jane" and others, and eventually settled on "Ladybird." Agnes was not particularly keen about being christened out of a nursey rhyme, which ran persistently in her head.

> Ladybird, ladybird,
>   Fly away home,
> Your house is on fire
>   And your children all gone;
> All except one
>   And that's little Ann
> And she has crept under
>   The warming pan.

There was another nursery rhyme which occurred to Agnes: the one about Mary's little lamb. She forbore to mention it; to be called "Lambie" would be even worse than to be called "Ladybird." Besides, Miriam might tire of that soubriquet.

3

It was a reasonable hope. Miriam might.

But Miriam didn't. And the worst of it was that behind the absurd name lay so much genuine kindness and affection that Agnes was half-ashamed of her own resentment.

The popover was gone now, and Agnes's cup empty. "Shall I ring for more coffee?" she asked.

"Not for me, thank you." No epithet at all these past few minutes. Agnes really was in disgrace.

In silence, the ladies left the breakfast table. In solitude and at leisure, they prepared themselves for church. Miriam had the car out of the garage and in waiting by the time that Agnes emerged.

Agnes slipped in beside her and submitted to the customary scrutiny. Miriam straightened the collar of her stepmother's silk suit, pulled her hat a little more to one side, tucked back a stray curl.

"You look very nice, Ladybird," she conceded.

So all was forgiven, on her side at least. There was no chance for Agnes in her turn to police Miriam, even if she had had the nerve. Miriam was perfectly groomed, as always. Everything would now proceed according to plan.

They parked half a block from the First Methodist Church of Antioch, Long Island. (There was, to be sure, no second or third.) The ladies walked to their accustomed seats; in a Methodist church there were no rented pews, but there was a recognized seating arrangement. The numbers of the hymns were posted. Agnes looked them up at once. Miriam did so after a slight pause; she never wished to appear overeager.

Agnes Costen had been born and brought up an Episcopalian. The Wainwrights had an Episcopal background; but it had pretty well receded into the distance. Agnes, how-

4

ever, was a reasonably good churchwoman; and when, as a bride, she settled in Antioch, it distressed her that there was no Episcopal church in town.

She compromised on the Methodist. After all, John Wesley never officially left the Church of England; he simply expressed the fear that some day the Methodist Church too would become rich and respectable—as indeed it had. So Agnes did not lack precedent for her behavior.

In these puzzling surroundings, her reflexes sometimes got the better of her at first. She had that strange feeling of being at home, almost; here in what should have been home, yet where she was not quite at her ease. She would bow toward the altar—or toward where the altar should have been —at the mention of the Trinity.

Just too late, she would realize that she had done so. Her momentary embarrassment meant very little. The other worshipers were so intent on their own devotions that they never even noticed her error, if error it was.

Later, Agnes learned to control her reflex, though possibly something of the original impulse remained. Also, she became used to the social session which followed each benediction. The restrained interchange to which she had early been accustomed, "Beautiful service, wasn't it?" had scarcely prepared her for churchgoing in which handshaking was practically a part of the ritual.

Now she enjoyed the feeling that they were all friends here. Church was church. It was a wonderful place to frequent. The fact that Agnes enjoyed it was nothing to anybody's discredit.

During their married life, Agnes's husband had usually accompanied her to church. He held that religion became a woman, and was entitled to some encouragement. Miriam

5

had inherited, or imitated, her father's indulgent attitude.

Musing and reminiscing, Agnes lost her place in the hymnbook. When it was time for the first number (which as she vaguely recollected had been one of her favorite processionals), Miriam reached over and found the place for her.

Agnes loved church. Agnes was no theologian; but she instinctively assumed that people were made for the church, and the church was made for people.

Ordinarily, that is. Today she really could not keep her mind on the service—and as for the sermon—!

It wasn't the clergyman's fault in the least. Agnes wasn't blaming him. She wasn't blaming anybody, not even herself. She was tired of blaming herself.

Or of being forgiven for things she hadn't done. Or of being treated as something between a retarded child and a senescent oldster. Or of having her lost place found for her in the hymnbook. Or of not being allowed to call it "hymnbook" or "hymnal," whichever she pleased.

Agnes stirred slightly in her seat; and Miriam, without actually glancing in her direction, managed to convey the effect of a well-deserved rebuke for squirming. That was the way things went with Agnes. She was a young widow with good health, her share of good looks, and a very neat income. She had all the material for a happy life except—and what an exception!—the right to call her soul her own.

The Reverend Mr. Crawford might have uttered the most shocking heresy. If it didn't actually stampede the congregation, Mrs. Wainwright would have remained totally unaware of it. Latent dissatisfaction with her life had come to the surface and was having its way with her.

An only child, and a late child, she had been the victim

6

of oversolicitous parents. They had died within a year of each other; and Agnes was still feeling lonely rather than free when Jerome Wainwright, a recent widower and nearly twice her age, came into the picture. He married her almost without her consent.

He had been all kindness and consideration. He insisted on doing Agnes's thinking for her; but doubtless that was natural enough under the circumstances. Their married life had been a picture of contentment, although in it Agnes had never experienced the delirious happiness of which she had dreamed as a girl. She had tried not to feel too disappointed; perhaps that sort of love existed only in books. Jerome had been a darling; she still missed him. And yet . . . and yet . . .

The sermon came to an end; the congregation rose for another hymn. It was, suitably enough, "Count Your Blessings." The Widow Wainwright would do well to take it to heart.

The usual after-church banalities raised her spirits somewhat. Agnes was a sociable soul, and found a simple pleasure in agreeing that yes, it was a beautiful day, and yes, the summer had been all too short. She remembered to thank Mr. Crawford for his sermon; it hadn't been his fault that his words fell on deaf ears. Come to think of it, they must often do so. That was one of the penalties of being a parson.

Home again, the Wainwright ladies changed clothes once more and settled down for half an hour with the New York Sunday newspapers. Agnes still subscribed to the *Times* because Jerome had always done so. Secretly she considered it rather heavy going, though she was forced to agree with Miriam that it was both full and authoritative. So, if you

7

came right down to it, was the New York telephone directory.

Dinner was served promptly at one o'clock, largely for the convenience of their domestic, Rosa Lee Montgomery. Rosa Lee was a pretty brown girl in her late twenties. She had every Sunday afternoon and evening off, and all day on alternate Thursdays. "Live in" servants were like that nowadays; you were lucky if you could keep a good one.

Miriam carved the roast lamb. Rosa Lee waited on the ladies, then brought in her own plate from the kitchen. She had learned to like lamb since she came North; but she never lavished on it the same loving care with which she handled ham or chicken.

Back in the living room after dinner, the ladies returned to the *Times*. Agnes studied the theatrical news with some care. Before long now, she and Miriam would make their semiannual pilgrimage to the Big City. It was an event to which Agnes always looked forward.

She was not so enthralled, however, that she could not brook interruption. This particular interruption, in fact, was welcome, though it was by no means a novelty. Sully, whose neat little real estate business was carried on under his official name of Walter Sullivan, was a chronic bachelor who often dropped in at the Wainwrights' on a Sunday afternoon. He was exactly Agnes's age, and it was primarily Agnes in whom he was interested; but he also enjoyed baiting Miriam.

He seldom came empty-handed. Today his offering was four paper-bound "whodunits." "These range anywhere from fair-to-middling up to good," he pronounced. "Reprints are generally pretty carefully culled, I've found."

Miriam's lips twitched, but she carefully refrained from

8

comment; she knew he was trying to provoke her. But the saucy Irishman persisted, still addressing Agnes, but for Miriam's benefit. "Want me to arrange them for you in the order of merit? That way you can save the best to the last."

This was too much for Miriam, who had long regarded such donations askance. She snapped, "I don't know what you mean by 'merit.' Detective stories are nothing but trash."

Sully smiled amiably, and inquired, "Don't you know you can't indict a nation, Maid Miriam?"

"I don't see the connection," retorted Miriam.

"There isn't any." Sully's grin broadened.

"Seems to me there is," put in Agnes. "You made a broad general accusation, Miriam."

On very little evidence, she might have added. How could Miriam know that all detective stories were bad, when she made a point of never reading any?

"The *roman policier*," Sully explained, "is a recognized art form."

" 'Art'? All that about killing?"

"There is no blood shed in such works," he explained. "Nothing but red ink."

"Then you admit that such a book is by its very nature a—a phony?"

"I admit nothing of the kind. A whodunit makes no pretension to be anything except what it is: a very ingenious type of puzzle."

"It's all of that," agreed Agnes. "Thank you very much, Sully. They will make good bedtime reading."

She took the books upstairs with her, hoping that by removing the tangible evidence she might also get rid of the subject. On her return, she found that her guest had in-

9

deed decided to behave himself. He switched to the news of the day; and although he and Miriam got into arguments about that, too, the discussion was on the whole amicable.

When at seven o'clock the three of them raided the refrigerator, Miriam even allowed Sully to carve the cold lamb. She set the dining room table, while Agnes made the salad and the coffee. Accompanied by plenty of toast and followed by snow pudding (also a leftover from dinner), it made a highly satisfactory Sunday supper.

Sully left at ten, after refusing "a nightcap." Most of the bottle of whisky which he had brought with him a week ago was still standing in a kitchen cupboard; but there were times when he preferred to do his drinking downtown.

The dishes were still in the electric dishwasher; Rosa Lee would deal with them the last thing tonight or the first thing tomorrow, at her convenience. She had her own key, too. Soon after the guest left, the ladies were free to withdraw to their bedrooms.

Agnes removed her make-up, brushed her hair a hundred strokes, donned a clean silk nightgown. She was just turning down her bed when Miriam came in to say good night. Miriam affected smart severe pajamas, which she changed religiously three times a week, although the worn ones were scarcely even wrinkled.

"So ends another Sunday, Ladybird," she proclaimed.

"So it does," agreed Agnes. "And on the whole a very nice one."

"You mustn't mind Sully," protested Miriam. And Agnes was just weak enough to let it go at that.

She applied herself to the first of the whodunits with a slightly bad conscience, which she soon forgot in the interest of the book. She was almost a third of the way through it when, quite unbidden, the thought flashed across her mind, *What a break it would be for me if one of these days Miriam should decide to get married! Because nobody could possibly expect me to turn into a resident mother-in-law.*

Agnes went resolutely back to her book. The idea was a chimera. Miriam was not much the marrying type. Anyhow, who was there to marry expect perhaps Sully? And Sully was most definitely not having any.

It was far more to the point to find out who had killed Sir Herbert, a most unpopular character; he had certainly deserved what he got. Agnes ought to be ashamed even to think of such a thing as getting rid of Miriam. Miriam was *so* devoted to her stepmother.

It was the basest ingratitude to resent such devotion. Young Miriam's collection of nursery rhymes had certainly not included the one about Meddlesome Matty. And the alliteration would hold just the same if a certain other name were substituted for "Matty."

"Astringent Agnes" wasn't too bad, either. Feeling relieved rather than guilty, Mrs. Wainwright went back to the pursuit of Sir Herbert's slayer. This time she read straight through to the end.

2.

Immediately after breakfast on Monday, Agnes consulted Rosa Lee Montgomery about meals for the coming week. It was her duty as titular head of the household. It was also a recurrent pleasure.

"The roast lamb was very nice," Agnes began. "We had it cold for supper, and that means—"

"Means lamb croquettes for lunch," Rosa Lee took her up. "But not before Wednesday."

"Exactly! You tuck into the cold lamb whenever you feel like it, *if* you feel like it." Agnes's dimples showed. "Wednesday or Thursday, whichever day we don't have croquettes for luncheon, we'll have fried chicken for dinner."

"Not too much fried in one day, Miss Agnes?"

12

"Not too much. I'll be looking forward to it. There isn't any other fried chicken quite like yours. With the necks and backs and things that don't fry well, you can make some sort of luncheon dish."

"It's a pleasure to cook for you, Miss Agnes."

"Maybe I'm a little too fond of my food. I haven't Miss Wainwright's self-control."

"Miss Miriam don't really care what she eats. Maybe she knows the diff'rence, but—"

Agnes suffered a convenient attack of deafness. She often had those when she was alone with Rosa Lee. The proprieties were thus preserved, without infringing on freedom of speech.

"Take a steak out of the deepfreeze for dinner tonight," Agnes went on. "We can have fruit for dessert." The tradition of washday dinners was one thing the born Wainwrights had in common with those who married into the family.

"I'll make a cake tomorrow," Rosa Lee promised herself as well as her employer.

Details could safely be left to her. Rosa Lee had been working here since before Mr. Wainwright died. That gave her, as things went nowadays, practically the status of an old family retainer.

"This next will be the Labor Day weekend," Agnes went on. "You'll want that off, of course."

"I could use it. But if you want to have company, Miss Agnes, of course I'll stay."

Agnes shook her head. "I'm looking forward to the quiet. All the people I know here will be leaving Antioch for three days. Most of them will wish they hadn't. Are you planning to go into New York, Rosa Lee?"

13

"I might at that, Miss Agnes." Rosa Lee's smile was flashing yet enigmatic. Agnes had often wondered what excitement there was here in Antioch for a comely brown girl, and indeed what Rosa Lee's precise idea of excitement was. But she contented herself with wondering. What Mrs. Wainwright knew about Miss Montgomery's private life was only what her employee chose to tell her.

Agnes took her departure from the kitchen premises. When she reached the front of the house, she found that the mail had just come. Miriam, preparing to distribute it, discovered postals addressed in the same distinctive hand both to her and to Agnes.

"Great-aunt Adelaide!" she snorted. "I don't see why she bothers to write twice. She never has any news."

"I think it's wonderful of her to remember me," Agnes asserted stoutly. "She's really your relative."

Mrs. Hammond was, as a matter of fact, the late Jerome Wainwright's aunt. She had lived her short married and long widowed life in the upstate town of Marshfield, where she was something of a personage. Her advanced age excused her from coming down here to the Wainwrights' home in Antioch; but on the occasions when Agnes had visited her, several times with Jerome, or Jerome and Miriam, and twice with Miriam alone, she had got on famously with Aunt Adelaide. The old lady was perhaps a little on the domineering side; but Agnes had never had to take her in large doses, and really envied her her independence.

Miriam scanned her postal; when Agnes presented hers for inspection, Miriam shook her head. She conceded, however, "You always think the best of everybody, Ladybird."

Agnes reread Aunt Adelaide's report that she was well and hoped Agnes was. The Japanese plums were almost

14

ripe, and Mrs. Hammond was looking forward to them. In a way, Mrs. Hammond hated to see the summer ending; they hadn't had too much hot weather. In another month she might be needing an open fire; that too was pleasant in a different way.

This might not be earth-shaking news. To Agnes, however, it spoke of a well-ordered life and a well-balanced temperament. Or did such things look that way only from the outside?

Agnes's only other mail was a small portfolio from the large New York department store where she carried her account. Altman's certainly believed in direct advertising. It was a boon to Agnes, who could thus shop by mail. But she looked through the leaflets this time with a view to buying some fall clothes there before very long now.

Miriam had some women's-club correspondence and a letter from an old friend at her women's college. Hers was a woman's world; but she had real standing in it.

Soon enough now, her days would be full and her evenings preoccupied. That would allow Agnes a certain measure of freedom. She felt slightly guilty at looking forward to it with such pleasure. Then a certain memory came back to her; and her pleasure fled before a deepening sense of guilt.

So long as Jerome Wainwright lived, Agnes had had a good excuse for not getting mixed up in Miriam's activities. Her year of mourning provided additional shelter. But last spring Miriam had urged, had indeed insisted, that her stepmother come out of her seclusion "and at least give outside interests a trial. American widows are not expected to practice suttee."

"Suttee" seemed a strong, not to say violent, word to apply

to placid housekeeping, puttering about the yard, reading, and embroidery. But Agnes allowed herself to be escorted (if she had used a violent word herself it would have been "dragged") to a women's club meeting.

There, unexpected disaster overtook her. The secretary had barely got halfway through the minutes of the previous meeting, when Agnes yawned. Two minutes later she yawned again. As the meeting proceeded, her yawns became more frequent. She struggled through somehow to the end. But she felt deeply apologetic toward Miriam's natural mortification.

Agnes herself asked for one more trial; she assured her stepdaughter that it would not happen again.

She got the trial. The yawns were, if anything, more overwhelming. Both the ladies refrained from comment that evening; and when Agnes felt in duty bound to bring up the subject next day, Miriam's reception of it was curt.

There the matter had rested. How long it would continue to rest there no one could predict on this particular Monday morning.

It wasn't that Agnes disliked people. If she had met some of these very same women when they were not clubbing, she would have got along with them fine. When she was marketing, for instance (she did her own marketing a great deal of the time, partly on principle, partly because she liked the job), she discussed the comparative merits of various vegetables with strangers. She cooed into baby carriages and complimented the women who propelled them. Some of these might well be the same women who, taken en masse, had stricken her into somnambulism.

Was it the mold rather than its contents that bothered Agnes? Perhaps with different molds her success would have

16

been greater. She had never been given a voice in their selection.

"Your club season starts right after Labor Day, doesn't it?" she inquired politely. As if she didn't know!

"Officially it does. The preliminary work is already under way. The Women's City Club has its fall luncheon a week from Thursday."

"Oh, yes!" agreed Agnes. She remembered reading over the cards which Miriam brought home from similar luncheons: the very dull menu, and a program built around a speech by some visiting celebrity of whom Agnes had never even heard.

"So much depends on getting the club year off to a good start. We have an inexperienced program committee this year. I would offer to help them out; but they might think I was interfering." Miriam looked faintly worried.

"They do say a new broom sweeps clean," Agnes consoled her. "But brooms are out-of-date now, aren't they, except as part of the witches' make-up on Hallowe'en?"

"You have an amusing way of putting things, Ladybird."

"But you don't care much for comedy?" flashed Agnes.

She regretted the words as soon as they were out. But she was spared the necessity either for taking them back or for explaining them, which was worse. The telephone rang just then; Miriam answered it, as Miriam usually did.

Sure enough, the call was for her. She listened more than she talked. She seemed startled, pleased, faintly embarrassed. This was a quarter-hour of surprises: Miriam worried, then embarrassed.

She wound up by saying, "I'm very much flattered. I still think you might have made a wiser choice; but I'll do my best not to let you down."

17

She hung up and turned to face Agnes. "That was the chairman of the Program Committee. She says they have talked the matter over at length, and decided that instead of getting in somebody from outside, they would like me to make the principal speech at the luncheon."

"My dear, that is very flattering!"

"It is and it isn't. They would have to pay an outsider, and they know they can get me for free."

All the same, Miriam was pleased. This was recognition right in a prophet's own country, even if it was also a good bargain for the members of the Women's City Club of Antioch, Long Island.

"You've been president, and before that vice president," Agnes enumerated. "You must know more about the club than almost anybody else does."

"There are many members older than I."

"But you've been to college, and you've been to Europe. And—and you always have so many ideas about everything."

"It isn't that so much. But I do try to think things through."

Agnes felt a sudden surge of sympathy for Miriam. That was her whole trouble, poor darling. She tried to think things through on the other fellow's behalf as well as her own; and the other fellow wasn't always any too grateful.

"There's your subject ready to your hand," said Agnes warmly. "Tell your fellow members what clubs are for. Not just their own particular club: women's clubs in general."

"But that's a huge subject, Ladybird! With only a little over a week to prepare my speech, how can I hope to cover so much ground?"

"You can try," said Agnes stoutly.

18

Miriam still shook her head. Her expression indicated that the Ladybirds of this world did not understand what the serious thinkers were up against.

All the same, late that afternoon she telephoned the Program Committee, in ample time for them to get it into the printed program, that her subject would be "Why We Are Here."

"That's much better than to make it a question, don't you think?" she said to Agnes—after the event, of course.

But Agnes agreed heartily. To phrase it "Why Are We Here?" would have been to lay the speaker open to the cynic's easy retort, "Why indeed?"

Miriam planned to work straight through the long weekend. She had little enough time, as it was, to prepare a speech only slightly less ambitious in its object than *Paradise Lost*. She aimed to justify, not the ways of God to man, but the ways of clubwomen toward other women—which might amount to pretty much the same in the long run, if that was the way you looked at things.

She was at Ladybird hot and heavy. But after the first day or two, Agnes realized that she was being used less as an audience than as a sounding board. She ceased to take much trouble with her answers; Miriam wasn't listening anyhow. If she was in love with the sound of her own voice—well, she was by no means the first person to be enchanted by those celestial strains.

Two other people in the vicinity, however, were making careful plans for the Labor Day weekend. Rosa Lee Montgomery baked a ham for Thursday dinner; there would be enough left over for six or seven lunches or cold suppers. She made sure that every household possession was in its exact place. She cleaned a house which was already spotless.

19

"Do you want me to leave a phone number where you can find me, Miss Agnes?" she inquired at the instant of her departure.

"I don't think it will be necessary. But if you'd like to call me, say around noon on Sunday—"

"About one o'clock? I sure will do that, Miss Agnes."

That very Friday afternoon, Walter Sullivan came in. "I'm a little early this week," he explained. "But this may be your last chance to gaze on poor old Sully in one of his comparatively sane moments."

Miriam gave him a glance which said plainly, *only comparatively sane.* Then she returned to a really interesting pursuit, thereby allowing the groundlings to amuse themselves in any frivolous way that suited them.

Left alone with Sully, Agnes inquired, "What does this mean, if anything?"

"A nice woman like you wouldn't know. A woman who pays her bills, and means what she says, and says only about half what she means—a woman like you really wouldn't know, gentle Agnes."

"I may be as gentle as all that. But I am not yet quite simple-minded."

"You certainly are not that. You're just too good to be true. You will understand why next Monday is called 'Labor Day.' The day when most people do not labor, and poor old Sully does."

"I am listening." Agnes looked stern. Or at least she tried to. It was a part in life for which she was poorly equipped. Not only was she cursed with a nice nature; the dimples kept breaking through.

"I have to stay here and show off houses. 'For Sale' or 'For

Rent.' I don't know which type of real estate is harder to handle."

"Tip me off when to cry. Meanwhile, would you mind getting along with your story?"

"Cruel charmer! You inherited this house. So far you haven't been driven to put it on the market."

"So far I haven't," Agnes agreed. "What are you talking about, if anything?"

"All this coming weekend, I am supposed to go around and show off real estate. Tell people what lovely homes these places would make for them. That's my job. An old bachelor like me!"

"What sort of old bachelor are you, Sully?"

"An accidental bachelor. Let's not go into that now. Here I am, with all these houses-for-sale on my hands, and all these supposititious customers."

"And a living to earn! Yes, Sully? Sully, you are tempted on both sides, aren't you?"

"Worse than tempted! Aroused, and at the same time bewildered. If the would-be sellers love their 'homes' (which I would naturally prefer to call 'houses'), why do they even consider putting them on the market?"

"But the would-be buyers?"

"They are worse, much worse. Most of them haven't the slightest idea of buying. They are out for a great, and a very cheap, pleasure; they want to find fault. They say to me things like, 'I wouldn't dream of living in a place with such old-fashioned electrical fixtures. If you have something a little better on your list, Mr. er . . . er . . . er . . .' "

"Go on, please. Don't you handle renters?"

"They are, on the whole, worse. The palaver runs something like this, 'If you will put in an air conditioner and a deepfreeze, we might consider renting it!' "

"It may be as bad as you say it is. But surely, Walter, you could earn your living in some easier way, such as digging ditches?"

Sully groaned, and then covered his lips with his hands and rolled his eyes, as if deprecating his next remark. But he went on clearly enough, "Somewhere there may be people who are looking for a good home, and can actually appreciate one. Enough for the moment, darling Agnes! Would you mind too much if I came over here Sunday afternoon?"

"Not much too much." For an instant, Agnes's dimples were really doing their best for her. "I'll expect you on Sunday then. You may have something more to tell me."

"Or something less. Thank you anyhow, Mrs. Wainwright."

He appeared on Sunday with his customary Sabbath offering. This time it was a newly published life of Michelangelo.

"This doughty chronicle would make Michelangelo turn in his grave," he reported. "I always suspected the old boy had some sort of complex; the way he left everything unfinished certainly suggests that. But I never supposed he was nothing but a tissue of complexes."

" 'A tissue of complexes'! Are you quoting, Sully?" asked Agnes.

"I'm improving. The so-called author of this tome couldn't think up as neat a phrase as that."

"Why bother to read it if it's all that bad?" inquired Miriam.

22

"Agnes will read it because while she's doing so she can look down her nose at all lesser wights."

"I can say, 'I don't read whodunits'?" Agnes asked.

"Better than that, say, 'I don't read fickshin.' Be sure you pronounce it 'fickshin.' That puts the dunces in their proper places."

"'Fick—'? Oh, you mean 'fiction'! But who on earth would say a thing like that?"

"Hundreds and hundreds of people. Perhaps thousands and thousands. You live such a sheltered life, Agnes."

"Do I?"

"People are inclined to spare your innocence, too. You have such a nice nature."

"Not as good as all that. Is it, Miriam?"

"Don't answer that one, Miriam," warned Sully. "It's a catch question, something like 'Have you left off beating your wife yet?'"

"Agnes has a nice nature," said Miriam tartly. "If she hadn't, she wouldn't put up with that Sullivan person."

"Or with the lady that's known as Miriam," Sully said all too sweetly.

"You let Miriam alone, Walter Sullivan." Agnes tried to sound severe, but she couldn't keep the laughter out of her voice. "She may not appreciate your particular type of humor; but she has more brains than you and I put together." She went on to tell him about Miriam's forthcoming speech.

"Well, I declare!" drawled Sully, completely unimpressed. "The audience will be ladies only, I gather. But perhaps you could smuggle me in if I disguised myself. When I was in college I played the leading part in a revival of *Charley's Aunt*. I was considered very good."

23

"And you admit it yourself," said Agnes.

Miriam looked puzzled. Her education had not included certain of the modern classics. Agnes felt compelled to explain that in the ancient and apparently imperishable farce, two undergraduates at Oxford are having their girls down for luncheon and a proposal of marriage; the party is to be chaperoned by Charley's aunt from Brazil. When she wires that she cannot make it, they disguise a pal in women's clothes and introduce him as Charley's aunt. The thinness of the disguise gets things off to an hilarious start; complications pile up, and the fun gets madder and madder.

"It was written in 1890-something," Agnes wound up lamely. "It must have added a good deal to the gayety of the Gay Nineties."

"Queen Victoria was still on the throne, wasn't she? In those days people were glad of any excuse to laugh." Miriam's elevated nostrils indicated what she thought of such foolishness.

"Sometimes a poor excuse is better than none, if it's uttered in a good cause," said Agnes with a flash of spirit.

"Of course, Ladybird, we can't always judge everything on high moral grounds," began Miriam at her condescending worst. Then all at once something inside her switched. She looked at Sully as if she had never seen him before, looked a second time, and suddenly burst out laughing.

Twice she tried to get her breath back; twice she went into another paroxysm. When she finally achieved coherence, she explained, "The very idea of Walter Sullivan's trying to impose on the members of the Antioch Women's City Club!"

"It might be good business if the imposture were detected," said Sully stoutly. "Show them that I'm not the

24

ordinary, run-of-the-mill, sit-on-his-seat-and-wait-for-customers real estate salesman."

"Did anybody ever accuse you of that?" demanded Agnes.

"That, my dear Mrs. Wainwright, is what is known as a rhetorical question. It does not require, nor expect, an answer." Sully drew the scene to a fine finish. Perhaps he had missed his vocation. Perhaps he should have been an actor. Perhaps he might have been, if it hadn't been for his prejudice in favor of eating every day.

Good old Sully! He could clown all he pleased; Agnes had never fallen into the habit of taking him for granted. Sometimes she had come perilously close to it. But today he had revealed a new facet in his many-sided character. He was, for the first time, looking at Miriam with real interest.

It was too soon to build anything on that. Still, a person could always hope. Then when hope was defeated . . .

Maybe she should have said "if" rather than "when." It didn't matter too much. Because when and if hope was defeated, a person could always go on and build up a fresh hope.

A person could? A person simply had to! Especially when that person was a nice enough, a well-meaning, possibly a weak-willed character known as Agnes Costen Wainwright.

Never, under her own volition, known as "Ladybird." Submitting but unconvinced. Unconvinced, but thus far submitting.

Thus far! Would it ever end? *The Rebellion of Ladybird*. That would make a much funnier farce than *Charley's Aunt*. It had yet to be written.

3.

Agnes would accompany Miriam to the luncheon, of course, even if they could not avail themselves of the escort of Charley's aunt. She would do her best to bear up under the deprivation.

Meantime, she found several ways to help out; the chief of them was to use her beautiful penmanship on the place cards. Miriam typed everything except her signature on bank checks. She had to type, if she expected anybody to read it. Her illegible scrawl was good enough for the one purpose, since it had the Wainwright money behind it.

This particular Thursday was Rosa Lee's day off; everything was very nicely cleared for the Great Event. Agnes went so far as to suggest that they call a taxi for the drive downtown. The double strain would be a little hard on Miriam; and Agnes herself had never learned to drive. During Jerome's lifetime, there had been no need for it; and a hint which she had thrown out to Miriam last spring had met with the prompt rejoinder, "I don't think you would be a very good driver."

Miriam hesitated just an instant, and Agnes moved toward the phone. She stopped when Miriam called out, "Never mind, Ladybird! I'm not in the least nervous, really."

Miriam was looking her sleek and handsome best. She drove competently, arrived in good season, found an excellent parking place. Agnes's carefully penned cards had been picked up Tuesday afternoon by the chairman of today's committee. She was already on hand; and she indicated to Agnes a table two ranks from the dais.

"It's an excellent location," she pointed out. "You will be able to see and hear everything." Perhaps she didn't mean that quite the way it sounded—as if she were giving every consideration to Old Lady Wainwright's failing senses.

It was too early yet to sit down; there was half an hour of new arrivals and greetings and gibble-gabble to be got through before they were free to take their places. Then came a typical public luncheon: broiled chicken, not too well cooked, cold mashed potatoes, peas almost innocent of seasoning. The ladies hadn't come here primarily to eat, of course; but Agnes felt that so long as they were going through the motions, it might have been made worth their while.

The stranger on her left took a gander at Agnes's place card and remarked, "Mrs. Wainwright? Any relation to the speaker of the day?"

"I'm her mother. That is, she was my husband's daughter by his first wife."

"Oh, stepmother!"

"Yes, the wicked character of the fairy tales. A stock character, like the wicked uncle, only more so."

She hadn't intended to sound biting; the other woman had been nothing worse than banal. Agnes was getting very touchy lately; such behavior wouldn't do either herself or Miriam any good.

But the woman on her left had now turned away. The one on her right was jawing away with some cronies. Agnes glanced up at the platform, caught Miriam's eye, smiled at her. Miriam smiled back. Mrs. Wainwright felt better.

The ice cream came, the cookies, the coffee. Thank goodness that was over! The waitresses began to clear away. Agnes's neighbor on her right, with whom she had a speaking acquaintance, engaged her for a few minutes in the exchange of commonplaces. Then Madam Chairman rose and called the meeting to order.

Her introductory remarks were too long; and there were two minor speeches to get out of the way. But at length Miriam's turn came; she rose, addressed the chair and the audience, and launched into her great effort.

The preliminaries out of the way, she reached the gist of her argument. "Organization is the modern substitute for genius. It is under better control than genius. It enables everybody to lend a hand. It works up to a real total.

"The result of combined effort amounts to the sum. The wisdom and experience of A and B and C, of Mrs. Brown and Mrs. Jones and Mrs. Robinson—or just as well of *Miss* Robinson . . ." She paused for a moment there, and was rewarded by a faint titter.

28

All well and good. Miriam was making her point. Then she must go on to elaborate it. "The sum remains a sum. The sum is an achievement. Toward that sum, each of us has contributed her share, she has made herself a factor."

And considerably more to the same purport. She wound up finally, and sat down amid hearty applause. She had earned it by the act she put on. Agnes was deeply and justifiably proud of her.

All the same, to Agnes's mind, Miriam had stopped short of the correct answer. To reach that, the sum should be divided by the number of the factors. The trip had been around Robin Hood's barn.

It just didn't make sense. Agnes really should have known better. For after all these years and all her experience, she still expected things to make sense.

Miriam in her glow of triumph was very sweet and appealing. Agnes reproached herself for even thinking that it would have been simpler, and to some of them at least just as satisfactory, if they had all stayed home in the first place.

Agnes attacked the home-cooked dinner with gusto, even if she had had to put the finishing touches to it herself. Miriam was too excited to eat much, even if her Spartan principles hadn't stood in her way. She kept reliving her speech and its acclaim, thinking of details that might have been improved, then reassuring herself about them, remembering what Mrs. So-and-so had said, what Mrs. Such-an-one hadn't. Everybody had been marvelous to her. "Everybody," she repeated firmly, meaning of course that there were exceptions, but she refused to dwell on them. Yet it would be a long time before she would undertake such an ordeal again. She wouldn't make a career of public

29

speaking, not if they paid her a thousand dollars a speech. "Which they aren't likely to," she added with a grin at her own fatuity.

"You wouldn't get more than nine hundred and seventy-five, most likely," Agnes agreed placidly.

All evening the telephone continued to ring; six or seven times Miriam received congratulations and plaudits. Then about eleven o'clock, the excitement ceased, while Miriam was still strung up.

"I've a good mind to go for a walk," she said. "Want to come along, Ladybird?"

"You'll find it more relaxing if you go alone." In this neighborhood, Miriam should be safe enough alone; Agnes was disinclined to stir. There had been no spotlight focused on her; but she too had had a big day.

She dutifully waited downstairs until Miriam returned. She offered a glass of whisky and recommended a hot bath. For once Agnes was ministering instead of being ministered to. She enjoyed the activity as well as the novelty.

Perhaps Miriam might go on to a really public career: one in which she was paid for her services. Or if she continued to act as a volunteer, perhaps she would continue along the path on which she had just taken a first step. In either case, she might learn to appreciate more highly Mrs. Wainwright's activities at home. In this way, too, Miriam might relish, and benefit by, an occasional drink. She might even reach the point where she would eat her meals.

There was a good deal of "perhaps" and "might" here, winding up in that fantasy of Miriam tucking into the fried chicken and even asking for a second helping. The idea lacked plausibility; but then, dreams often did.

At that, dreams sometimes came true. Not often. Not

30

always in the exact form which they had originally taken. But it could happen. A rainbow-tinted "perhaps" could be transformed into a pleasant fact.

Enough of Agnes's brief authority remained next morning to enable her to say, "I'm going to write Aunt Adelaide all about your speech at the luncheon yesterday. I'll call on you if I'm not sure about anything."

"You needn't go to all that trouble," Miriam demurred. "I can type out a letter. That will take much less time."

"I don't grudge the time," Agnes assured her. "You may write too, of course. But you'll be much too modest. I'm going to let Aunt Adelaide know just how splendid you were."

"I'm afraid you're prejudiced, Ladybird." All the same, Miriam was pleased. At the bottom of her heart she felt that she had indeed been very good.

Agnes wrote for the better part of an hour, with a few pauses for reflection. Then she read over what she had written. She had given the gist of Miriam's speech, not too unfairly; but she had laid stress on how pretty and appealing the girl had been.

It would never do to get caught in such a statement. Agnes added a hasty paragraph about their coming trip to New York; could they buy anything there for Aunt Adelaide?

She signed and sealed the letter, drew a long breath, then waited for Miriam to finish telephoning before she said, "Perhaps you'd like to read over what I've written. I've already sealed the letter; but of course I can tear it open."

Miriam would very much have liked to see what her stepmother had written; but she did not suspect Agnes's duplicity. The Ladybirds of this world are assumed to be incapable of circumventing the deep thinkers.

31

"Never mind," said Miriam. "I'll write her a note myself, but perhaps not until tomorrow. She wouldn't get it until Monday anyhow."

"You might wait, then," said Agnes. "It would be nice if she got our letters different days. Something in every mail, I mean. I don't suppose she has many correspondents."

"We'll get her postals Monday anyhow. I must be sure to warn her just how long we'll be away. Unless you've already thought to do that, Ladybird?"

"I'm afraid I haven't," said Agnes. "Afraid" of course was an understatement; she knew quite well that she hadn't. She had been in a hurry there at the end, for reasons of her own which she was not divulging.

Miriam wrote the letter, and got it off her mind. Presumably she didn't say much about her speech; she didn't take the time.

She spent what remained of the morning and all the afternoon largely at the telephone, with occasional excursions to the typewriter. She had not only to alert herself for the New York trip; she had also (a much more important and time-consuming task) to get her interests in order so that she could leave.

"I declare, Ladybird," she fussed at the dinner table, "I don't see how I'm going to spare the time; but I won't have you disappointed."

Agnes faltered that she could go alone. "I'd miss you, of course, but—"

"You have no idea of the responsibility involved in making arrangements for such a trip," cut in Miriam the indispensable.

"I can't learn younger," said Agnes. Then, ashamed of her own curtness, she had to backwater and assure Miriam,

32

"You have all the trouble and only half the fun. I do appreciate that, Miriam. Don't imagine for an instant that I do not."

Miriam, mollified, announced, "If you have any special preferences, Ladybird, you have only to let me know about them."

The one preference Agnes felt, she had just hinted at; she could not in common decency proceed farther along that line. She said vaguely, "Oh, I'm sure everything is going to be just fine!"

The little brush put Miriam on her mettle. "I hope we can make this year's trip a trifle different. The whole idea is to give you a change. I've an idea how it may be done."

She didn't share her idea, of course. In the kindness of her heart, she was preparing a surprise.

That evening she again went to the telephone. She called a New York number and talked for some time. Agnes tried not to eavesdrop on the conversation; and such fragments as penetrated her consciousness left her none the wiser.

Miriam wound up by making an appointment. To Agnes she reported, "I'm going into New York tomorrow to look the situation over. It's too much to expect that I should succeed on the first try. Still, it can happen."

Planning helped out on luck, thought Agnes. That is, other people's planning did. Perhaps there was another helpful characteristic: self-assertion.

Miriam went into New York the next day. She came back radiant over her success.

"It turned out just fine," she reported, "though not quite in the way I had looked for. I happened to remember that Clelie Durand and her husband go abroad every fall; I had thought that we might rent their apartment furnished.

33

They are going all right, but not for another month. However, they put me on the track of some friends of theirs who leave Monday. So it's all settled."

"You've rented a furnished apartment—from strangers?"

"All the better if I did! Clelie would have wanted to let us have their place as a favor. This way it's a business transaction."

"Yes, of course."

"We'll pay pay less rent to them than our hotel rooms would cost us. Meals will probably amount to more; but we should come out just about even. This will be a nice change from staying in an hotel, and give us a lot more privacy."

Agnes enjoyed the bustle of hotel life. Besides, who wanted privacy except honeymooning couples? It would be a change, yes. But another year—

Another year Agnes would be thirty-four instead of thirty-three. Surely by that time she would be on her own at intervals. Even now she would have been quite safe, and by no means lonely, if she lived unchaperoned at a respectable New York hotel for two weeks.

She still hoped for a slip-up. But it was a very faint hope.

On Sunday afternoon, Sully failed to show up. When his usual hour came and passed without bringing him, Miriam snapped, "He might at least have telephoned."

"Who might?"

"You know as well as I do. Walter Sullivan."

"He isn't such a fixture as all that."

"But he knows we're leaving this week."

"It may have slipped his mind."

Miriam's exasperation showed a trace of amusement. "I declare, Ladybird, you would make excuses for the Devil himself."

34

"Especially for the Devil," said Agnes. "It must get very monotonous, having to stay everlastingly in Hell and torture all those poor lost souls."

"The Devil too is a victim? I suppose that's one way of looking at it. But Ladybird, how do you think of such things?"

"It's a talent," said Agnes, dimpling. "If it were a secret that could be imparted, I'd give it to you. But it isn't."

The talent had served its purpose; it had deflected Miriam's wrath from Sully. It also kept Agnes from missing him too much. Agnes would give Sully his due quite as readily as she would give the Devil his. Sully was good company.

If she had been in love with him, his unexplained absence would have verged on the intolerable. Agnes might have been driven to do something foolish, such as trying to get in touch with him. As it was, she figured that an overdose of Sully would be worse than no Sully at all. Sully in just the right amount was the proper prescription. The only difficulty was to determine what was just the right amount.

To determine—yes, and to get it. Walter Sullivan knew that he was always welcome here. But very likely the Wainwrights' was not the only household where he was welcome.

The telephone rang twice in quick succession. Once it was a wrong number; the other time a fellow clubwoman wanted some information from Miriam. Agnes finally decided that she'd better give up. She should have arrived at that decision sooner.

It would have made all the difference if she had had an interesting book. An interesting *new* book, to provide surprise as well as delight.

She plowed steadily ahead with the *Life of Michelangelo*. She might have to report on it to the donor one of these

35

days; best get it out of the way in advance of her New York trip.

The book succeeded in being dirty and at the same time dull: an unusual feat, and to Agnes's mind scarcely worth the effort. It might be true to most of the surface facts; Agnes was not scholar enough to know. But that the over-all picture was correct she never for a minute believed. Michelangelo might not be exactly like one's next-door neighbor in Antioch, Long Island. But he couldn't have been all that queer.

Agnes returned to the book after supper, took it up to bed with her, somehow managed to stay awake until she had reached the long-deferred final page. It must never be said that a Wainwright—or even a Costen—could not finish whatever was once fairly begun.

A consideration altogether beside the point. This Costen's whole trouble was in starting things.

4.

Miriam got Monday morning off to a good start by proclaiming, "Other years we've left on Friday for New York. But this time we haven't any hotel reservations to meet, so I think we'll try to get away on Thursday. That way we'll have more time to get settled for an interesting weekend."

She was, as usual, ready and willing to do Agnes's thinking for her. Also as usual, she had reason on her side. There was nothing Agnes could say except, "I'm sure you're right, Miriam. I can be ready to leave Thursday."

She took their Thursday departure for granted when planning the week's meals with Rosa Lee, and realized, just too late, that she didn't know whether leaving a day earlier would mean that they also returned a day sooner, or that

37

they were awarding themselves an extra twenty-four hours in the Big City. Miriam had already steamed off downtown, so the information was not at once available. Agnes evaded the point, and Rosa Lee did not press it.

Miriam returned in good season with their railroad tickets and the facial expression, at the same time satisfied and apprehensive, of the born executive who is getting ahead with arrangements, but remains constantly aware of manifold responsibilities. After luncheon she betook herself to the telephone. She was the type that keeps lines busy. What a lull there would be at the Antioch exchange while she and her stepmother were in New York!

Agnes ransacked her wardrobe, decided which clothes to take with her, laid aside some to be given away, began to list the new things that she would need to look for in New York. This part of the preparation was real fun; and she still had plenty of time for second thoughts.

At the dinner table, conscience compelled her to bring up the question as to when they were planning to return. "Return?" echoed Miriam. "We haven't started yet."

"Then you didn't buy return tickets?"

"Not this time. They would tie us down, and the saving is really very little."

Miriam was honestly in search of change. That augured well. The immediate difficulty had been solved, too: Agnes now knew what to tell Rosa Lee. Everything augured well for the success of their trip. Agnes could not explain to herself her underlying feeling of apprehension.

Am I developing nerves? she thought. Better put it down to that, anyhow, and try to forget about it. Why should she spoil her own pleasure by wanting her own way, and at the same time accuse Miriam of bossiness?

38

Wednesday evening, Sully telephoned that he would drive the ladies to the station on Friday. This was a brand new attention; but he should have made the offer sooner. Miriam, who answered the phone, informed him curtly that they were leaving Thursday.

He was sorry he hadn't known that earlier; he was tied up all day Thursday.

"You could have found out easily enough," Miriam pointed out. "Thank you for asking." Then, and only then, did she put Agnes on the phone.

"Her Nibs is nibs-ing," drawled Sully. "After all, I have to make a living, and I am in the real estate business. I can't always take time off even on Sunday to act as a Squire of Dames."

"I missed you," said Agnes. "That book couldn't quite take your place."

"Having read the book, I resent your statement. I call it damning with faint praise."

"Alexander Pope!" cried Agnes. "You do read something besides whodunits and rotten biographies, then?"

"Or did, when I was in school. Send me a card, won't you? If you remember to put your New York address on it, I'll retort in kind."

Agnes gave her promise, bade him a cheerful farewell, inquired whether he would like to say "Goodbye" to Miriam. "Not even 'Au revoir,' " Mr. Sullivan answered.

Agnes hung up, nerved herself a little, and turned to Miriam. "You sounded amused," said Miriam drily.

"Well, why not?"

"Why not, indeed!" Miriam shook her head. "All that Irish blarney!"

"Blarney usually is Irish, isn't it?"

Miriam did not try to answer that; and Agnes felt that, unimportant as the skirmish was, she had come off victor. During the brief time that the interchange lasted, Miriam had not once called her "Ladybird."

The ladies departed on schedule. Rosa Lee Montgomery was left behind to clean house at her leisure and then take half her vacation. "Have some of your friends in for a bite and a drink any time you like," Agnes bade her in a private farewell. "It won't do for you to get too lonesome."

"I won't get too lonesome, I promise you, Miss Agnes. But I'm going to miss you," said Rosa Lee, with just the slightest emphasis on "you."

A man from the garage picked up the car at the station; it would be overhauled while they were away. Two well-upholstered members of the Women's City Club saw the Wainwrights off, and presented them with magazines to read on the train. The arrangements were perfect; the ladies were free to enjoy themselves. Indeed, it was their duty to enjoy themselves, after all that preparation.

Yet Agnes was strangely subdued. She dutifully leafed through a magazine, inspected the other tenants of the chair car, gazed out of the window. Miriam placidly read on and on, making every minute count. The magazines were more to her taste than to Agnes's, anyhow, instructive rather than entertaining. The old adage forbade the recipients to look a gift horse in the mouth. But mightn't it be a good idea for the donors, at least once in a way, to take a glance at the horse's teeth?

Miriam presently finished her magazine, offered to exchange with Agnes, then added politely, "But perhaps you hadn't finished?"

Agnes had had all she wanted; she could just as well neglect the second magazine as the first. She let it lie open on her lap, and began to dream of New York expeditions which she and Jerome had made while Miriam was away at college.

Sometimes she had joined them for a truncated weekend, chiefly when the opera season was on. Miriam "adored Wagner," and when she was with them, Wagner was what all three Wainwrights attended. Agnes enjoyed the excitement and the air of festivity at the Metropolitan. She would have found even Wagner not too bad if she had been allowed to listen to the music instead of being required to understand it.

Most of the Italian operas she loved; but her great favorite was *Carmen*. The music that thrilled her most in that great opus was the "Habanera": that melody, and that sense of expectation, of listening for the first quick click of the castanets. And at the end, though in a sense Carmen had asked for what she got, Agnes always found herself regretting that so much gayety and vitality should be snuffed out.

It affected Jerome, too. Throughout *Carmen* and during most of *Faust*, he dropped the American male's pose that he allowed himself to be dragged along to the opera only because it pleased his womenfolks.

The opera season wouldn't begin for some time yet, so perhaps Agnes was wasting her nostalgia. She wasn't unduly sentimental over Jerome; sometimes she had a guilty feeling that she didn't miss him half enough. But today, for some strange reason, he seemed very close to her, and at the same time very far away. It was a really widowed feeling: fainter by far than she had felt immediately after his death, yet oddly poignant.

The furnished apartment which was to be their nesting

41

place for the next two weeks or so did nothing to raise Agnes's spirits. It was advanced modernistic, all shiny chrome and slippery leather and angles either so acute that they looked like pincers or so obtuse that they yawned. None of the chairs accommodated to the human frame; and the colors were at once strident and icy.

To Agnes's eye, the place had all the homelike charm of an especially antiseptic funeral parlor. But Miriam seemed impressed. "Interesting, isn't it?" was her comment. "And different."

With that second proposition, at least, Agnes could agree. It was indeed different.

They unpacked and went out to lunch. Agnes's spirits rose at once. She was *here;* and even with her visit conditioned as it was, to be in New York was a treat.

She would cheerfully have spent the entire afternoon meandering; but Miriam had some duties to get off her chest. If Duty was "stern daughter of the Voice of God," Miriam was certainly a favorite niece.

There were "Off Broadway" tickets to pick up, though Agnes would have been satisfied with "On Broadway," or even a first-run movie. In each case, Miriam sized up the neighboring restaurants; they might dine in the vicinity when they planned to take in a play, and thus avoid hurry and congestion. She had been given the address of "a good cheap dressmaker," too; and although she shared Agnes's suspicion that the two adjectives more or less contradicted each other, Miriam must look up the establishment, just in case they decided to give it a trial. She was not favorably impressed, so Agnes was spared further anxiety on that score. She would have hated to waste any of her precious New York hours on fittings and refittings.

42

Toward the end of the afternoon the errands were finally accomplished. Miriam agreed to go for a ride on the Fifth Avenue bus; and when the lights began to come on, they left it for a stroll. Such leisurely pursuits were very much to Agnes's taste; but they would be rationed out sparingly in the course of what she was ungrateful enough to term to herself "the Wainwright Endurance Race." She could have had such a good time if she were only left to her own devices!

Agnes's father had been an architect up in Massachusetts. Reared in that atmosphere and tradition, Agnes had soaked in a good deal. She judged by conservative standards. The various styles which she saw in New York fascinated her; and the blend of incongruous styles, though it was often distasteful and sometimes shocking, contributed to the charm which made New York unique among cities.

"You may disapprove of a lot of things here," she summed up. "But New York gets you. It really gets you."

"It gets you, yes," Miriam assented grudgingly. "But enough is enough; and so often here in New York there is just too much."

That was Miriam for you. If there was a fly in the ointment, Agnes could acknowledge that fact and make allowances. Miriam characteristically would set to work to get rid of the fly; until she had done so, she could not relax and enjoy the ointment. For all practical purposes, the ointment did not exist until she had worked off the responsibility.

Even after she had done so, the memory was likely to rankle. In such a case as this, she was considerably at a loss; it was scarcely feasible for her to redesign and rebuild New York City. Perhaps she couldn't help the way that she was made; she was a born reformer. Such characters have their

43

uses. But milder and more acquiescent souls would be better pleased if they did their reforming at a distance—and if they omitted it altogether when they were on what was supposed to be a vacation.

Agnes chuckled suddenly. Miriam looked at her inquiringly; but Mrs. Wainwright couldn't very well explain the joke. This was a case of the proverbial pot and kettle. Miriam was the fly in Agnes's ointment; and it was just too bad if Stepmama concentrated on it to the partial ruin of her visit.

Because there was so much for her to see and do and enjoy! Shopping at Altman's: these big New York department stores offered a free pageant as well as articles that their customers might want to buy. At the Metropolitan Museum of Art, they trudged through gallery after gallery, and looked and looked until they could no longer see what they were looking at. They spent one afternoon in the art dealers' shops along Fifty-seventh Street.

That was the day when Miriam had her moment. "There's a famous Russian restaurant the other side of Fifth Avenue, Ladybird," she said. "Let's go over there and treat ourselves to an early dinner."

"Fine!" Agnes agreed. "For once, let's quit while the quitting is good."

They were seated at a good table, and the cocktail-and-wine card put before them. Ordinarily they did not indulge. But they disliked to proclaim themselves bluenoses. "I think for once in a way, a cocktail would taste good," proclaimed Miriam. "Since this is a Russian place, why not try something made with vodka?"

In their inexperience, they had to trust the card. Each of them ordered something known as a "vodka perfect."

44

The drinks arrived. The ladies tasted, hesitated, took a second sip. Then they caught each other's eyes, and Agnes raised her eyebrows. "If this is a vodka perfect—"

"I'd hate to try a vodka imperfect," Miriam finished for her.

Agnes contemplated her glass without offering to touch it. "Think the habit might grow on us?"

"Habit?"

"Shall we drink this to save it? We're going to have to pay for it anyhow."

"Let's not pay two ways." Miriam beckoned to the waiter, and ordered two martinis.

They went to three Broadway plays, two of them in the evening, one at the midweek matinee. The matinee crowd was almost entirely women; but Agnes, who disliked assembled women when they listened to committee reports and passed resolutions, found this particular audience a pleasant change. The play happened to be very much to her taste, too; it was lively, it dealt with likable people, and it made no attempt to point a moral.

"Off Broadway" rated four shows to "On Broadway's" three. One was engaging; it had a lot of hopeful young people in it, and the friendliness of the atmosphere made up for any technical shortcomings. The second was in the "almost" class: just good enough to exasperate because it wasn't better. The third was acceptable; it didn't arouse much feeling one way or the other.

The fourth was Anton Chekov's *The Three Sisters.* "More things Russian?" asked Agnes, examining her program.

"This time with malice aforethought," said Miriam. "I

45

read the play years ago; I wonder how it will appear in production."

She had the advantage of her stepmother. If Agnes too had read it, she might have found an added interest in the play.

An addition which was badly needed. The play droned on and on and on. It was laid in Russia in 1900, in a provincial town where dullness seemed to be varied only by disaster. Perhaps that was what life was like there and then. But why bother to bring it up here and now?

The final curtain descended. In silence, the ladies walked to Fourteenth Street, which Miriam deemed the best place to get a taxi. While they were waiting, Agnes ventured, "Maybe this is heresy. But if those three sisters wanted so much to go to Moscow—"

"Why didn't they go to Moscow?" Miriam agreed.

It wasn't until after she was in bed that night that Agnes reflected, it must be the multiplication of the theme that made it so appalling. An only child might hesitate to make a break. Might very understandably hesitate. The fact that the situation was simpler might well make the tie, and the resultant hesitancy, stronger.

Having slept on it twice, the only child—or rather the senior only child, for of course Miriam was one too—ventured to inquire, "Don't you think that for a change we might separate for a day? Each go on her own, and then later compare notes?"

Miriam looked taken aback; but after an instant's hesitation she replied, "Of course, Ladybird, if you would prefer it that way. I wish you had mentioned it earlier. We haven't so very much time left now; and I've tried to get everything into our schedule."

The schedule! That Frankenstein monster which Miriam first created and then submitted to. A schedule might be desirable, might even be necessary, if you were running a factory or planning a campaign. But why should two independent Americans on pleasure bent burden themselves with those fetters?

Such questions are easier to ask than to answer. Agnes gave in. She tried to console herself by reflecting that, had that extremely unlikely plan gone into effect, her trivial "notes" must have withered away altogether under Miriam's exacting scrutiny.

Miriam might be a martinet by nature, too; but the rigidity of her training had done nothing to soften her. Those "bright college years" when she might almost as well have been marooned on some island inhabited by Amazons had been varied by conducted tours. *Europe as we require you to see it.* Our aim is travel, which is broadening, and culture, which you are going to acquire whether you like it or not. Enjoyment is not the idea; you must take advantage of your opportunity while you have it. As for straying and dallying, perish the thought! It wasn't for the thought of such heathen delights that your parents laid down so much good money.

Miriam had suffered three conducted tours to Agnes's one. The wonder was not that she lacked suppleness, but that she had come out reasonably understanding and considerate.

Perhaps Agnes's one European tour offered no fair basis of comparison. Her parents had died within a few months of each other; and she was still in a state of shock when a puzzled elderly uncle who was practically a stranger to her had shelved the problem by buying her (with her own

47

money) a three-month European tour which was guaranteed to be comprehensive and at the same time luxurious.

At first, Agnes had been diverted, if somewhat bewildered. Then, when she was required to do too much in too short a time, it all became a blur of cathedrals and crooked streets lined with medieval houses.

Worse even than an overcrowded day at the Metropolitan, and no respite on the morrow. Punishment instead of pleasure. This might be good for you, as they used to tell you in your youth that oatmeal was. But at least when you had eaten your oatmeal, it was over for the day. You were not forced to have it choked down your throat hour after hour.

She hadn't yet recovered from that numbness when Jerome Wainwright, an old but casual friend of Uncle's, met and married her. Jerome had conducted their married life, too. But that hadn't been any such fantastic whirl. Indeed, there had been times when ungrateful Agnes could have wished for a little more momentum.

Miriam was right, of course. Their remaining days in New York, lived carefully according to plan, were full to bursting. Their fall wardrobes had to be filled up, though the novelty of shopping had worn off. They must make their decision about a present to be dispatched to Great-aunt Adelaide: that ticklish gift for the relative who has everything. They took in one concert. For a second time, Miriam accompanied Agnes to Vespers at old Trinity, that historic church which sat so sedately at the head of Wall Street, and proceeded according to program, even when there were more persons in the choir than in the congregation.

The last day came too soon; it always did. Agnes, sorting as she packed, discovered that she had accumulated three standard U.S. postals from Great-aunt Adelaide and two

48

picture postcards from Walter Sullivan. Miriam had destroyed hers when she answered them. A wise precaution; it prevented their adding to that end-of-vacation feeling.

"So goodbye to this modernistic apartment," said Miriam, testing a suitcase for fullness and reopening it. "Next time I think I'll take a look before I lease."

Agnes hadn't held Miriam to blame for the oddities of their camping place. Not too much to blame, that is. She held her tongue.

"Modified modernistic would be all right," Miriam went on. "But this rigid scheme is upset if you bring so much as a wastebasket into it."

"And there's no place for the old things to which a person has become attached."

"Indeed no!" Miriam grimaced. " 'So much rubbish!' the High Priests of *moderne* would say. 'Away with it!' "

" 'Heave it out, to make room for something we can charge you two prices for!' " Agnes amended.

Miriam nodded, but she was only half listening. "I think some day, if I had a little place of my own—" she began, and paused.

Agnes held her breath, waiting for Miriam to go on. After a minute's silence she encouraged, "Yes, if you had a little place of your own—?"

Miriam looked startled. Perhaps she was not aware of having spoken aloud. She bent over her packing, got that first suitcase to her satisfaction, opened a second, then straightened abruptly. She was once more the sergeant major when she said, "Can I help you there, Ladybird? I had planned on an early lunch. There's nothing I hate worse than having to rush for a train."

49

5.

GETTING HOME WAS ALWAYS A BIG THRILL; AND AFTER A modernistic apartment and over two weeks of eating in restaurants, a substantial, pleasant house and Rosa Lee Montgomery's cooking made the wayfarer agree that indeed there was no place like this.

The new clothes had to be sorted and installed. The trip must be reported on. Agnes inspected Rosa Lee's house-cleaning, and Rosa Lee expressed her pleasure with her dozen pairs of nylons. (Unlike Great-aunt Adelaide, Rosa Lee was easy to buy a present for.)

Then Agnes experienced a letdown. The trip to which she had looked forward so long was now a thing of the past. Her housekeeping duties could have been performed by a child of twelve. Church came only once a week; and Sully, although he was the best of friends, was about as novel as the back of one's own hand.

She must have gone through sieges like this before. She had, of course; she remembered them. But that wry consolation served only to remind her that doubtless she would go through more such sieges in the future. Agnes groaned aloud.

Miriam was busier than ever, making up for lost time. "I declare, Ladybird," she said more than once, "I had no business to go gallivanting off to New York when I was needed right here at home." She was too preoccupied to notice how listless Agnes seemed. That was so much to the good.

That expression so common nowadays, "the foreseeable future," had long puzzled Agnes. How could anybody possibly foresee any of the future, let alone differentiate between the discerned segment and the mighty unknown that lay ahead?

Well, she was learning now. The next few months lay spread before her like a landscape viewed from an eminence: a pleasant enough landscape, but dull. Not as dull, of course, as the provinces in Russia in 1900. On the other hand, Agnes, though she had some money and at least technical freedom, was not at all certain in which direction Moscow lay.

Tedium is a very inexact measurer of time. The hours that dragged their weary length along appeared to do so for months. Actually, however, very little of the calendar had dropped into the abyss after things were settled for the winter when they began to come unsettled.

The upset started right here at home. Miriam never had

even an ordinary cold, and was somewhat disposed to look askance at sufferers from the commoner woes of the flesh. They deserved what they got, in her opinion, though she didn't say it in so many words. She didn't need to. She implied as much by the hints she gave, and by the good example she set the weaker sisters.

Yet Miriam, Arch Priestess of Hygeia, practitioner of her own gospel: Miriam, who ate sparingly, exercised regularly, got a proper amount of rest, was the one who came down with a virus attack which descended on her out of the blue.

Of course, nowadays they called everything "a virus." That didn't disguise the fact that Miriam was a very sick girl. She groped her way through a pre-dawn darkness to bid Agnes send for a doctor. After that she tossed in a high fever and answered questions, when she answered them at all, by nodding or shaking her head.

Agnes was frightened out of her seven senses. But when the doctor brought up the question of hospital and Miriam gestured toward her stepmother, Agnes took her decision instantly. Sick or well, Miriam was not to be turned out of her own home.

Fortunately, there was very little sickness around; a day nurse and a night nurse were promptly to be had. The household had to be reorganized around them—while Miriam the organizer herself lay prone and speechless.

After three days the situation stabilized itself. The "miracle drugs" performed their office. Miriam was pronounced out of danger. The night nurse was no longer strictly necessary, though Agnes insisted she must stay until the end of the week.

"Everything has gone beautifully so far," the doctor pronounced when Mrs. Wainwright showed him out. "Convalescence is the real test."

Agnes didn't know what he meant by that. She soon found out.

Miriam, now that she was no longer sick, expected to be able to resume her usual pursuits at once. Yet she was barely able to totter to a chair, even with the nurse's assistance. After half an hour there, she was glad enough to get back to bed. The second day, she insisted on sitting up longer. This time, on her return trip she lost her balance, and might have dragged the nurse down with her if Agnes had not sprung to their assistance.

The third day, in answer to Agnes's counsels of prudence, she snapped, "It's all very well for you to talk. But when I think of the thousand and one things I should be doing—"

Then she cried, apologized, cried some more, turned her face to the wall, and refused to get up at all that day. Agnes was worried and wanted to send for the doctor. The nurse reassured her. That crankiness was only a part of the usual picture.

Miriam was the victim of her own sense of responsibility. All those pursuits of hers! Agnes sometimes wondered whether they were so called because she pursued them; it did seem as if, on the contrary, they were after her.

The fourth day, the nurse was again allowed to make ready a chair on the other side of Miriam's bedroom. Agnes was in anxious attendance when Rosa Lee Montgomery beckoned her out of the room. A telegram had just arrived. Would she please sign for it?

A telegram which was delivered instead of being phoned! That could mean one of only two things: congratulations

53

or a death message. And nobody under this roof was in a position to be congratulated.

Sure enough, the wire was from Marshfield: "MRS. ADE-LAIDE HAMMOND DIED LAST NIGHT IN HER SLEEP. FUNERAL ARRANGEMENTS INCOMPLETE. WIRE HOUR WHEN YOUR TRAIN ARRIVES. WILL MEET."

That was the way it read when you put in the period every time it said "STOP." It was signed W. R. Kent—whoever he was.

Miriam might know; and Agnes had the happy idea of asking, even before she produced the telegram, "Did you ever hear of a W. R. Kent, Miriam? The name Kent isn't common; but I can't quite place him."

"W. R. Kent? Right here in Antioch?"

"No, up in Marshfield."

"Marshfield? You've heard from somebody in Marshfield? Then Great-aunt Adelaide is—dead?"

That instant's hesitation somehow touched Agnes. Great-aunt Adelaide had always been a part of Miriam's background. A childhood memory had come back, however briefly. This, too, at the moment when Miriam was least able to deal with it.

Agnes produced the telegram. Miriam read it, blinked back the tears, said with a faint wry smile, "The telephone still works, doesn't it?"

It did. Agnes long-distanced Marshfield and talked to Dora Dean, Great-aunt Adelaide's housekeeper. She learned that Mr. Kent had been Mrs. Hammond's lawyer, that he was being very helpful, that provisional arrangements for the funeral had already been made.

"Tell everybody to go ahead. I'll get there as soon as I can. Thank you very much, Dora."

54

Agnes caught a half-stifled sob before Dora managed to say, "Not at all, Mrs. Wainwright" and hang up. People were awfully sweet, really. They were much kinder than they got credit for being.

Agnes made two local calls, one to the railroad station, one to the bank. She telegraphed Mr. Kent. She gave a few brief orders to Rosa Lee. She took the nurse aside, and for once talked more than she listened.

Then she faced the interview with Miriam. "That I should have to let you go alone on a hard trip like this—I can't tell you how I feel about it, Ladybird—I can't begin to tell you!" Miriam's features contorted. She made a strong effort of the will, and then realized that this time no effort would avail her. She was in the hands of strong forces.

Agnes felt apologetic toward Miriam, for no very good reason. At the same time, some other feeling was arising in her bosom. In the flurry of departure she could ignore it, and did. Maybe later on . . .

The flurry mounted as the moments sped. Miriam kept interrupting with suggestions which had to be met or parried. The nurse acted as an unwilling Mercury. Fearful of offending her, Agnes made several trips to the sickroom. She finally begged off, sending word that she was afraid she might miss her train. That was not to be thought of; no Wainwright had ever missed a train.

Agnes got off with almost half an hour to spare. The garage man drove her to the station. He refused to take any pay for his services; but Agnes tipped him ten dollars. It was her own money she was spending; and this time there was nobody to watch her spend it.

At the station, her freedom went further to her head. Leaving her bags in charge of a porter, she went into the

55

drugstore across the street and bought four brand new paperbacks, whodunits every one of them. This time Walter Sullivan could not be held an accessory to the blameworthy deed. Nobody would be. What some people didn't know wouldn't hurt 'em.

Mrs. Wainwright left Antioch in a frame of mind most unsuitable for a person who was on her way to a funeral. On her way from a sickbed, too. This was in sharp contrast to her low spirits on her recent journey to New York. She hadn't yet had time to realize that Great-aunt Adelaide was gone; and the absence of the family Mentor gave Agnes that beginning-of-vacation feeling. Not everybody is grateful for good counsel. It might, indeed, be classed as one commodity much more likely to bless him that gives than him that takes.

Agnes read steadily all the way into New York City. Resettled for the journey up the Hudson River, she glanced around the chair car, which was almost full. Then she studied the thronging traffic on the platform. All these people going somewhere on their various errands: what a lot of business, and of pleasure too, went on in this great world while the Widow Wainwright stayed holed up in the wilds of Long Island!

The chair next hers to the rear of the coach stayed empty until the train was just about to start. Then a man took his place there. A casual glance informed Agnes that he was about her own age or a little older, good-looking in a smooth, dark way, and apparently intelligent. With that much knowledge she would remain satisfied. Her new-found freedom scarcely entitled her to scrape acquaintance with strangers.

They were off. That curious part of New York City which lay north of Grand Central Station slipped past Agnes's window. Some time she would like to investigate the district. She had been through here times enough; some day she would like to stop and poke around.

Now they came in sight of the Hudson River: not an exciting stream, but mighty, sightly, storied. Agnes relaxed in her chair. She could remember being read to before she was old enough to read for herself; in her father's voice she heard that wonderful opening line, "Whoever has made a voyage up the Hudson River must remember the Catskill Mountains."

That was *Rip van Winkle*. Rip took his historic nap a long time ago; it was years, indeed, since small Agnes had listened to his story. She could still repeat it almost word for word. Perhaps it was time for her to get back to something fresher. Agnes produced the paperback of which she had read the greater part on the first leg of her journey, and made fairly short work of the rest.

She had closed it and was reaching for a second volume when a man's voice asked quietly, "Good?" It was her neighbor, the latecomer.

"I enjoyed it; but I'm rather easily pleased."

"I shouldn't have suspected that."

Agnes shot him a look. He had just right amount of self-assurance. "See for yourself," she said, and offered the volume.

"Oh, thank you! But are you sure I'll have time to finish it? You're not getting off soon?"

"Not for some time," said Agnes, and looked away.

For as much as half a minute, she was proud of her own cunning. Then she realized that she had given him the perfect pretext for renewing the conversation.

He renewed it sooner than she had expected. Only a third

57

of the way through *Dire Darling*, he marked his place with his finger and leaned over to say, "All right if I stop now and guess?"

Agnes, marking her own place, elevated her eyebrows. "I'll tell you whether you're right or wrong. But you don't want me to give the plot away, surely?"

"Not for worlds!"

He began to guess. He gave reasons for his conjectures. He was right so much of the time that Agnes, who been misled by one false lead after another, was astounded.

Then he was right once too often. She tumbled. "You've read it before," she said sharply.

"Not this one, dear lady, but many, many others. There's a strong family resemblance."

He kept his face straight enough; but the twinkle in his eyes betrayed him. Trying to sound severe, she asked, "Do you think that's honest?"

"Not honest, maybe, but fair enough."

"All right, then, you're on a train trip and you want somebody to talk to. You know we'll never see each other again. Yet for an hour or so, here and now, we might exchange our news and views."

This time he did smile. "I was only waiting for that word. Very well, then. I no longer travel in the smoking car. I've heard all those stories before."

"A family resemblance there, too?" suggested Agnes.

"Worse than that. Not merely kinship: twinship."

"That's almost a pun. Keep it 'almost,' and I may forgive you."

This time he gave her an appraising look. It was brief; but clearly he was more interested than he had expected to be.

58

Then he began, "My name is Tom Jones. And it really is Tom Jones. My mother must have been reading novels before I was born, or she would have named me for my uncle Harold, who was supposed to have money."

"Did he?"

"If he did, he still has it. I wouldn't know. In college I roomed for one semester with a fellow named Jack Smith."

"Interesting," mumured Agnes.

"You don't believe that one, either?"

"Does it matter what I believe?"

"I am legally free at the moment," he went on. "My wife didn't appreciate what a bargain she had."

"What difference does that make? You appreciate it."

"You don't play fair," he complained. "I'm the one who is taking the risk. Your husband may be a large, strong, insanely jealous man who will get on the train at the next station with a horsewhip in his hand—"

Agnes dimpled, and resigned herself. It was time this nonsense ended; the wonder was that she had been able to keep it up so long.

"I'm Mrs. Wainwright, and the name really is Wainwright," she said. "My husband is dead. It was not his habit to stalk me; and he seldom carried a horsewhip."

"It's a good name: the kind that nobody would make a joke about. Are you traveling much farther, Mrs. Wainwright?"

"To Marshfield."

"Good! I go one station beyond that. Will you have dinner with me presently?"

"Thank you, I will. Now may I finish my book?"

"Yes, indeed. And if you can furnish me with one that I haven't read, I will put in a fruitful hour."

59

It was any man's guess what might have happened if Agnes had bought only the two books. As it was, she produced two others and gave him his choice between them.

Over the dinner table, she revealed what was bringing her to Marshfield. He showed proper concern. "I never knew Mrs. Hammond personally; but she was more or less a legend around this part of the country. Are you staying on after the funeral?"

It was a natural enough question, but it brought Agnes up short. She had not yet thought as far ahead as the funeral, let alone planned beyond it.

She hesitated, and Tom Jones perceived his blunder. He fished for his wallet and produced a business card. "I can phone and find out," he said. "I live only one station beyond Marshfield."

The card described him as "T. H. JONES, PRESIDENT, ROSEMOUNT POTTERY WORKS, ROSEMOUNT, NEW YORK." "If you're bone lazy," he explained, "the smart thing to do is get yourself born into a family where the foundations are already laid. My grandfather started the business and my father expanded it. My hardest job is to listen to old faithful employees. But I can always manage to spend a good deal of my time out of town."

He had made good his footing before he presented his credentials. Agnes realized that she was going to like Mr. Tom Jones. In fact, she already liked him more than a little.

"Write your home telephone number on the card," she suggested carelessly. "Not that I ever call anybody up. I intend to all right; but procrastination gets the better of me."

"You sin in good company," said Tom Jones. "Good for a dining car meal, isn't it?"

60

"It helps to pass the time," said Agnes demurely.

Back in the chair car, she resumed her book rather ostentatiously. Some minutes later she glanced up and caught Tom watching her over the edge of his. Agnes dropped her eyes. This wasn't the time or the place for a pickup, even if she had been the type.

The next thing she knew, the porter came for her luggage; they were pulling into Marshfield. Tom thrust his unfinished book back at her. Their brief exchange of her offer to let him keep it and his refusal lasted just long enough so that Agnes was still crowding the bone of contention into her handbag when she was helped to the station platform.

Mr. Kent was waiting for her: Mr. Kent, the old-fashioned family solicitor, complete to graying imperial and obsequious chauffeur. He apologized for even asking her to do so when she must be tired from her trip; but if Mrs. Wainwright felt up to stopping at the undertaker's on her way to the house, funeral arrangements could be completed that night.

Agnes felt scarcely equal to "doing so"; even a lifetime of acquiescence had not prepared her for so much falling in with whatever was expected of her. She said wearily, "Not tonight, please."

Gone was her entertaining encounter with Tom Jones, utterly gone and ready for forgetting. If it had ever happened at all, it had happened to somebody else. She answered Mr. Kent's inquiries about Miriam's health. She made a polite speech of thanks about all that he was doing for her. She said yes, he was quite right in assuming that she would be more comfortable at "Mrs. Hammond's home" than at an hotel, in spite of "the sad associations."

The associations were not sad; Agnes was groping in a

61

fog of unreality. It lifted only when they stopped at that hospitable mansion. Their arrival had been awaited. The front door came open, and a substantial form emerged to await them on the front porch.

It was Dora Dean, Great-aunt Adelaide's housekeeper of many years' standing. She took Agnes into her capacious embrace and cried out, "You had to come alone!"

Then, and only then, did Agnes realize what had happened.

6.

Great-aunt Adelaide was "more or less a legend," Tom Jones had said. So she had been, to outsiders. To Agnes she had been the most interesting of family connections, an understanding older friend, and something of an enigma.

Now it came sharply home to her that Mrs. Hammond was gone. Never again would she and Miriam come visiting together, and be ceremoniously installed in those great southern guestrooms, each with its dressing room and bath. That spacious, gracious way of living was gone. Time, which devours everything, had finally got the better even of Adelaide Hammond.

Mr. Kent's chauffeur had taken Mrs. Wainwright's bags upstairs. Mr. Kent arranged to call the following afternoon, "unless you would prefer to remain undisturbed." The funeral would be at ten in the morning the day after tomorrow. "Be sure to let me know if I can be of the slightest service."

He left, and Agnes came to herself. She ought to be the consoler instead of the one consoled. Aunt Adelaide's passing had shaken Agnes; but for Dora Dean it was the end of life as she had known it.

Agnes managed a shaky smile. "Can't we sit down somewhere?" she asked.

She had managed to do exactly the right thing: give Dora a chance to be of service to her. "There are fires laid in the sitting room and the library," Dora informed her eagerly. "Maybe you'd like a nice cup of tea?"

"The sitting room will be fine," said Agnes. "Tea will be, too, provided you'll join me."

Dora turned on lights in both the library and the sitting room: overhead lights in huge gas-and-electric chandeliers. In the sitting room, she turned on two side brackets, each of which impersonated a small candelabrum, and a table lamp which had clearly started life in the days of kerosene. Dora touched a match to a wood fire which lay ready in the grate; then she departed in quest of tea.

Agnes strolled through the two rooms. She remembered so much, and remembered it well. On the other hand, it was strange to find how many details—significant details, some of them—she noticed now for the first time.

For instance, the library walls were lined, except for the necessary intervals occupied by fireplace, doors, and windows, with tall glass-fronted walnut bookcases. At the fireplace end of the room low open bookshelves had been set in front of them for later additions; and two large library tables,

64

balancing each other at opposite ends of the room, not only displayed new books and current magazines; their lower shelves were crammed tight with surplus volumes. It was a room from which nothing was ever discarded, though additions had constantly been made.

There was stability here, and very likely inertia, too. Was? There had been. Creeping change had outflanked even this high citadel. The old order was gone and, except for the occasional student or sentimentalist, pretty well on its way toward being forgotten.

Back in the sitting room, too, rosewood formed a background for various other kinds of furniture; and the knick-knacks had assembled themselves over the years. After all, this was not a stage setting, although it was more interesting than most of those Agnes remembered. It was somebody's home.

It was. It had been. The dire note of *gone, gone, spent and gone* kept reiterating itself.

Dora came back presently with a tea table, then on a second trip fetched the ready-set tray. "Lucky the girls have both gone to bed," she chuckled. "I've taught them to wait at table fairly well, though generally as soon as I get a girl taught that, she quits. But the tea table is beyond them. Of course they don't get much practice. When Mrs. Hammond is here alone, I serve her myself."

She spoke in the present tense. Involuntarily? Or deliberately, to see what Mrs. Wainwright would make of it?

Agnes motioned Dora to a seat, then devoted herself to pouring. "There are still two girls employed here?" she asked quietly.

"Off and on there are, though I suppose we've been luckier than most. One girl and more help by the day might get the work done better; but they do keep each other company."

"It's a responsibility for you either way," said Agnes quickly.

"It takes a responsibility off of Mrs. Hammond's shoulders." Dora Dean stirred her tea, started to lift the cup, set it down so hastily that it slopped into the saucer. "I mean it *did*. For so many years I tried to think of her and plan for her. I just can't realize that she's gone."

"You were a great help to her all those years," Agnes consoled. "I know Mrs. Hammond was very fond of you."

"Not any fonder than she was of you," said Dora Dean stoutly. "Just in a different way. She told me quite a while back that if she had ever had a daughter, she'd have wanted one exactly like you."

Agnes stared with her mouth open. Dora couldn't possibly have made that up. Yet why should anybody take such a liking to her amiable but insignificant self? And of all people to take a liking, the powerful, reserved, almost austere Adelaide Hammond!

Dora fetched a cloth and wiped up the tea. Agnes, having had greatness thrust upon her, advised, "Go ahead and begin your tea. I'm sure you need it. We can talk awhile afterward."

Dora was famished. While Agnes nibbled at a cookie and sipped half a cup of tea, Dora drank three cups of tea fortified with sugar and cream, and ate what amounted to a substantial supper.

"I didn't know how hungry I was," she explained halfway through.

"Of course you didn't. You weren't thinking about yourself."

66

Dora finished her meal and tidied the devastated tray. "You have somebody working for you, haven't you? I hope she realizes how lucky she is."

"We get along all right. Sit still a minute longer and get your breath back. You must have had an awful day."

Dora nodded. "It was one of the girls who found her. She went all to pieces; the other girl had her hands full with that one. I had everything else to see to. Maybe it was all for the best, at that. I didn't have the two of them to fall over every time I turned around."

"You knew what Mrs. Hammond's wishes were."

"I did, and I didn't. I tried to do the best I could. I left the choice of the casket to you, Mrs. Wainwright. You'll have to see to it tomorrow."

"Oh, yes! Yes, of course." Agnes blinked away a slight fog. It was not the first time she had performed that dismal office. "Mr. Kent must have been a big help to you."

"Mr. Kent is always a big help, when the family has enough money," said Dora tartly. "It all goes down in the bill."

This was more like it. Agnes listened to details about the day's events and prognostications about tomorrow. Then, while Dora washed up the tea things, Agnes had a chance to draw a long breath. What was the funny Southern expression that Rosa Lee used? Oh, yes, "take a blow"! At first that had sounded to Agnes more like an idiom suitable to pugilism or to whaling. But perhaps in a hot climate after prolonged exertion you got your breath back very audibly.

Dora accompanied her to the guestroom, turned down the sheets for her, and bade her "call me in the night—any time in the night—if you want anything."

There was nothing Agnes could conceivably want in the

67

night that wasn't right there at hand. She knew her way around the house anyhow; and she was years younger than Dora Dean. The poor thing wanted to be wanted; that was all. Her Mrs. Hammond was gone. Who was to take that vacant place?

Agnes did ask to be called at seven. Then she arranged herself comfortably in the bed, and discovered that she was brutally tired, but not in the least sleepy. She was accustomed to a nightly dose of whodunits: as habit-forming, surely, as any tranquilizer which could be bought on the other side of the drugstore. Yet to have recourse to one here and now seemed in highly questionable taste.

But did bad taste matter all that much if nobody found out about it? And when you came right down to cases, what possible good could it do the late Great-aunt Adelaide, the invalided stepdaughter Miriam, Agnes herself, or anybody else under the canopy, for Mrs. Wainwright to lie here twisting and turning?

Agnes got out of bed and fetched the book. She thought briefly of Tom Jones: a self-conscious character, like Sully, but pleasant enough for a change. She discovered that she had picked up the wrong book; this time, not to risk making the same mistake a second time, she brought all three of the others with her.

Thus fortified, she began again the book which she had just condemned as the wrong one. The next thing she knew, she waked, shivering a little, with the lamplight full in her eyes. This time she settled down and consciously lost consciousness. A blissful experience; too bad it always had to be so frightfully brief.

She was officially awakened by Dora Dean, who prudently remained in the room until Mrs. Wainwright was out of bed.

68

Dora was solicitous as to how Agnes had slept. Her answer to Agnes's return inquiry was borne out by her appearance. She was still sad and shaken; but she was again on her way to being the Dora Dean that Agnes remembered. Her hair had gone gray in Mrs. Hammond's service; and years of good living had put added weight on what must have been a substantial figure to begin with. But she was still apple-cheeked, clear-eyed, almost unwrinkled: a capable and reliable woman whose very appearance inspired confidence.

Dora's greeting ushered in one of those crowded days which keep the newly bereaved from feeling the full impact of their loss. Immediately after breakfast, Agnes was driven to the undertaker's by Great-aunt Adelaide's chauffeur-gardener; he was an elderly widower who lived in the second story of what had once been the stable, and, like Dora Dean, he appeared to go with the property. He explained carefully that he would have enjoyed meeting her train last night; but Mr. Kent thought that as a mark of proper respect he should be the one to do that, and of course he used his own car.

"Thank you, Eustace," said Mrs. Wainwright. She proceeded with a little speech of condolence, which did not interfere with her thinking that to extend courtesies and manage at the same time to get it all down in the bill was really pretty close to being a selfish man's dream of Heaven. Jerome Wainwright had been a lawyer, too, and a successful one; but he had been nothing like such a good schemer. Agnes felt the first faint stir of reluctant admiration for Mr. Kent.

At the undertaker's, she selected a simple, beautiful, and very expensive coffin. "Casket," the undertaker called it. That was part of his trade jargon, doubtless. In his vocabulary, people never did anything as crude as dying; they

69

"passed away." And they weren't buried; they were "laid to rest." As a matter of fact, even up here in Marshfield, undertakers themselves no longer did business under the old trade name; they now styled themselves "morticians."

Must there be so much fraud attendant on a deathbed? Or was the fraud, as in Mr. Kent's case, actually attendant on the money?

The coffin matter disposed of, Agnes nerved herself to say, "Now, if you please, I'd like to look at Mrs. Hammond." This was what she had been dreading; it was to her mind far the worse ordeal of the two.

It proved to be nothing like as bad as she had dreaded; in its way it was almost consoling. Mrs. Hammond was wearing a beautiful gray lace dress which she had brought back from Paris years ago: one of those lovely things which never go out of style. She looked very handsome, and singularly young. Perhaps the "mortician's" art was in some degree responsible, but not altogether. The healing touch had already been laid here by the Great Reconciler.

A wave of compunction came over Agnes. She had always got on famously with Great-aunt Adelaide. But she could have done more than she had done to show her affection and appreciation. *She wished that she had had a daughter like me! If I had known! If I had only known!*

It was the same old cry that the survivors had been uttering down through countless centuries: the cry of natural but bitter self-reproach. Because in a sense we did all know it. One of these days one of us would not be here any more. Sometimes the one would go, sometimes the other. We all knew that. More or less, we all disregarded it. Reiterate. Think the thing through. Resolve to do better in the future. Or if not better, at least differently. We all make mistakes.

70

But why should the same human being, supposedly sane, keep making the same silly mistakes over and over and over?

Agnes had a caller before lunch: a very dignified white-haired lady, survivor of a generation when morning calls were actually made in the morning. Her presence did something toward restoring Mrs. Wainwright's composure. An excellent lunch helped, too: waffles with fried chicken, topped off by more waffles with butter and honey. Hattie, the second maid, waited on table. But it was Dora Dean in person who brought in another helping of waffles. Dora's cooking was superb; and like all true artists, she liked to display her talent.

Two other ladies came soon after lunch. They were followed by the rector, who came to consult her about the funeral. He knew more about Great-aunt Adelaide's taste in hymns than Agnes did; between them they worked out a reasonable choice, "Abide With Me," "Rock of Ages," and "Ten Thousand Times Ten Thousand." They would have a vested choir, of course. What was Mrs. Wainwright's preference in voluntaries?

Agnes declared for "One Sweetly Solemn Thought." It had been sung at Jerome's funeral, and would take her back almost too vividly. But Agnes was not sparing her own susceptibilities; she wished only to do honor to Aunt Adelaide's memory.

The rector took himself off when Mr. Kent arrived. He wished to read Mrs. Hammond's will aloud to Mrs. Wainwright and the servants: tomorrow afternoon, if Agnes felt that she would have sufficiently recovered from "the services." If not, the day after tomorrow.

The servants? Oh, yes, Great-aunt Adelaide would have

remembered them in her will. Dora Dean certainly had more claim on her than her relatives did, even if Mrs Hammond had been blessed with more and closer relatives.

"Tomorrow will suit me perfectly," said Agnes. "I'd like to have everything in good shape before I leave for home."

"Naturally," agreed Mr. Kent. "I think you will approve of the way Mrs. Hammond set her affairs in order. She was an excellent businesswoman."

"Some women enjoy business," remarked Agnes. "I suppose they have a certain ability to begin with."

"Ability, yes. Then add training and character. Character is not the least ingredient in any recipe for success."

This time Mr. Kent had really said something. He was a windbag, yes; but he would scarcely have gone on working for Aunt Adelaide all these years if he had been a windbag and nothing else.

After he took himself off, Agnes long-distanced Miriam. "I've been waiting all day for you to call," said the invalid reproachfully.

Once more she was putting her stepmother on the defensive. But this time Agnes had her answer ready. "It has been a full day; and I saw no point to calling until I could give you a full report."

"Perhaps not; but it would have eased the strain. You've no idea, Ladybird, how I have you on my mind."

If Agnes had no idea of her position on Miriam's mind, she was too stupid even for a ladybird; she had been told times enough. But she again tried to make allowances for a convalescent's natural peevishness; as soon as sick people began to get better they began to behave worse.

Agnes went into some detail about today's activities and

72

the arrangements for tomorrow. She submitted to cross-examination, but stuck to her story. She was scolded for telling Mr. Kent that he could read the will tomorrow; she could give no answer to the question, "Why does he insist on reading it to you, anyhow?" Miriam could not remember that Papa ever did a thing like that. The possibility that he might have done so without informing his daughter never seemed to cross Miriam's mind. Neither did the idea that the ways of Tweedledum are not the ways of Tweedledee.

Agnes got rid of her finally. Perish the thought; but it almost seemed to her that Miriam resented her stepmother's ability to manage this crisis without a born Wainwright's help.

Agnes brushed her hair and changed into a housecoat. Then, realizing that this frivolous pale-blue garment might be considered a failure to show proper respect for the dead, she changed again, this time into a black afternoon dress which was the soberest thing her wardrobe afforded.

She had her trouble for her pains. Nobody came to the house that evening. Agnes was left to her own reflections; and they had their share of strangeness.

She deserted the cheerful side of the house where she felt so much at home, and crossed to the great front and back parlors. They had changed very little since Agnes first saw them; but it struck her tonight that there must have been one change there before her day.

A large, heavily framed, and obviously expensive portrait of Mr. Hammond hung over the mantel in the front parlor. A similar portrait of Mrs. Hammond occupied a similar position in the back parlor. Obviously they were companion pieces; they must once have hung together. But after her husband died, Aunt Adelaide had removed her effigy from the vicinity of his. Was there significance in that act? Or was Agnes getting fanciful?

It's almost as if she felt that he belonged inside a frame, thought Agnes. *A rigid man by his looks, even when he was paying a painter to flatter him.*

Dora Dean chanced to enter the room just at that moment; and Agnes started guiltily. But Dora was no mind reader, and she came on a simple domestic errand. She had told the maids that they might go to their rooms. Was there anything she herself could do for Mrs. Wainwright?

"Nothing, thank you," said Agnes. "You may go to your own room if you wish to, Dora. You must be very tired."

"We all have a trying day ahead of us," said Dora. But she lingered as if she would like to keep Agnes company.

"You knew Mrs. Hammond very well, didn't you, Dora?" asked Agnes.

"I knew her, and I loved her," said Dora simply. "But if you mean, was I close to her, no, I wasn't. I don't think anybody was ever very close to Mrs. Hammond."

Agnes had found out more than she bargained for. She suddenly realized that she was extremely tired. Worse still, she was bitterly depressed.

"I'm going upstairs myself now, Dora," she said. "Will you see to everything, as usual, and call me in good season tomorrow."

"At seven, Mrs. Wainwright."

"At seven, yes. That ought to work out just fine."

Undressing slowly in the dressing room, and then making her way to rest through the great lonely bedroom, Agnes

74

felt a dank inner chill unlike anything she had ever known before. When you came right down to it, was anybody ever really close to anybody else? And in spite of the brave show that many of us put on, was anybody ever really happy?

7.

ON THE DAY OF THE FUNERAL, THE SHAFTS WOULD HOLD UP the horse. All the arrangements had been made, and the professionals took over. All anybody had to do was follow orders.

Agnes had one bad moment while the mourners were being seated. As official representative of "the family," she had naturally invited Dora Dean to sit with her. The pew immediately behind theirs was allocated to the two maids; the gardener-chauffeur sat across the aisle from them. All at once it came over Mrs. Wainwright that here at the end of a long and exemplary life, Great-aunt Adelaide was being attended only by strangers.

Dora Dean was more friend than servant, to be sure. Agnes

76

was the daughter Aunt Adelaide wished she had had. But they were neither of them kith and kin. The one surviving relative had been detained at a distance. The essential loneliness of death cast a melancholy light back upon what must have been a lonely life.

Agnes shuddered, and Dora Dean glanced at her apprehensively. Agnes laid a reassuring hand on Dora's arm, and in her turn gained confidence. It was not for Mrs. Wainwright to put on a show of grief. Not in the face of Dora's loss, which was so much greater than hers. Not in the purlieu of the Episcopal Church.

All at once the Church took over. Agnes, glancing discreetly about her, had a sudden sense of being at home. She was grateful to John Wesley for his Methodists. She respected everybody's religious belief. But she felt, as she hadn't felt in years, the warm sensation of belonging.

The music took over in its turn, and the beautiful Burial Service. Everything went off without a hitch; and Agnes was soothed almost into numbness.

The church part of it was over now. They were ready to accompany Great-aunt Adelaide on the final stage of the journey to her last long rest.

Mrs. Wainwright and Dora Dean prepared to follow the coffin down the aisle. The maids stood ready to fall into step behind them. Then all at once a piercing shaft of awareness shot through the mantle of Agnes's slumbrous serenity.

Directly behind the two maids stood a man alone. A tall man. A handsome man. Agnes thought for an instant that she had seen him somewhere before. Then she realized that she hadn't. Not this man, nor anybody like him.

Her impression subsided during the Committal Service, with its beautiful words of final peace and reconciliation.

77

At its close, Agnes spoke a brief sentence to the clergyman. She was careful not to look at anybody else.

Then, strangely enough, it was all over. In a few minutes more they were back at the Hammond mansion. Dora was suggesting that Mrs. Wainwright have a nice cup of tea; that is, if she thought it wouldn't spoil her lunch.

Agnes didn't especially want tea; but she suspected that Dora would like to make it. She enjoyed ministering to people; and the busier she kept, the less time the poor thing would have to realize that the days of her ministry under this roof were numbered.

"A cup of tea will be fine," said Agnes. "Nothing with it please, Dora. And go a little light on lunch. We have a good deal of the day still ahead of us."

They changed clothes, freshened themselves, sat down together. The cup of tea, combined with the companionship, brought back Agnes's memory in all its normal keenness. Old Demon Curiosity raised its two-pronged head.

"Dora," she said, "who was that man sitting just behind us in church? A large man, rather nice-looking. I don't remember ever meeting him."

For an instant, Dora looked puzzled, as well she might. "Rather nice-looking" was a furious understatement.

Then Dora remembered. "That was Dr. Sheridan, Mrs. Hammond's physician. The young doctor."

" 'Young' doctor?"

"That's what people often called him, to distinguish him from his father, who took care of the Hammonds for many years. That was Dr. Frederick. This one is Dr. Hugh."

"He was alone in church, wasn't he?" Agnes bit her tongue too late; the words were out. What had ever possessed her to let on that she noticed Dr. Sheridan's solitary state?

78

"His wife died about a year ago. They never had any children."

"If he stays a widower after the first year or two, it will be from choice. That is, unless Marshfield is different from any other town I ever heard about."

"It isn't. There are plenty of women who have no objection to being a second wife. Oh!"

This time it was Dora who bit her tongue. For the moment she had forgotten that Agnes Wainwright was a second wife.

Agnes herself had all but forgotten it. The first wife's legacy now sprang to mind again. Agnes went to the telephone, long-distanced Miriam, and reported on the funeral.

Miriam was pleased at her promptness. Gratified too, perhaps, that Ladybird had learned her lesson and did not again keep her preceptress waiting all day for a phone call. She let Agnes off with less than the usual number of questions, though not without a reminder that she expected another report when the afternoon's conference was finished.

It was with an easy conscience that Agnes sat down to Dora Dean's idea of a light luncheon: homemade beef broth, chicken salad, popovers, and icebox cake. If it had been at all feasible, Agnes would have liked to stay here and see what Dora served for a real meal: Thanksgiving dinner, say.

Just as well that it was out of the question! That much more of Dora's cooking would have made Agnes hate to face not only her special censor, but the very scales themselves.

Agnes was curious as to the contents of Great-aunt Adelaide's will. In the whodunits, the wealthy aged relative always had strange testamentary fancies, and the putative heirs had urgent if discreditable reasons for hastening the rich old so-and-so's demise. That had no resemblance to the present situation. Mrs. Hammond had been the least in the world subject to caprices; and what few heirs she might have were highly respectable as well as solvent.

Yet that afternoon's tableau had every quality which characterized similar scenes in detective stories. It also suggested that morning's grouping at the funeral. This time, Dora Dean sat slightly to the rear of Agnes; but the two maids were behind them, as aforetime, and Eustace Smith opposite them at a decent distance. Mr. Kent had brought along his legal acolyte, too; and his professional manner when he faced the little group was strongly tinged with the pontifical.

As soon as Mr. Kent began to read, however, the scene was transformed. Agnes was no longer reminded of the police romance. She felt that she was present at an episode in a regular novel. Not a very recent novel, either.

The document began as all wills did begin, and probably had to. A will was drawn to serve a definite purpose, not as a literary exercise. I, Adelaide Wainwright Hammond, being all that my countless predecessors have been, do publish and declare this as my last Will and Testament, hereby revoking . . . I direct my executor to pay all my just debts and funeral expenses. That will take care of the mortician.

Now there should be a bequest to church or charity. There was. Ten thousand dollars to St. Andrew's Church, Marshfield, New York. Liberal but not lavish. Which was as it should be; St. Andrew's had not appeared to Agnes to be greatly in need of funds.

Now began the personal bequests. Five hundred dollars

each to any maids who should be in Mrs. Hammond's employ at the time of her demise, and an additional hundred dollars for each year they had been in Mrs. Hammond's service. One of the maids caught her breath at that, and the other shushed her.

To my driver and gardener, Eustace Smith, the sum of five thousand dollars, provided that he shall still be in my employ at the time of my demise.

To my faithful friend and housekeeper, Dora Dean, the sum of ten thousand dollars outright, three thousand dollars a year income from the proceeds of a trust fund to be set up in her behalf, "and that painting of the Lakes of Killarney which she has always admired." No mention here of being still in Mrs. Hammond's employ. Some things could always be taken for granted. Dora stirred in her chair, but made no sound.

To my great-niece, Miriam Wainwright, the sum of twenty-five thousand dollars outright. Good as far as it went (Miriam was too young to have a trust fund established for her). But if Great-aunt Adelaide really was a wealthy woman, wasn't this being a little niggardly toward her next of kin?

Then came the climax, that "All other property, real and personal, whereof I die possessed." Agnes thought her hearing had suddenly failed her. Or if she had heard, she had failed to understand. The bulk of the estate was left to "my nephew's widow, Agnes Costen Wainwright."

That was the name. The address was given, too. But Agnes Costen Wainwright was just too bewildered to take it in.

There was one further clause, the usual threat to anybody who contested the will. Agnes barely heard that one; she had turned a little sick and giddy.

81

She began to stammer, "I don't deserve . . ." But did she utter the words aloud, or did she merely frame them in her mind? Nobody else seemed to hear them.

Dora Dean patted Agnes's arm and said, "I told you she thought the world of you." Mr. Kent shook Agnes's hand and said, "A very judicious will. I wish I could say the same of more of them." The acolyte began to put papers together. The maids slipped out; Eustace had already vanished. The great Third Act was over. But was the curtain about to rise on another drama?

"There are a few questions I'd like to ask you, Mr. Kent," said Agnes.

"At your service, dear lady," he assured her. "Dear lady" was condescending, perhaps; but Agnes did not resent it. She had no claim to being a second Portia.

"This house belongs to me?"

"Indeed it does. There are certain formalities to be gone through with, of course. But this house was left to you."

"The house in Antioch belongs to me, too," Agnes pointed out.

"That's your home, of course. You may find that you wish to sell this house. There's no obligation to keep both of them, though you could well afford to do so."

"Sell a house like this?"

Agnes meant that such a sale would betray a tradition and upset an established order. But Mr. Kent assumed that she referred to financial possibilities. "There's not much market for a house like this," he warned her. "Too large, and too expensive to maintain."

"Things don't balance very well, do they?" said Agnes. "A house like this belongs to a family which is running out; but a poor man with six children has to be satisfied with a hovel."

"He might have thought of those things before he had six children."

Agnes wondered what Mr. Kent himself had done along that line, but didn't feel that she could very well ask. It was left to him to go on, "This has quite taken your breath away, hasn't it, Mrs. Wainwright?"

"I'm still gasping," Agnes confessed. "It was lovely of Mrs. Hammond, of course. But I'm not sure I ought to take all that. Is it really Wainwright money?"

"Very little, perhaps. There's Hammond money, too. And a good deal of it Mrs. Hammond made herself. She had every moral as well as legal right to leave it as she saw fit."

"I still don't see why she saw fit. Don't misunderstand me, please. I'm truly grateful. It will take time to settle the estate?"

"A year or more. You can always come over here again, or we can come to see you. But if you could manage a few days, or even weeks, here right now, that would make things simpler for everybody."

"I'll stay, with pleasure. I have no definite plans." Plans of my own making, she thought. Perhaps she needn't always be bound by the plans that other people made for her.

"There are many matters which must be taken into consideration," Mr. Kent went on. "There are inheritance taxes, to begin with. They will be heavier in your case because the kinship is not close."

Dora Dean had gone out of earshot at the beginning of the interview. The acolyte was officially deaf. Agnes drew a long breath, and decided to test her powers as Mrs. Hammond's heiress.

83

"I had promised to telephone my stepdaughter about the will," she said. "I wonder if you would do that in my stead? The whole thing is still far from clear to me."

"That is an excellent idea," said Mr. Kent. "We had expected to write Miss Wainwright, of course. But this is Saturday afternoon. It will be much better if we get in touch with her at once."

He signaled to the acolyte, who wrote down Miriam's phone number. Then he rose to take his leave.

"Congratulations and condolences, Mrs. Wainwright," he said. "This bequest will make you a rich woman. As things go in Marshfield, that is. I'm not judging by New York standards."

A rich woman by Agnes's own standard, surely. She wasn't exactly a pauper to begin with. To her that had, more was being added. But it wasn't the money alone that mattered. Much more important was the prospect of vastly changed circumstances.

She assured Mr. Kent that no, he need not call her back after he had talked to Miss Wainwright. She set him on his way, and turned to face a changing future.

For an hour, she sat alone in the garden. Then on her way upstairs to freshen for dinner, she sought out Dora Dean and said, "Do whatever you think best about tomorrow and the maids' time off. It's too early yet to make plans; but for the present, we'll just go on as we are."

"Thank you, Mrs. Wainwright. There are bound to be changes. She—Mrs. Hammond—I can't realize yet that she's gone."

Dora's lips twitched and she blinked away the tears. But before Agnes could make up her mind to attempt consolation, Dora was again the ministering one. "Wouldn't you like to lie down for a while now, Mrs. Wainwright? I can call you whenever you say; or dinner could be put back, if you'd rather."

"Go ahead just as you had planned, Dora. I'll have some suggestions later on, probably, but not until I get my breath back."

"Took you by surprise, didn't it?" Dora was gratified by this final proof of her late employer's astuteness. "She was a great one to keep her thoughts to herself, Mrs. Hammond was."

Agnes's bewilderment persisted all during dinner. She had one moment of almost too great clearness, when the telephone rang and she feared it might be Miriam in search of an accounting. But the call proved to be a wrong number; and Agnes decided that she was wasting perfectly good worry. There were some things that simply were not said.

She did remember to inquire about Mr. Kent's marital status. He was a married man with two daughters, both of them married; he had one grandson. Another dwindling family with means; a further contrast to the penniless oaf with six children.

Not that Agnes planned to seek out such a person and endow him. Beggars never needed to be sought, anyhow. Mrs. Wainwright had always had plenty of chances to give money away; and when word of this new bequest got around, there would be added throngs eager to help her into Heaven through their own special needles' eyes.

After dinner, Agnes strolled through the house, feeling afresh its atmosphere and charm, yet unable to realize that it was now hers to alter or destroy. To preserve it as it stood was out of the question. Even if it had been feasible, a home preserved in that spirit was a home no longer. It was a museum, cold, sterile, pervaded by the stench of embalming fluid.

In the back parlor, Agnes stood for some time, gazing up at the portrait of Mrs. Hammond. It seemed to her that Aunt Adelaide was in a sense actually here; what they had laid away in the cemetery was only a simulacrum. Yet how get in touch with that spirit? How divine the secret intentions of a woman who even in life had been noted for keeping her own counsel?

She had trusted Agnes, and Agnes wouldn't let her down. Beyond that, everything was hazy.

There was no need to go beyond that while the whole thing was still so new and strange. Sleeping on it would help. Later on, there might be people who could cast a little light: the rector for one, and the doctor. She must get to know them both better, for their own sakes as well as for what she might be able to learn from them.

Agnes had recognized the difficulty; that was the first long step toward solving it. She concluded her tour and went upstairs. To the guestroom; but she was a guest no longer. What a difference a little time could make in anybody's circumstances! This was almost as great a change as that little ten minutes in church which had transformed Miss Agnes Costen into Mrs. Jerome Wainwright.

The one shift was contingent on the other. If she had never become Mrs. Wainwright, she would not now be pondering . . .

Hold on! This was getting nonsensical; she must relax. Agnes undressed, took a hot bath, and, on her way back to bed, picked up a paperback. Her slight sensation of guilt was natural but irrational. If she had tackled a devotional manual or a philosophic treatise, it would have been beside her own purpose; and it couldn't have done Aunt Adelaide any good.

The unpopular millionaire was just nicely on his way toward becoming "the body" when a knock at the door heralded Dora Dean with a covered plate in her hand. "I brought you a little something just in case," she explained. "Mrs. Hammond always liked to keep a plate of cookies on her bedside table, in case she was to wake in the night and feel hungry."

One more proof that Agnes was now the mistress here. The position had its privileges as well as its responsibilities. At a moment like this, the privileges were what counted.

Agnes found the cookies a wonderful addition to the whodunit. She wondered a little at their being offered on a plate instead of in a jar. Had it been Mrs. Hammond's custom to finish them all at a sitting? Or was it more what Dora Dean expected of Mrs. Wainwright?

But it was not for Agnes to look a gift snack in the mouth. It was her own time she was wasting, her own digestion she was imperiling. She was neither a young idiot nor an old fool. Nicely balanced between those two extremes, she spaced the physical provender and the mental food so that they would be likely to come out even.

Two-thirds of the way through both, she suddenly realized that the one thing now essential to her sense of well-being was a glass of milk. No one would be any the wiser, or any the worse off, if she were to sneak down and help herself to one.

She was halfway out of bed, with her hand stretched toward her dressing gown, when it came over her that there was no need for her to sneak. This was her house. The kitchen was her kitchen. If her money hadn't exactly paid for the milk, at least she was legally entitled to it.

She drank one glass standing in the kitchen, and carried a second up to bed with her. That gave her one thing more to enjoy, and to space.

The milk slightly outlasted the other two. They came out even; the plate was emptied, and all but licked clean, by the time the gyves were clapped on the least likely suspect.

Agnes swallowed the last sip of milk, and reached up to turn off the light. She forbore to look at the clock. It was late. It might even be very late. Just how late made no difference to her. What mattered was that the complicated and amazing day had finally ended; and Time the all-powerful, Time the Archenemy, the Great Destroyer, was for once in a friendly mood. At the instant that Agnes turned the light out, Time was her foremost ally.

8.

SUNDAY, A SHARP REACTION SET IN. AGNES WAS TIRED BUT restless. She could not very well go to church the day after Aunt Adelaide's funeral. A drive into the country might have helped; but here too the proprieties stood in her way. It came over her for the first time that here in Marshfield she was not a private citizen; she was the representative of the Hammond family.

Later on, she would get used to the situation: would face up to the responsibilities of her new position and take advantage of its privileges. But it would take some doing.

Perhaps what really ailed her was stage fright. She had spent too many years as a clinging vine, though she had never been completely reconciled to the role. But now that

89

she was to be put to the test, she might not find it so easy to stand on her own feet. Had she the toughness of fiber to gain strength by exercising her new power? A question much easier to ask than to answer.

Late in the afternoon, she had a visitor. Dora Dean, announcing him, smiled as if she had invented him. Agnes's heart beat high, and she felt herself blushing like a schoolgirl. Yet what was there to get so excited about? It was only natural that Dr. Sheridan should come around to pay his respects; and for all that Agnes could tell at the moment, their first meeting might well be their last.

He was waiting for her in the front parlor. Agnes fancied that there was a shade of wistfulness in his manner when she joined him in the familiar surroundings. He might well feel regretful. Not only had he lost a good friend; Aunt Adelaide's death marked the passing of the old order.

She was at her ease with him almost at once; and she presently found herself confiding something of her perplexity. It was news to him that Aunt Adelaide had left Agnes the bulk of her property.

"I'm sure she made a wise choice," he said courteously.

"If you're sure, it's more than I am. I'll try my level best; but the whole business is complicated." Agnes smiled suddenly. "When news about the will gets around, won't tongues start wagging!"

"They've already started, or I miss my guess. Even in her lifetime, Mrs. Hammond was something pretty special. Now—!"

"Now people will wonder why she practically passed over her next of kin in favor of a little sillybilly like me."

"Let them talk; she had her reasons. Mrs. Hammond was not a person who acted from caprice or prejudice."

90

"But my stepdaughter is the executive type. She likes to make decisions."

"So I've gathered from Mrs. Hammond." Dr. Sheridan did not quite keep the dryness out of his tone.

Agnes had her answer. She wasn't the only person who resented Miriam's bossiness.

He stayed only a few minutes longer. His visit had done Agnes good. She got up her nerve now and telephoned Miriam that she was prolonging her stay indefinitely. Would Miriam ask Rosa Lee to pack more of Agnes's clothes and send them to her by express?

"Perhaps you'd better talk to her yourself," Miriam snapped. "Why don't you call her tomorrow?"

"She will naturally consult you," pleaded Agnes. At heart she knew better. Rosa Lee disliked having Miriam interfere in any affair that concerned herself and her beloved Miss Agnes.

Rosa Lee Montgomery was a Johnny-come-lately compared to Dora Dean. At the thought of that faithful retainer's present desolation, Agnes's heart sank again. Dora was being well provided for in a material way, but the ending of her long years of devoted service must leave her with a terrible sense of loss.

On an impulse, Agnes went looking for Dora, and asked to be shown that painting of the Lakes of Killarney which had been important enough to figure in Aunt Adelaide's will. Actually, Agnes knew where it was. She wanted to draw Dora into talk of the dead woman; in it she might find some consolation. Agnes herself would be better off listening than moping. Her attitude this morning had been a form of ingratitude; and that came pretty close to being the cardinal sin.

Soon after breakfast on Monday, Agnes called the house in Antioch. Rosa Lee answered the phone. Evidently she had not been told that she might expect the call. She acted surprised and delighted to hear from her Miss Agnes; and when the nature of the commission was made known to her, she laughed aloud. "Planning to stay awhile?" she inquired.

"Are you so pleased to be rid of me?"

"Lordy, no! Speaking for myself, Miss Agnes, I wish you were here this very minute telling me to fry the chicken."

"It makes your work easier to have me away."

"It makes less chicken to fry, that's all."

Clearly, Rosa Lee was not enjoying a session of Miriam in control. Agnes took time off to inquire about Miss Wainwright's recovery. She was sitting up every day now, it appeared, and was beginning to talk of letting the nurse go.

"Tell her I inquired," said Agnes. "About my clothing, Rosa Lee, you might send along enough for two weeks. I may not be here that long, but . . ."

"Nobody know where nobody be in two weeks," Rosa Lee pointed out. She dropped into dialect only when it suited her purpose; a vague foreboding shot through Agnes's mind. But Rosa Lee promptly shifted to details.

For the next five minutes, both women enjoyed themselves. Then Agnes wound up, "That ought to do very nicely. You can phone the expressman to call for the package."

"Sure you don't want me to get on the train and bring it over to you, Miss Agnes?"

"There isn't that much hurry. But any time you want to come over and see me, Rosa Lee, I shall be delighted."

"Any time?"

"Any time. You needn't warn me in advance, either. This is a big house, with three indoor servants falling over one

92

another to wait on poor little me. We can always stretch to a cup of tea, or even a sandwich."

"Or a cup of tea *and* a sandwich," amended Rosa Lee. "Thank you, Miss Agnes. I'll take you up on that one of these days."

With Antioch off her mind, Agnes phoned Mr. Kent's office. She was answered with professional caginess; a strange woman's voice might herald anything from a charitable appeal to a personal hard-luck story, and after all, his time was worth something. But as soon as she identified herself, Mr. Kent in person came on the wire.

Agnes stated that she would like to come down to his office and talk to him. He offered to come to the house. Presumably he was moved both by courtesy and cupidity: by sympathy for the bereaved, and by the fact that, like a doctor, he could charge double for house visits.

She refused. She was curious to see The Kent on its native heath. Also, she wanted to get out of the house, to do so on an errand which could pass muster anywhere. There was something to be said for the old days in which the horses had to be exercised. "My driver," Aunt Adelaide's will had dubbed Eustace; Agnes liked that.

"I realize that a busy lawyer's time is taken up in advance," Agnes sailed on. "I'd appreciate it, however, if you could get me in tomorrow. Either morning or afternoon; I can suit your convenience."

"I can make it this afternoon, if you can," said Mr. Kent. "I had intended to go to court for a time; but I can send Mr. Loomis in my stead."

Mr.—? Oh, yes, the acolyte! Agnes protested. Mr. Kent insisted. Finally, the appointment was made for three.

So much accommodation made Agnes uneasy for a

93

moment. Was Aunt Adelaide's estate due to be swallowed up in costs, like another Jarndyce-and-Jarndyce? Then common sense came to her aid. Hers was not the only breast in which curiosity ever stirred.

"How do I get word to Eustace that I want the car this afternoon?" she asked Dora Dean.

"He's always come in for orders after he had his breakfast. Then he could plan his work for the day. Of course, if something came up later on, he was usually somewhere around the place."

"We'll have to go hunting him, then?"

Dora grinned. "Not today you won't. He's still cluttering up my kitchen."

Agnes sent her orders through Dora. Then she settled herself in the sitting room and began to go over in her own mind the points on which she desired enlightenment.

The legal side of the situation could be easily clarified. Or no, "clarified" wasn't the proper word. Lawyers made their money by befogging an issue, not by casting light on it. But Agnes could learn from Mr. Kent the essentials of the technical question, and make due allowance for his if's, and's, and but's.

It was the human element on which she needed light: these unknown or little-known people who had been, in a sense, thrust on her hands. How much could Mr. Kent help her here? How much would he?

She would do her best to get him interested, to learn all that he knew or could find out for her. After—oh, let the "after" wait its turn!

W. R. Kent, Attorney at Law, occupied a spacious suite on the third floor of the First National Bank Building. Agnes was received there by a prune-faced woman who looked as

94

if she might have been selected for the job some twenty-five or thirty years before by Mrs. W. R. Kent in a jealous mood. But Agnes remembered from Jerome's day that competent law stenographers were pearls of great price; willingness to sit on the boss's knee was no part of their qualifications.

Indeed, a young and pretty girl would have been out of place in these surroundings, where all the furniture and fittings were so good that they just wouldn't wear out. They took on at worst a monied shabbiness, like a coat of first-class Irish tweed.

Mr. Kent received her in the second of two waiting rooms. He showed her around the establishment at once: the law library, "storeroom" worthy of Dickens, Mr. Loomis's minor office. Then he ushered her into his own private office.

Agnes was really impressed. Everything here spoke of worth, dignity, a settled order. Those qualities were not the same as supernatural wisdom. Not the same as magnanimity and loving kindness, either. But they had solid merits of their own.

Facing Mr. Kent across his desk, Agnes explained, "I'd like to read over Mrs. Hammond's will. I was so startled Saturday that I didn't altogether take it in."

Mr. Kent rang for a copy of the will. It had been made out in quadruplicate; one copy had been deposited with "the bank" and he had two here; the fourth must be somewhere among Mrs. Hammond's papers.

"I haven't looked," said Agnes. Indeed, it had not occurred to her that she was now free to rummage among Mrs. Hammond's papers.

The bank was to act as executor; that fact had escaped her. Mr. Kent and Mr. Loomis had signed as witnesses. So had one Hazel R. Scofield, presumably the acidulous secretary.

95

The will was dated last January; for the better part of a year, Agnes had had "great expectations," and been none the wiser for them.

"You are offering this for probate soon?" she asked. The question was in the nature of a nudge; lawyers hated to do anything soon.

"Yes, very shortly," Mr. Kent assured her.

"It takes some time to settle an estate. Until that is done, how do I manage about running expenses?"

The bank would take care of all that. Mrs. Hammond had been not only a depositor but a substantial stockholder.

"That's fine," said Agnes. It was about what she had expected. Someone could always be found to handle business details for her; what couldn't be deputized was the human situation.

"I'm staying on here for a while," she said. "Once I get the hang of things I'll find it easier to make plans. Right now I'm still at a good deal of a loss."

"It isn't strictly necessary," said Mr. Kent. "But if you conveniently can remain in Marshfield, it might be advisable."

"I don't have to suit anybody's convenience but my own," said Agnes. In her own ears it sounded like a reckless statement. But it was true—or she could make it true. She was faced with the chance of a lifetime.

Mr. Kent accompanied her down to the bank and into the president's private office. She was treated there with deference. Agnes was beginning to enjoy this heiress business. It was such a pleasant change from being Ladybirded.

Her business was presently concluded, and Mr. Kent escorted her to her car. The one touch wanting was some Sir Walter Raleigh to lay down his coat and let her walk

96

on it; but in these cement and asphalt days, that would really have been superfluous. "Home, Eustace," she directed. Yes, just like that, "Home"!

She sat in smiling silence until they were clear of the business section. Then it occurred to her to ask, "How often did Mrs. Hammond pay you?"

"Every week, generally on Friday."

"I'll see to it this coming Friday, when you have two weeks' pay coming to you," Agnes promised. "That is, if you can afford to wait that long. You aren't in debt, are you?"

"Debt?" Eustace echoed the word as if it tasted bad. Then another thought occurred to him. "You're not giving me notice, Mrs. Wainwright?"

"Hardly," answered Agnes. "I don't drive. Anyhow, we can't let the lawn and garden go to rack and ruin."

"It's good to hear you say that. Lots of young people don't appreciate a fine old place."

Aunt Adelaide thought I would, flashed into Agnes's mind. The reasons for her bequest were becoming increasingly clear. A fine old place. Fine old family retainers. Mrs. Hammond had felt that Agnes could be trusted with them. Agnes intended to justify that trust. She believed that she would find the task much to her liking.

Dora Dean greeted her as if Agnes had returned from a long journey. "Make tea for the two of us, if you please, Dora," Agnes ordered. "There is something I want to talk to you about."

Agnes was halfway up the stairs when she realized that that might have sounded as if she had some fault to find. Well, it was said, and there was no taking it back. Next time she might have a happier inspiration.

Ten minutes later, Agnes came downstairs, considerably

cleaner and beginning to be a little bit hungry. She established herself in the sitting room. "The" sitting room. It used to belong to Mrs. Hammond. It now belonged—or almost belonged—to Mrs. Wainwright. If she didn't do the honors of it, who would?

She poured the tea carefully. She sipped her own. She complimented Dora Dean on her cinnamon toast. Again Dora was being treated here as a guest.

Then Agnes sat back in her chair and began, "This whole thing has come over me rather suddenly. I've spent a full afternoon, but I hope a profitable one. What I would like to consult you about, Dora, is your future plans."

Consult was a good word. Maybe it was the one that broke Dora Dean down. Her lips quivered. She tried to smile, tried not to cry, finally managed to gesture for another cup of tea.

"Mrs. Wainwright," she choked, "I simply haven't any!"

Agnes very carefully poured the tea. Then she said. "Don't you want to tell me about it? Tell me that right now and here. Here, where you have been at home so long."

Dora Dean took two small sips of tea, stared at Agnes, and blurted out, "I wish I knew what I was going to do."

"You are in the same boat with me," said Agnes softly. "Go on."

She couldn't even be certain that Dora Dean heard her. Dora stammered on, "Mrs. Hammond was always so generous! So much more than generous! She left me so much of everything! So much more than I need—or want! But you're right, this place has been home to me so long! I hate to see a home broken up."

All these exclamations from the usually placid Dora told Agnes more than did the words themselves. Her astonish-

98

ment must have betrayed itself in her looks, for Dora added hastily, "I didn't mean to complain. I should count myself a very lucky woman."

"I asked, didn't I?" said Agnes.

There was a short pause, during which the two women avoided each other's eyes. Then Agnes looked up and said quietly, "I'm staying on here for the present. I don't know just how long; but it may be several weeks."

"You're staying here?" Dora repeated incredulously. "Right here in Mrs. Hammond's house?" Then, at the sound of her own words, she flushed with embarrassment and added, "But it's your house now, isn't it? What ever made me forget that?"

Agnes smiled. "I'm not yet used to the idea myself. It's going to take some time."

Dora returned Agnes's smile. "If there's anything I can do to help you, Mrs. Wainwright, you have only to say the word."

"There will be plenty later on. Tonight just give me one of your good dinners. After that we can both relax."

"I had planned on steak."

"I see no reason to change such a good plan as that."

"Perhaps you'd like a glass of wine with your dinner? To celebrate, sort of."

Just what she was supposed to celebrate was not quite clear; but Agnes agreed to the glass of wine. She was looking over Aunt Adelaide's cellar with respect and some bewilderment (Agnes was not much of a connoisseur), when she was summoned to the telephone. Her sense of guilt led her to ask, "Is it Miss Wainwright?" though there was surely nothing that Miriam need call her about.

"No, it's a man," the maid reported. "He says he's Mr. Jones."

The man had good reason for saying that he was Mr. Jones. It was her train acquaintance, Tom, calling from his home town. He professed himself delighted that Agnes was still in residence at Aunt Adelaide's. Would it be all right if he came over to visit her for an hour or two this evening?

"Better make it tomorrow," said Agnes.

It wasn't until after they had agreed on an hour and hung up that she realized what had happened. She had merely made the conventional response expected from a well-brought-up girl of her generation; proper young ladies did not accept last-minute dates. But to find herself actually accepting a date after all these months of Sully with his tepid and divided attentions—that experience took her breath away.

She had all evening to get it back. After the steak and a glass of imported claret, Agnes bethought herself of Aunt Adelaide's record collection, which was housed in a series of cabinets in the back parlor; an ancient Victrola flanked it on one side, a fairly recent three-speed player on the other. The collection was carefully indexed. The sight of so much system gave Agnes an idea: she would play through all the Beethoven symphonies in order. It would take some time, to be sure. But the evening was yet young; and if Agnes chose to sit up half the night hearkening to the strains of the Great Master, she need answer to nobody for her choice.

What she failed to reckon with was her own inability to absorb more than a certain amount. She lasted beautifully through the magnificent *Fifth*, and of course the *Sixth* was easy going. But after that her attention began to lag; and when she was finally faced with the climactic *Ninth*, Agnes repented of her own rashness. The *Choral Symphony* might rank as one of the greatest human achievements; but so far as Mrs. Wainwright was concerned, it could wait.

It could wait, and it did. Agnes yawned her way upstairs, and was asleep as soon as her head touched the pillow.

9.

Tom Jones appeared with a handful of whodunits. "These have great sentimental value," he explained. "It was their like that brought us together in the first place."

"I've heard of people who were introduced by a cinder in the eye," remarked Agnes.

"Meaning—?"

"Meaning thank you very much, Mr. Tom Jones. It's kind of you to remember me."

They were standing in the great front parlor. Agnes laid the books on a small table, and motioned her visitor to a seat.

He looked around him with some curiosity. "So this is the great House of Hammond."

"Exactly." Agnes's eyes began to twinkle. "At present

102

I'm curator of the museum; and I'm a frightful greenhorn."

"But surely this is your future home?"

"I still feel like a guest here. But let's get going. Perhaps you would like to have me show you over the house? Or perhaps a glass of wine would refresh you after your journey?"

"What stately language we use in this stately mansion! I know you are going to enjoy living here."

Agnes's defenses collapsed. "All right, then, take both! After a conducted tour, you'll be ready for a drink. We'll begin with Mr. Hammond, there, gazing down at you from his frame."

"Which becomes him as perhaps nothing else could."

Agnes shot him a glance. Perhaps he was only talking; perhaps at some time over the years he had heard things. "Meaning just what?" she asked a trifle sharply.

"He doesn't look like a man whose ghost would walk."

Agnes felt a pang of contrition. Mr. Hammond had lain quiet in his grave for years. But with Aunt Adelaide scarcely cold in hers, Agnes had no right to be enjoying herself even thus mildly. Not here of all places. Not here and now.

Agnes had long craved independence; now she saw that it meant having nobody to turn to. Yet that was the state in which Aunt Adelaide had lived for many years, and had at length died.

Unless in some curious way she was now turning to Agnes. Perhaps a ghost did indeed walk here, and only she could lay it. She turned eyes of distress on Tom Jones.

His flippancy fell from him instantly. "You've been through a lot lately, haven't you? Perhaps you'd rather I went away now, and came back some other time."

If he left her now, he would never come seeking her again;

and frail as the tie between them was, he was company, and she liked him.

"I want you to stay," she said. "It has all been sudden and startling. But I must try not to cross any bridge until I come to it."

"Try not to cross two bridges at the same time," advised Tom Jones.

He's almost as silly as Sully, flashed through Agnes's mind. When would she see Sully again? There were times when she thought him plumb foolish; right now, she caught herself missing him.

She began a circuit of the room, calling Tom's attention to feature after feature. He was duly appreciative, though not enthusiastic. In the back parlor, however, he stood for some moments looking up at the portrait of Aunt Adelaide. His only comment was, "She must have been very lonely sometimes."

Agnes's eyes and his met briefly; there passed between the two of them one of those communicative flashes which tell more than words do. He too had been married. He had witnessed the death of love, which must be even worse than the death of the body. He wanted her to know it.

They continued their tour on the same terms as before until they came to the dining room. There Tom Jones suddenly took over, and showed not only highly specialized knowledge but real enthusiasm. He was of as well as in the family business; he knew all that there was to be known about china.

It was the same in the butler's pantry, until he brought himself to a sudden halt. "I've been delivering quite a lecture, haven't I? Suppose we call this the end."

104

"The intermission, rather," suggested Agnes. "Your throat must be very dry."

"Indeed it is. Almost as dry as the matter which has been pouring from it."

Agnes started to call for last night's bottle, but changed her mind. This was neither the time nor the place for cheese-paring.

"Wouldn't you like to look at Mrs. Hammond's cellar?" she suggested. "It's fairly large; I've an idea it's good."

"You're willing to trust me in there?"

"I'm out for any information I can pick up. I offer to buy you a drink. That's a fair exchange, isn't it?"

"Probably not. It shows you have a nice nature; but I knew that already."

What happened in the wine cellar was a further surprise to Agnes. Tom Jones surveyed it, walked the length of the room, turned to her, and said, "It is a true wine cellar. I didn't suppose there was one like this in all Upper New York State."

"How about what's in it?"

"What's in it may be worthy of the setting. My own choice would be to stand right here while somebody brings me a whisky and water. I'm a guest, though. I'm not giving orders."

The guest's wish was the same as an order. Agnes had Dora Dean fetch him his drink; she also bespoke a glass of wine for herself.

Tom Jones was still nursing his drink when they returned to the ground floor and he took his leave. Agnes picked up his offering of paperbacks. She was halfway to her bedroom with it when she remembered that the *Ninth Symphony* still awaited her pleasure.

105

It would have to wait a little longer. Agnes had other matters to mull over.

Actually, she did very little mulling. She fell to on Tom Jones's offerings. They were seven in number. Was that because he knew or guessed that she had had four on the train, and determined to go her several better? Walter Sullivan's number was often four; but there was no way Tom could know that.

The first whodunit dealt with a "private eye." Eye though he was called, his foresight appeared to be largely hindsight; but the amount of physical punishment which he could take was extraordinary—not to say incredible.

Agnes sweetened his exploits with the cookies which Dora Dean had faithfully supplied. She saved a few for the second book. But when it proved to be about another private eye who, after he had been treacherously kicked downstairs, required no repairs beyond a hair-comb and a clean shirt, Agnes decided that a second such hero was rather a test of endurance—the reader's as well as his own—than a bedtime treat. On top of all this, half a glass of milk was enough to send her to sleep.

Wednesday saw the arrival of a large package from Antioch. It contained not only many and varied articles of clothing, but the pictures of her father and mother which Agnes was accustomed to keeping on her dressing table, and a small shabby dictionary to which she had clung for years. It was apparent that Rosa Lee expected her to be away for some time.

That morning also brought a partial return to sanity. Agnes went down to the wine cellar and took a good look.

When Tom Jones paced it off last night, it had appeared baronial in extent. It was indeed a brooding cavern; but it was only about as large as the two pantries put together. The stock which had so awed her consisted of only six or seven dozen bottles, most of which looked as if they had been here for a long time. There were between five and eleven bottles each of four different kinds of liquor; they appeared much newer.

The obvious inference was that Aunt Adelaide had inherited the one and purchased the other. There were a great many inferences around this place. Agnes was a little easier at heart today. She might not be the world's greatest wizard at the solution of problems; but once the problem was fairly stated, she had at least a chance.

Just before lunchtime, she called Miriam. She acknowledged receipt of the package and inquired about her stepdaughter's health. Possibly Agnes put the two things in the wrong order; anyhow, Miriam sounded decidedly snappish when she went on to inform her caller that she was "having a meeting here this afternoon. An important committee meeting."

"Taking advantage of my absence?" asked Agnes.

Her faint facetiousness was lost on Miriam, who retorted, "Certainly not! I'm so far behind with things that I had to start catching up."

"In a few more days you'll be out and around as usual," Agnes reassured her.

"I'm sure I hope so. When I assume an obligation, I do my best to live up to it."

"You do all that one woman can do," Agnes asserted warmly.

At last she had managed to say the right thing. "Thank you, Ladybird," answered Miriam. "It's kind of you to say so.

One of these days, when I'm a little caught up with things, I hope to run over and see how you're making out."

"There's no hurry," said Agnes hastily. "I can always phone you if I need help."

Miriam ignored that one; there was something else she wanted to get off her mind. "I've been thinking things over; and I've decided that while you're away I'm going to assume all the household expenses here."

"That isn't necessary," said Agnes. "You've always done your share; there's no call for you to go beyond that."

"It's what I prefer." Miriam had the last word, as usual. Agnes, hanging up, thought, *There goes Rosa Lee's fried chicken.* Poor Rosa Lee: a great artist condemned to play to empty seats!

Dora Dean was, in her different way, just as much an artist. Agnes had already sampled some of her specialties, and was to become acquainted with others as time went on. Dora particularly enjoyed serving Mrs. Wainwright with meat pie, stewed chicken and dumplings, devil's food cake with caramel frosting, hot biscuits, homemade preserves. If Agnes gained weight on this diet, she could always buy herself new clothes. Doubtless, the day of reckoning would come; meanwhile she might as well go ahead and enjoy herself.

The rest of the week passed pleasantly, and almost too fast. Thursday morning, Agnes had a household conference with Dora Dean; nominally, Mrs. Wainwright took over the reins of authority, but she was careful not to pull them too tight.

That afternoon she had Eustace take her for a drive in the country; when they reached a particularly inviting lane she made him wait while she went for a stroll. Exercise, when nobody ordered it, was really fun. So many things were, if you did them of your own free will.

That evening Agnes finally got around to listening to the *Ninth Symphony*. Her duty done, she returned to her real favorites. Nothing could beat Fate Knocking at the Door; but the *Pastoral* made a really delightful topping.

Friday morning, Tom Jones called her from his office. He was leaving that afternoon for a weekend in the Big City. Could he do anything for her there?

"Give my regards to off-Broadway," said Agnes flippantly.

" 'Off—'? Bless my soul, the little woman is a wit!"

"Only half one, really. But maybe she's just as happy as if she had good sense."

"Could I persuade you to meet me in New York, say on my next visit there? We needn't stay at the same hotel, of course; but we could do the town together."

"It sounds delightful." Agnes tried, not too successfully, to keep the eagerness out of her tone. "We'll see about it when the time comes."

"I'll be looking forward to it. This is all for the present, then?"

"It will have to do."

"The Queen's mandate! Take it easy, Your Majesty."

"There isn't much of any other way to take it, is there?"

"Not in the Hammond Mansion, I suspect. Oh, I was forgetting! It's the Wainwright Mansion now, isn't it?"

"It isn't, and you know it isn't. You were right the first time."

That afternoon, Agnes went for another drive, this time in the other direction. On her return, she told Eustace that she would not want the car again until Sunday morning.

109

Outings, above everything, should not be allowed to become routine.

Saturday, Agnes went for a stroll downtown. She was really beginning to learn her way around. Several strangers smiled and looked as if they would like to speak to her. Only one actually did, and that was an older woman. Another time, Agnes might take the initiative—or at least act encouraging. For the present, things were going well. What more could any reasonable person ask?

That night she went upstairs early but read late. She finished Tom Jones's seventh—and final—offering. Finished it with very mixed feelings. It was merely the nature of the reading matter that confused her. She had already decided that she liked Tom Jones.

She went to church Sunday. Agnes attended the eleven o'clock service. Dora Dean had already been to early Communion. Eustace, who was a Presbyterian, had plenty of time to go to his own house of worship. Agnes was free to keep her mind on her devotions.

She did, until just after they ended. She rose from her final blessed moment of silent prayer, and waited for the final voluntary. Just as it was beginning, she turned to encounter the eyes of Dr. Hugh Sheridan.

She found him waiting for her outside the church. He made the gesture of helping her into her car, which Eustace had at the curb only a few steps down the street. This encounter was something which Agnes had both hoped for and dreaded, and had never consciously faced even in her own mind.

She had an impulse to invite Dr. Sheridan to "take pot luck" with her. She checked it, wished she hadn't, assured herself that the worst he could have done was to say "no." Or perhaps the worst would have been for him to come along and then have the hospitality fall flat on their hands.

Perhaps she had done the right thing—or refrained from doing the wrong. Above all, she must avoid the impression that she was giving him a rush. Again he had had that oddly disturbing effect on her. Again she relived the experience in retrospect, and half-wished it hadn't happened, and wouldn't have missed it for the world.

That made Sully's appearance in the middle of the afternoon all the more welcome. Agnes was grateful for it anyhow. In Antioch, the Wainwrights' house was a convenient stopping place for Walter Sullivan, Real Estate (on the Sundays when he had no potential customers to show around). Today he had taken a real trip to see her.

Also to satisfy his native curiosity, of course. He gave the house a once-over, and scarcely waited to be asked for the verdict.

His professional opinion was that the Hammond Mansion could be remodeled into apartments, and would be a real income-producer. "You could even have a special apartment for yourself laid out on the ground floor."

"I could, maybe. But why should I?"

"It would give you a handy refuge any time you felt that you wanted to get away from it all." He pronounced those last words with a lingering inflection. "It all" was lofty but rather vague language for what an urchin would have called "The Boss."

There was something in the idea; Agnes perceived that at once. She even envisioned a small apartment for Dora Dean: a place made to Dora's order, and adjacent to Mrs. Wainwright's own.

111

But the solution was just too pat. "A consummation devoutly to be wished." Yet something—or somebody—was sure to come along and upset it.

"This is the wrong time of year to start rebuilding," Agnes parried.

"Who said it wasn't? You'd have to clear the place out before you could even start. That would take some time, provided you were already committed. Think it over first."

"Good advice. Who rushes in 'where angels fear to tread'?" Agnes asked.

"That adage turns, as so many of them do, on the word 'fool.' "

"So many such adages, perhaps, because there are so many fools?"

"No 'perhaps' about that one. There just *are*. But the number does not include my dear friend Mrs. Wainwright."

"Thank you, sir. Now suppose we sit down somewhere, and ring for a drink, and I'll consult your expert knowledge on another problem."

While Dora Dean was bringing them a drink, Agnes fetched the paperbacks which she had been reading. "So many of these deal with a 'private eye,' " she reported. "A— what else do they call him? A 'shamus.' "

"Misunderstood Gaelic, my dear. That's a slight mispronunciation of the Irish for 'James.' "

"Are these private eyes a really recent invention, Sully?"

"My guess would be that they are not. They are descendants of Sherlock Holmes, who, you will remember, was an old bachelor."

"Just like—?"

"Did you change the subject, Agnes, or didn't you? Yes,

112

I'm a chronic bachelor; but I assure you that these private eyes are not even distantly related to me."

"The man-against-odds is an admirable hero," Agnes pursued.

"Agreed. Take David and Goliath."

"Or to come a little farther down to date, take that fellow in Dumas, for instance, Bussy d'Ambois. Wasn't that his name?"

"Take almost any Dumas hero, for that matter," Sully agreed. "The reader accepts his deeds of prowess, adores him, wants the story to go on and on."

"In Dumas, yes. But in these private-detective romances, I boggle just a little at these independent practitioners who are so much smarter than the regular police, who take an incredible amount of punishment, who do without food or sleep, and who drink so much and so steadily that it's hard to see how they can recognize the culprit even if they happen to fall over him."

"Agnes, my child, you're analyzing. That way lies the death of all entertainment."

"Oh, dear!" sighed Agnes. "I suppose one of these days I'll have to go back and read something good."

"I'm afraid so. There should be plenty of such around."

"There is. Better than that, there's time to read it, and a lovely feeling that if you don't choose to stick too closely to your book, you can always depend on Dora Dean to supply you with a plate of cookies."

"That's it!" Sully underlined. "There's something about a combination of physical ease and mental activity—if the mental activity isn't too great—that adds up to real contentment."

Contentment was not happiness: not by a long shot. But

113

it was a very great deal; and it was much rarer than it should be.

Agnes contented herself with contentment. Until Sully's departure early in the evening, she and he kept safely to impersonal topics.

10.

Tom Jones telephoned Tuesday afternoon and came over that evening to report on his New York safari. This time his offering was a flask of Chanel Number Five. Nice he had laid off the whodunits—and opportune. Agnes had found in Aunt Adelaide's library a complete set of the works of Robert Louis Stevenson, and had decided that, the Fates permitting, she would read them all in the coming months.

She began with *Treasure Island,* just as she had begun in her childhood when she first made the acquaintance of the great Tusitala. She was in a position now to appreciate the craftsmanship of that deceptively simple story, though the suspense was nothing like the same.

115

On her first perusal, indeed, the suspense had been her undoing. She had just reached the point where Jim Hawkins lay hidden in the apple barrel and the pirates had begun to conspire in his hearing, when bedtime came for small Agnes. Mother was very firm on that subject; and to do her justice, she generally had to be. Also, the event generally justified her discipline: the little girl went to sleep with just enough to dream about.

That was far from being the case tonight. Not only was Agnes's curiosity aroused; so was her alarm. Something terrible threatened Jim Hawkins and his good friends; the fact that she didn't know what it was made her all the more uneasy.

Agnes grew constantly more wakeful. She turned and twisted. She tried to reassure herself: it would come out all right. It must do so. She would learn all about it tomorrow. But she was no longer living in her own bedroom in her own safe happy home; she was living in the story. The magic of the tale-teller's art was in this case black magic.

Finally she gave in. She left her disordered bed, and without even waiting to put on dressing gown and slippers, fled rather than walked down the stairs.

The apparition of her barefoot darling, rumpled and distressed, naturally alarmed Mrs. Costen. "Are you sick?" she cried, and opened her arms to the waif.

Even the haven of Mother's lap had less than its usual calming effect. It was some moments before Agnes could give a coherent account of her distress.

When Mrs. Costen understood, she was naturally relieved; but she was almost proportionately annoyed. "It's just a story," she proclaimed. "It's nothing to be so upset about. Now be Mother's good girl. I'll take you upstairs and tuck you in. Then you'll forget all about the bad men in the book; and you'll go right off to sleep."

But instead of being a good girl, Agnes stiffened and began to yell her head off. Her father, who had been watching the scene over the top of his book, decided that the time had come for him to take a hand. He came across the room, stooped over Agnes, and began softly to pat her head.

Her crying gradually subsided. He dried her eyes on his own big handkerchief, then held it for her to blow her nose. "There are times when it's just as well to make an exception," he said quietly.

Mrs. Costen's wifely retort was, "I'm supposed to make her mind; yet you take her part against me." But she allowed him to lift the little girl away from her and lead the way upstairs.

There he stood waiting while her mother made her comfortable. When the time came to restore her book, he gestured to Mrs. Costen to go ahead. She insisted that he do so. Their little tiff was over. Agnes's only interest was in retrieving her prize; she wished they wouldn't waste so much time being polite to each other.

The bitter had turned to sweet. Agnes smiled when she recalled that long-ago experience. Then, just perceptibly, she sighed. Some things could come only once.

Some things didn't come even once. Doubtless it was the part of wisdom to learn to do without them. Agnes just wasn't that wise. Not yet, at any rate. Not in the depths of her. Not here alone with herself.

Hugh Sheridan's face and figure flitted before her eyes. A man she had seen but three times. A man she might not even like if she came to know him better. Why should he haunt her like this? Just when things were beginning to go so beautifully for her, too! With determination rather than gusto, Agnes returned to her book.

She woke in a much better frame of mind. The possibilities here in Marshfield were endless, most of them unexplored, some scarcely even glimpsed. She could give herself up to them unreservedly. Antioch and all the Wainwright concerns there were off her mind.

That was what *she* thought. But on Saturday morning Miriam called her from the old home town.

Her tones were crisp, not to say snappish. "I'm sorry if you consider this bad news, Ladybird. But I'm having to let Rosa Montgomery go."

"*You*'re having to—?"

Miriam disregarded the emphasis. "She never did know her place; and since you left, she's been growing more and more uppish."

"But you—" began Agnes, and bit her tongue. She suddenly remembered that Miriam had assumed the running expenses of the household in Antioch! Agnes had assumed that it was a generous impulse, and as such not to be gainsaid. Now she saw it as one more grab for power.

"Good servants are hard to get nowadays," Agnes faltered.

"I am looking the field over carefully," Miriam assured her. "Very carefully."

There was nothing more to be said. Agnes would have liked to speak to Rosa Lee. (Miriam hadn't even accorded her the courtesy of that name.) But she knew it would be useless to ask. Miriam had spoken in the present tense; but undoubtedly, before she put in the call she had sent Rosa Lee packing.

Once she had got over the first shock, Agnes realized that this wasn't too bad. She had lately been sympathizing with

118

Rosa Lee's frustration over having only Miriam to cook for. Just a little, she wondered what standards Miriam would use in looking the field over carefully. And would "the field" look right back at Miss Miriam Wainwright?

Tom Jones had already dated Agnes for Saturday evening. It was his treat this time, he specified. But he would not disclose the nature of his plans beyond asking, "If I drive over to Marshfield, you won't be afraid to get into my car with me, will you?"

"Oh, no!" responded Agnes. It wasn't until after he had snickered that she realized she had said it almost too promptly.

Her answer fitted the facts of the case, however. What Tom suggested was that they drive over to his home town, "where we can take in a Saturday-night movie without having every old hen in the neighborhood say that you aren't showing proper respect for your aunt Adelaide's memory."

"How do you know they would say that?"

"I don't, of course. I'm just not taking any chances."

On this occasion there was no gainsaying him. Agnes was not much of a gainsayer, anyhow. She went right ahead and enjoyed the movie.

She hadn't been to many movies since—well, since her marriage. It made her a fresh audience: not immature exactly, but naïve. As for showing proper respect, that could be done in its turn. Respect was a Sunday morning quality; and Agnes had every intention of going to church.

After the movie they had a quiet drink in a nearby bar. When Tom suggested a second round, Agnes nodded. But with her glass standing untouched on the table, she said, "It's been a lovely evening, Tom. But you know what the crowning charm of it is?"

119

"There is a crowning charm? Go ahead and tell me."

"Nobody knows where I am!"

"Nobody knows—or cares?"

There for the first time she had a real clue to Tom Jones. Under his apparent bravado, and his very real charm and kindliness, he was a lonely man. He, and Hugh Sheridan, and . . .

Agnes thrust all such considerations from her. "Or cares! Why should people? This minding my business for me presupposes that I'll stand for a great deal of interference."

"Do tell!" said Tom Jones, and picked up his drink.

Agnes picked up hers. She didn't need to tell. A single evening of happiness shared added to the sum total of human enjoyment. That total was never so large that it couldn't stand an addition.

On the drive back to Marshfield, they talked about Stevenson. Here Agnes had the advantage; and she wasn't slow to let Tom know it. He had read *Treasure Island* and *Kidnapped* and *The Strange Case of Dr. Jekyll and Mr. Hyde*. So had everybody else. But how about *The Dynamiter?* How about *The Beach at Falesá?* How about *The Wrong Box?*

He had to plead ignorance; but he got her point so neatly that he turned it back on her. "The case must be parallel to that of Dickens. Everybody reads Dickens. Everybody admires him, more or less."

" 'And those who came to scoff remained to pray,' " quoted Agnes.

"Exactly. The professed admirer is an initiate. But there may be other degrees above his. A reader may be a devout Dickensian without being a Droodian—Dickensians who specialize in *The Mystery of Edwin Drood.*"

120

"That's the novel that was left unfinished when Dickens died. Oh, yes!" said Agnes.

And said no more. Tom chuckled.

"All right, then, Mister Smarty Tom Jones!" Agnes retorted. "But as sure as shooting, if Aunt Adelaide has *The Complete Works of Charles Dickens* in her library—"

"Any 'if' about that?"

"When I was young it was considered rude to interrupt." Agnes barely managed to get that far before her laughter overcame her. When she got her breath back she went on, "Have it your own way. I'm going to reread *Edwin Drood*. Then if I still like *Bleak House* better, come around and tell me I'm hopeless."

"It isn't that. Other novelists have left an opus unfinished. Didn't your idol do something of the kind?"

"Stevenson left more than one, I'm afraid. He was a great beginner."

"It's largely a matter of luck, I should imagine. On this one point Charles Dickens had all the luck. His fragment broke off at exactly the right point."

Agnes was startled to see how late it was when he landed her home. This evening, Time had simply scuttled away. It was too late to ask Tom in, even if Agnes had been willing to risk an anticlimax.

It was not too late, however, to locate *Edwin Drood* and lay the book on top of the other Dickenses. That was in the nature of a memorandum, "Agnes to Agnes." Not that she would need much reminding. When people were really interested, they remembered well enough.

Then here came Sunday morning again; and this time she was more on the alert than she had been a week ago. During the voluntary, Agnes had felt somewhat conspicuous, sitting all alone in that prominent pew at St. Andrew's. The Hammond heiress would unavoidably be the object of discreet curiosity. Agnes couldn't blame it; she realized that if positions had been reversed, she herself would have taken an eyeful. Yet that well-bred scrutiny made her uncomfortable.

She forgot it at the first note of the processional. Apart from religious conviction or upbringing, such music was in itself a good enough reason for attending church.

Her enjoyment actually increased during the prayer-book service; it folded its wings for a rest when she sat down for the sermon. She maintained the appearance of attention, and would have supposed that she was attending, if sharp eyes had not caught her out.

Children are not hypocrites; and they know instinctively which grown people have a fellow feeling for them. St. Andrew's had a mixed choir; the men and women sat on the far side of the church, but the boys were directly in front of the old Hammond pew. Midway through the sermon, one of them suppressed a yawn, caught Agnes's eye, and grinned at her. Naturally, Agnes grinned back.

The rest of the sermon was completely lost on her. A shining new idea had flashed into her mind and taken possession.

Details could wait. The salient fact was this: the urchin was willing to make friends with her. If Agnes wanted that too, it was up to her to give him the chance.

When she began to make her way down the aisle at the conclusion of the service, her bright idea cast its first ray across her immediate path. At ease in his presence for the first time, she inquired of Dr. Sheridan, "Were you a choir boy in your extreme youth?"

122

"Alas, no!" he replied. "I could carry anything except a tune. I was allowed to march in the procession all right, but only so long as I kept my mouth shut."

"You mean you wanted to march in the procession?"

"That's where my gang was. I wanted to stay with my gang, didn't I? All boys do."

There was a second directing ray. Already the thing was beginning to come into focus. "I may want to talk to you one of these days," she said.

"Any time you like, of course. I shall be delighted."

There was a warm glow at Agnes's heart when she waved goodbye to him from the window of her car. What was all that nonsense she had dreamed up about glimpsing a rich happiness in Dr. Sheridan's direction, only to have it denied her? She was no Mariana in the Moated Grange, prey to a dank spirit as well as a damp atmosphere. " 'He cometh not,' she said. She said, 'I am a-weary, weary, I would that I were dead.' " Who would want to come to a woman who moped like that? Just an old sourpuss, who might much better have turned her mind (if any) to getting some decent plumbing installed.

The Widow Wainwright was not a disappointed old maid. (Mariana . . . Matty . . . Miriam . . . Oh, forget it!) She was an extremely lucky person. It was up to her to share her good fortune.

It was also up to her to display a little common sense. She was going to make a friend of the Widower Sheridan. He hadn't too many real friends. Nobody had. Most people had some sort of ulterior motive.

Mrs. Wainwright herself had, though it was not too ulterior. Too ulterior? She was using the adjective "ulterior" as if it admitted of comparison. She would take that up

123

some time with some amusing male companion, if and when they ran out of other things to talk about.

Meanwhile, her not-too-ulterior motive was that she genuinely desired Dr. Sheridan's advice and assistance with making some little boys a trifle happier. Well-placed little boys, well brought up. They might be lucky that their gang hung around church. They were lucky, indeed. But they were just a little pitiful, because they were so young.

Agnes was duly set down at home. It was "home" to her in a special sense, because she was becoming more and more interested in it. At the rate her plans were beginning to shape, it bade fair to become the center of her life.

She had a walk in the country that afternoon, and took *Edwin Drood* to bed with her. She succumbed to the magic of the great story-teller. She saw that the *Mystery* really was one. It tantalized, because there were so many possible solutions, yet not one that was obvious. But all the while, another stratum of Agnes's mind was busy with the idea of making boys happy.

Monday morning, she dawdled a little over the mail. There were no letters, only some circulars and Sunday's *New York Herald Tribune.* That was Aunt Adelaide's newspaper, and Agnes had continued to subscribe to it, just as back in Antioch she had kept on with Jerome's *New York Times.* Here in Marshfield she had the big Sunday newspaper to herself, even if it was a day late; and she really enjoyed making her deliberate way through it.

(It was different with the *Wall Street Journal.* That kept coming; but it was duly opened, glanced at, and laid aside. An authoritative publication, no doubt; it just was not for Agnes.)

She sought Dora Dean presently, and after a little per-

124

functory attention to housekeeping plans, inquired, "Did Mrs. Hammond ever entertain children here?"

"Oh, yes, Mrs. Wainwright! When the younger ladies came to tea, they sometimes brought their little girls with them."

"But didn't children ever come by themselves?"

"Not in my time, ma'am. Indeed, I think little girls might have felt maybe stiff and strange around Mrs. Hammond."

This was positively Victorian quaintness, and Victorian charm—yes, and Victorian constraint. Agnes could well imagine the careful coaching before Mama's darling was produced upon the scene, every curl in place and her polite speeches well rehearsed. The chosen little girls must have felt very important but somewhat uneasy. And had Aunt Adelaide felt really at home with them?

Little boys did not seem to come into the question. That told Agnes something she needed to know. It was also proof, if proof were needed, that it was high time things changed around here.

Agnes went toward the front of the house with every intention of phoning the rector. She remembered in time that a clergyman was supposed to have Monday pretty much to himself, to recover from the strain of his Sabbath duties. She could hardly wait to get started; yet one day more up in the clouds would be an added boon to her.

Actually, what had she to be so cheerful about, here in a house of mourning and with the future very much unsettled? A little boy had smiled at her—and undoubtedly forgotten all about her inside of the next minute.

She hadn't forgotten; that was the point. She, Agnes Costen Wainwright, who had been so long on the receiving end, was now in a position to give. To give pleasure where it counted for the most: to appeal to the unjaded palate of childhood.

In pleasing a child she would please herself. Or perhaps disappoint herself; common sense whispered that maybe she was no better fitted to deal with little boys than Aunt Adelaide had been. In that case—

Agnes pulled herself up short. "Perhaps" was a word which had been too often on her lips, or in her mind, since she migrated to Marshfield.

She marched to the telephone. The rector couldn't do anything worse than say, "No."

As a matter of fact, he seemed pleased to hear from her. He had "promised himself the pleasure of calling on" her. He welcomed her suggestion of a cup of tea Tuesday afternoon.

Of course "here" was the Hammond Mansion. But Agnes mustn't let herself get into the habit of thinking that everything which came her way was deference due to the Hammond money. That was simply snobbery in reverse.

She didn't invite the rector's wife; she wanted to talk business. They set the hour, and rang off. Then Agnes went in quest of the omniscient Dora.

"What does Dr. Follansbee like for tea?" she inquired.

"What doesn't he?" asked Dora. "When is he coming?"

"Tomorrow."

"Shall we spoil his dinner for him?" Dora twinkled. She was remembering.

"Do, please." Agnes twinkled back. This augured well. The shadow of common sense might have fallen here for a minute, but it hadn't lingered. Mrs. Wainwright was in no mood to lure it back.

126

11.

DR. FOLLANSBEE CERTAINLY ENJOYED HIS HOT BUTTERED TEA-cake and caraway-seed cookies. All consumed along the line of his duty, too. Agnes ate her share, just to show him that the food wasn't poisoned. If they both spoiled their dinners, she wouldn't have to account to anybody for it. With Mrs. Follansbee's feeling about the subject, Agnes was not immediately concerned.

She had had her second cup of tea, and the rector his third, when the subject of the interview finally had to be dealt with. She had sought the interview; he had met her on her own ground. Yet Agnes was disconcerted by what seemed to him, doubtless, the easy and indeed obvious solution.

Dr. Follansbee simply suggested that she join the Choir Guild. Seeing her hesitate, he amended it to, "If you do not feel in a position to do that right away, won't you at least work with them for a time?"

Why should Agnes feel taken aback? Obviously that was the easy and natural way for her to get acquainted with the little boys.

Her dread of women's organizations probably had a good deal to do with it. Worse than that, however, was Agnes's fundamental ignorance. She was an Episcopalian at heart, doubtless; but her training had been more than a little partial and one-sided. In their small church deep in New England, their music had been sung by a quartet, all grown, all volunteers. The Costens' congregation had had no real organization, largely because they had needed none.

Her hesitation was noticed, but only in a passing way. The rector reassured her kindly, "You do not have to give me an immediate answer. Think it over. You know I am always at your service." He refused a fourth cup of tea, but managed to put down several more cookies before he finally left.

When Dora Dean came to clear away, Agnes complimented her on the excellence of her teacake. Dora acknowledged the compliment, then added with a touch of complacence, "You can't beat a good old Sally Lunn. And if I do say so myself, Mrs. Wainwright, I make as good a Sally Lunn as anybody."

Sally Lunn was presumably an Englishwoman who had originated that particular delicacy. Other names have come down in history with far less reason.

"Did you bake enough to last you and the girls for your—?" began Agnes. Then, realizing the fatuity of the

128

question, she broke off with a simple, "I hope you and the maids enjoyed your tea."

"Almost too much, Mrs. Wainwright. Will you be wanting your dinner put back?"

"Make it late and light. Dr. Follansbee wasn't the only person who spoiled his dinner."

Agnes had planned to talk to Dr. Sheridan: to talk to him in this very connection. Yet now that the opportunity offered, she hesitated. Would he think her a nincompoop who could not make up her own mind? She had resented being treated as one, but perhaps she was. People always tried to excuse their own failings.

An hour later, when the teacake had begun to wear off, the simple answer occurred to her. What she wanted from him was not advice, but approbation. To gain that, she must give him something to approve of.

She called him, and announced, "Here I am, so soon! There's no hurry, of course; but any time that you feel like listening to one more silly woman, I'd like to see you."

"My evening office hours are supposed to end at nine," he said. "If I came over after that, would it be too late?"

Agnes felt a little thrill. He was coming as soon as he got his daily duties off his hands: coming with a free mind, prepared to relax. Just for an instant, she felt sorry for Mariana; the Lady of the Moated Grange had had nothing like that to look forward to.

Agnes had a salad and a cup of coffee at eight o'clock. Perhaps coffee on top of tea was too much stimulation. When she went upstairs to change for *his* coming, her hands shook, and beneath their light coating of rouge, deep natural color burned in her cheeks.

When she heard him announced, her self-control returned. For a flash, she feared that she might be disappointed. But only for a flash; the instant he entered the back parlor, Agnes felt a lovely glow at her heart.

She offered a drink, and joined him in it. Then she began to explain about her decision—her near-decision—to join the Choir Guild.

"I don't know how long I'll be in Marshfield," she went on. "But while I am here, shouldn't I take advantage of—of everything?"

"While you're here, you *are* here."

"Exactly. Even if I should decide to stay—" (her heart beat high at her own daring when she uttered those bold words) "—joining the Choir Guild is not like being married. There's no 'till death us do part' involved here."

As soon as they were out, she regretted those last words; they must remind him of his own loss. She hurried on, "I don't work well in organizations."

"You mean that you haven't so far? Perhaps you haven't been introduced to the right organizations."

If that was a guess, it was a shrewd one. Yet of course he was familiar with Aunt Adelaide's opinion of things—and people.

"I fancy I'll try it," Agnes concluded.

"I fancy you fancy correctly. Now, what else have you been doing with yourself?"

She told him about going to a movie in another town, so as to avoid observation. "Now was that sneaky? Or was it prudent?"

"It was prudent, if you and your escort weren't seen there. If you were, you'll set tongues wagging."

Agnes looked startled for an instant, then showed all her

130

dimples. "That's a new one on me. Maybe in future I'd better stay home evenings."

"There are worse things to do with one's time. You like to read, don't you?"

"Love it, especially late at night. To get into bed with a clean nightgown and clean sheets and a new book—"

"Which needn't be too clean."

"Taking that chance is part of the fun. Then to be able to read as late as I like, and not to have to answer to anybody for it! That is luxury! That is—" she choked on the word "—freedom!"

"That is also therapeutic," Dr. Sheridan pointed out. "A relaxed body and an alert mind make a combination that would be hard to beat."

Tom Jones's verdict in different words! Agnes dimpled. "How nice it is to grow up! In my early youth, when they were urging my cereal on me with the usual promise of benefit, I once exclaimed, 'Everything that you don't like is "good for you!" ' I couldn't see why they laughed. Now I find that you may like a thing, yet have Those In Authority approve of it."

Dr. Sheridan smiled back. "You betrayed me into presenting you with a professional opinion, free-gratis-for-nothing. You're welcome. Keep the change."

They passed to further talk of books, glanced at politics, paid their respects to a juicy scandal now being reported at length in the newspapers. They agreed that such affairs should not be given so much publicity; but they had both followed it closely.

The hour passed quickly. It had stretched almost to two when he rose to go. "Come again soon," invited Agnes. "Don't wait for my next problem."

131

"I'll wait only for an invitation," Dr. Sheridan assured her. They shook hands as if they were ratifying a bargain.

It had all been wonderful. Agnes went upstairs in a mood of smiling content and, as a bonus, she took to bed with her that very lovely early Stevenson, *An Inland Voyage*. Naturally, after all of that, she sank into a sweet deep sleep.

But along toward morning she began to dream. She was in a car being driven down a side street which was strange to her, though Agnes felt that she had been in this neighborhood before.

A street not only strange to her, but strange in itself. It was paved with cobblestones, and was so narrow that the small car practically filled it. They passed on their right the side of a small house. Its entire back yard was occupied by a flower garden, and all the flowers were in bloom.

"And all white!" gasped Agnes.

"Yes," agreed her driver, at whom she had not even glanced.

The scent was almost overpowering: one fragrance after another, each lovely in itself, yet blending, then separating again, in a most perplexing way.

Then they passed a second garden, still on the right. It too was crowded with white flowers, this time including pansies. But the pansies did not run true; colored ones kept intruding, and that distressed Agnes.

She had alighted from the car by this time. Someone whom she vaguely knew but could not quite place, a woman, advanced to her rescue. It was she who handed Agnes white pansies to substitute for the colored.

Here the dream broke off. Agnes never saw the driver, a man; nor did she remember alighting from the car. She had simply found herself in the second garden.

132

She woke suddenly in great distress. She turned on her bedside lamp, but the light failed to dispel her strange emotion. The details returned to her again and again with startling vividness.

When things had cleared up a little, it struck Agnes that this might well have been a premonition-of-death dream. No earthly flowers ever grew that close together, and with all varieties blossoming at the same time.

Agnes sat up in bed, helped herself to a glass of water, looked around the room which had been so familiar and friendly earlier that very night. Now she felt oddly forlorn here.

That must be what it meant, this imagery of being driven by an unseen man and succored by a strange woman. Everything was done for her, yet she dwelt in loneliness. Her much-desired freedom served only to show her what she was missing.

She had planned to make the best of what was within her reach; now here she was crying for the moon. A woman loving yet unloved: surely that was common enough in practice, even if convention still looked askance at it. This was no Mariana situation. "He" had come, and stayed, and they had enjoyed themselves. If at the end he had gone away, what was so terrible in that? He would come back before too long; he had promised to.

Agnes had argued herself out of the feeling of nightmare; but its shadow lingered. Enough was enough; she must ward off a recurrence. She went back to her book, and read until, with the advent of daylight, the *Voyage* ended.

She fell asleep then, woke much later with a start, and found that she was late for breakfast. Or would have been, if there had been a breakfast hour in her present household. As it was, Dora Dean simply greeted her, asked whether she would prefer grapefruit or orange juice, and went back to the kitchen to start the coffee and the bacon.

The first thing to be done today was to write Dr. Follansbee. That would be much better than phoning; and there was no point to suggesting a second interview, when all she needed to do was tell him her mind was made up.

In quest of stationery, Agnes set herself to explore Aunt Adelaide's big desk: an extremely business-like desk, with deep drawers for filing, and shallow drawers for supplies, and a typewriter which could be swung out of the way when it was not in use. The very sight of all this system and order was disconcerting. Agnes simply ran away from it.

She remembered noticing in Aunt Adelaide's bedroom a lovely little buhl desk: a lady's desk, such as Adelaide might have used while her husband had been still living. The room had been left just as it was; the task of going through Aunt Adelaide's clothes and intimate personal belongings still lay ahead of Agnes.

Now she was briefly glad that it had not been undertaken. Right here time had stood still. Agnes wasn't the Hammond heiress, faced with responsibilities and perplexities. She was young Agnes Wainwright, here on a visit to a beloved if not-very-well-comprehended aunt.

Under the shelter of that feeling, she opened a small drawer. It contained keepsakes: Aunt Adelaide's wedding invitation, a small package of letters—love letters, by the look of them—a sprig dried beyond recognition, but still tied with a white ribbon and attached to a card which read, in Mrs. Hammond's writing, "Lavender from Juliet's tomb, Verona," and the date. A honeymoon souvenir, doubtless. Herbert and Adelaide had been so young then, and joyous,

134

and hopeful. The lavender was not the only thing which had faded.

Agnes closed the drawer rather abruptly. She had come to look for stationery, not for memories.

She found it in the drawer where she might have expected to find it: social stationery, some of it old, all of it good. There were three fountain pens of various vintages; Mrs. Hammond pretty well kept up with the times, but like many rich people, she never threw anything away.

Agnes wrote her letter: short, to the point, and, she hoped, cordial. She decided to have it delivered by hand, noted that fact on the superscription, and gave it to Dora to give to Eustace.

Back at the big business desk, Agnes went just far enough to assure herself of her own ignorance. Then she called Mr. Kent, and got through to him with a minimum of delay.

"I want to find out more about Mrs. Hammond's business affairs," she explained. "Would it be a good idea if I went through her securities?"

"A very good idea, indeed," approved Mr. Kent.

It was also a very obvious idea; but let that pass. "I shall need help with them."

"That is what we are here for. Shall I call the president of the bank, and make an appointment for you?"

"Yes, please," said Agnes. "The sooner the better, too. I have so much to learn!" That's it, Mrs. Wainwright! Be all wide-eyed inexperience, but hustle them off their dignified feet. They won't dare procrastinate too much in the face of the Hammond money.

Mr. Kent called back to say that Mr. Estabrook would be

at her service this afternoon, but Mr. Kent himself would like to help, and he couldn't make it until tomorrow.

There was really no point to having Mr. Kent charge up his time whenever Mrs. Wainwright turned around. In his way, however, he was a shrewd old cove. Agnes agreed to the appointment as suggested.

This time her accommodating nature did Agnes no harm; for who should come dropping in at the Hammond mansion that afternoon but Rosa Lee Montgomery, once in Mrs. Wainwright's employ in Antioch, and fired therefrom by Miss Miriam Wainwright. So she didn't hold her unemployment against Agnes!

"I can't tell you how glad I am to see you," Agnes greeted her. "If I had had any idea how things were going, I'd have come over to Antioch and tried to straighten them out."

"Tried to" was possibly a slip. Still, the limitations on Agnes's authority in "her own home" were no news to Rosa Lee.

"Don't let that worry you for a minute, Miss Agnes. I'm going South and visit my relatives. This way I can stay as long as I like. You're looking fine."

"Meaning I've gained weight?"

"If you have, it's your own weight, isn't it?"

"It's my own business, too." Agnes spoke half under her breath, and Rosa Lee had a convenient attack of deafness.

"I want you to meet my present housekeeper," said Agnes, and sent for Dora Dean.

The two sized each other up for an instant; than they both smiled. "I've heard about your fried chicken," said Dora.

"My pecan pie is good, too," returned Rosa Lee. "Used to be, that is. I haven't had much practice with it lately."

136

It was Agnes's turn to pick up the ball. "Dora, do you want to get tea for the three of us while I show our guest over the house? Or would you rather have something stronger to drink, Rosa Lee?"

"Tea will be fine, Miss Agnes. I still have to get back to New York tonight."

They began their guided tour. Halfway through the second floor Agnes suggested that they sit down for a brief rest. "It's a big place, isn't it?"

"It's a fine place: a place for quality."

"I sometimes think I'd like to live here always," said Agnes. "Yet have I any real right to be here this minute? There's Miss Miriam alone in the house in Antioch, just getting over a serious sickness, and trying to do all that club and committee work."

"Miss Miriam can get along fine till she finds somebody who suits her," said Rosa Lee dryly. "You have a very good can opener, Miss Agnes; and it's always easy enough to undo a package of crackers."

Agnes rose and resumed the tour. If made exhaustive, it would also prove exhausting. She gave Rosa Lee barely a glimpse of Mrs. Hammond's bedroom, and bypassed Mr. Hammond's. Had they always possessed separate bedrooms, Agnes wondered. If so, how long had they occupied them as such? Surely they were not on distant terms in the long-ago days when they brought back a sprig of lavender from the tomb of Juliet? Poor Juliet, who had occupied the same chamber as her young husband for only a few hours!

Dora had not gone to the extent of baking a Sally Lunn; indeed, how did she know that she would have time to do so? But she had thoughtfully added to the tea tray a decanter of sherry and three glasses.

137

Agnes poured the tea, dispensed the sherry, and left much of the conversation to the two domestics. Dora explained that she had never been in the real South. Rosa Lee said, "It's a good place to come from."

Dora pounced on that. "A good place to go back to?"

"For a visit, yes. But if I'd been satisfied there in the first place, wouldn't I have stayed there?"

They passed to the subject of recipes. Dora Dean followed most of hers strictly. That is, cake recipes, and—and—

"And you always measure when you make coffee?" Rosa Lee finished for her.

"Indeed I do. But you can't carry strict rules too far. Isn't there an old saying, 'The proof of the pudding is in the eating'?"

"If there isn't, there ought to be. Though I must say I don't care much for puddings, Miss Dean. I'd much rather have me a good piece of pie any day."

They did not discuss employers. They scarcely needed to. The ex- of one and the now of the other was sitting right there with them and taking in every word.

The session ended presently. Agnes insisted that Eustace drive Rosa Lee back to the station. (She had arrived in a taxi.) Agnes accompanied her guest to the front door; and while they were waiting for the car, Rosa Lee said suddenly, "You live where you're happy, Miss Agnes. You're not beholden to nobody."

She was very much in earnest; she had not been in the habit of doubling her negatives. Nor, for that matter, of venturing unsolicited advice.

"It's a free country, and I'm over twenty-one," Agnes agreed. "Well over!"

138

"The best years of your life are still ahead of you." Rosa Lee spoke both in consolation and in warning.

Agnes agreed cordially. Yet when Rosa Lee, safely ensconced in the Hammond car, leaned over to wave to her from the window, and Agnes waved back, she still experienced a lingering doubt. Maybe she should go back to Antioch, at least for a time, and see what she could do to help—or appease—Miriam.

Back in the sitting room, however, she speedily realized her own absurdity. She considered herself obligated to go back and help Miriam out? Agnes—help—Miriam?

She was headed for another nightmare if she kept on with this absurdity. This time the nightmare would be neither beautiful nor strange. It would be purely ridiculous, though of course easy enough to interpret.

The nightmare which Agnes could foresee, and which she had no intention of undergoing, would show her, high on the deck of a ship, in full possession of power and authority, recognizing Miriam's flounderings and taking pity on them, and throwing her stepdaughter a lifeline. Well!

12.

Under the eyes of the two men, Agnes glanced through Aunt Adelaide's thick bundle of securities. She reshuffled them for a second scrutiny, after which she looked up with a half-smile.

"Much of this is beyond me," she confessed.

Mr. Kent looked wise. The omniscient male; and then, of course, a lawyer was in duty bound to let on that nothing was beyond him.

Mr. Estabrook nodded sympathetically; but he could not—or did not—quite keep the dryness out of his tone when he remarked, "It might well be. Mrs. Hammond was a woman of independent judgment."

"She read the *Wall Street Journal*," said Agnes. "You mean she didn't take it for gospel?"

"Exactly. And when she came to me for advice about investments, she listened to all that I had to say on the subject, then went ahead on her own."

"She had every right to." Mr. Kent put in his two cents' worth. "It was her money."

Mr. Estabrook shrugged.

Agnes picked up the ball. "Didn't she sometimes lose through not following your advice?"

He grinned. "She did. We never indulged in post-mortems; but we made out her income tax returns, so that once a year I had a chance to check on her capital gains and losses."

"Couldn't she lose on purpose, in order to cut down her taxes?" asked Mr. Kent.

"She could, of course. But is it likely that she did?"

"Not likely, perhaps, but possible. A brilliant woman, yet still a woman."

Agnes had had as much of the omniscient male as she could take. She asked very sweetly, "Didn't you tell me, Mr. Kent, that over the years Mrs. Hammond had made a good deal of money?"

They both rushed to assure her that Mrs. Hammond had done that very thing; and Mr. Estabrook had the grace to add, "Money is money, whether it's made on or against my advice."

This was more like it. Agnes was not a brilliant woman, but she could learn. It was high time she set about doing so.

"My husband bought 'blue chip' stocks," she explained. "I'm very glad he did; most of my income is from dividends on his stock, though I inherited a few securities from my father. Otis Elevator is one of them. I remember his telling me that he had inherited Otis from *his* father."

141

"There you have it!" said Mr. Kent triumphantly—though what he had to be so smug about was a little hard for Agnes to see.

"To buy stock in basic American industries and then hold it is conservative policy," said Mr. Estabrook. "But, on the whole, a sound policy: one that pays in the end."

Now he was the one who sounded like a pompous ass "on the whole." Very much the wide-eyed innocent, Agnes asked, "But is it as much fun as speculating?"

To ask a banker such a question was blasphemy, doubtless. But it did put him in his place.

Having achieved that result, Agnes proceeded to get down to business. She handed Mr. Estabrook the stocks and directed, "Please read me the names of these firms. If I say 'Yes,' lay the certificate in one pile; if 'No,' in another."

It was a quick way of separating the sheep from the goats. Any stock which Agnes could easily identify went into the "Yes" pile; those which were strange to her or doubtful were classified as "No."

Only once did Mr. Estabrook venture an observation; that was when he reached a certificate for one hundred shares of International Business Machines. Then he said, with respect in which there was perhaps a trace of envy, "She bought this years ago, when the enterprise was comparatively new. It has not only paid dividends right along; what with stock splits and one thing and another, it is now worth twenty times what she paid for it."

"She was a brilliant woman," repeated Mr. Kent. This time he sounded as if he had invented Aunt Adelaide.

They finished their sorting. Agnes gave the pile of good little stocks a pat. The others she shoved back to Mr. Esta-

142

brook. "Could you have a list of these made? Two copies, please, one for you and one for me."

"Certainly, at once. How about those others?"

"Dividend checks will be coming in from those. I'm in no danger of forgetting them."

While the stocks were being listed, Agnes inquired about endorsing dividend checks. Some had already arrived; she produced them from her handbag.

"There's also the matter of inheritance taxes, isn't there?" she asked.

"Alas, yes!" said Mr. Kent. "There are the other legacies, too, and a trust fund."

"That will all be taken care of," Mr. Estabrook assured her. "You may have to sell some securities of those that finally come to you."

"You will have to," chimed in Mr. Kent.

"That's what I'm afraid of," said Agnes. "The ones I want to sell may be the ones that nobody else wants to buy."

Mr. Kent enjoyed her little joke; but Mr. Estabrook assured her, "It can't be quite that bad."

"I'll take to reading the companies' reports," Agnes promised him. "I'll pay more attention to the *Wall Street Journal*, too, though I don't know how much good that may do me. But I'm going to have to rely principally on you for my information, Mr. Estabrook."

This was the proper feminine attitude. Both the gentlemen beamed at Agnes.

It had been on the whole a highly successful interview. Agnes was still in a glow from it when she reached home. This seemed, then, like a good time to call Miriam.

The telephone in Antioch was not answered. Obviously Miriam was off again on her appointed rounds.

143

"Shall I keep trying?" asked the operator.

"Try again at half-past five," Agnes directed.

By half-past five she was feeling distinctly deflated. With all those other claims coming ahead of hers, many, if not most, of those stocks would not even belong to Agnes. Those two men had been indulging her all along. They would let the little woman go ahead and talk; the law and finance would grind on in spite of her.

She was grateful for the delay, however. All she now needed to tell Miriam was that she was getting the business affairs started.

That was what she did tell her when she finally got through. "I'd no idea it was going to be so complicated," she went on.

"Of course, Ladybird, you're inexperienced. You must trust older and wiser heads."

Come, this was something gained! Miriam wasn't trying to take over the direction of the whole affair. Not yet, at least.

It was time to change the subject. "You must be very busy these days," said Agnes. "It's hard on you, with all your outside interests, to have to do the housekeeping, too."

"Oh, I've arranged about that! I have somebody coming in tomorrow."

"That is quick work. Live-in servants aren't always so easy to get."

"They can be had, if you put your mind to it. Most women make too much fuss about such things."

Agnes agreed heartily. At this distance, she found it extremely easy to agree with Miriam.

She inquired about Sully. "He came over for a while Sunday," Miram reported. "The proverbial bad penny."

"Miriam, why do you say such a thing? I think you like him."

"I'm used to him. You're the one he really likes."

Just a hint of jealousy there? Not that it would signify if there were; the facts of the case were on Miriam's side. People liked Agnes, though Miriam was the one whom they respected.

"The next time you see him, give him my regards," requested Agnes.

Miriam laughed shortly. After that, there was really nothing more to say.

On Thursday morning, Agnes attended her first meeting of the Choir Guild. Dr. Follansbee was there to receive her. After he had introduced her around, he withdrew; and the president of the Guild, Mrs. Egan, instructed Agnes in her new duties.

At this meeting, all that the ladies had to do was get the vestments in order: brush and if necessary mend cassocks, press ties, make sure that fresh cottas had arrived from the laundry and last Sunday's been taken away. Her fellow members stood ready to help out her inexperience; and beginner though she was, Agnes didn't do too badly. After all, this sort of work was something every housewife did right along, or turned over to a competent servant.

When the session was over, Mrs. Wainwright learned that nothing more would be expected of her until half-past ten on Sunday morning. She took notice of which cars drove in her direction, and which members were doubling up. The time might come when she would offer some of them a lift.

Friday afternoon, Agnes took a long walk downtown. Several times she spoke to friendly strangers; twice she was greeted by name. Not by her own name both times; but the person who replied to her as "Mrs. Hammond" had at least made the identification.

Tom Jones had telephoned that morning to make an appointment for Saturday evening. When he showed up and again suggested a movie in his home town, Agnes repeated the caution which she had received.

"The darling old tabbies!" drawled Tom. "Just wait until we make our New York trip! That will give them something to talk about."

"Tom Jones, you don't really suppose I would go junketing off to New York with you!"

"You are to meet me there. Isn't that our agreement?"

"I wasn't aware that we had an agreement."

"You're aware of it now. Later on, you can name the day. That's the woman's privilege, isn't it?"

Agnes refused to commit herself about a New York trip. But after that, she almost had to yield about tonight's entertainment. Tom Jones was really an excellent strategist. He must have had a great deal of practice.

Agnes was a novice; and this was much more complicated than Choir Guild duties. Or than law and finance, for that matter. They proceeded according to recognized principles; but in the field of man-and-woman manoeuvring, the players made up the rules as they went along.

Still, she could learn. She might even enjoy learning. Tonight she rather thought that she would.

The evening itself she thoroughly enjoyed. When at its end Tom ventured to suggest that they "do this again a week from tonight," Agnes said demurely, "I don't make fixed dates."

This time she was the one who had scored. He hadn't

146

actually suggested that they spend all their Saturday evenings together; but he had taken the first step in that direction. She liked his nerve. Not even Agnes was as green as all that.

Sunday morning was wonderful. Agnes brushed choir hair and tied choir ties diligently if awkwardly; and the lad who had started this whole business for her recognized her with a prompt, "Hello."

Entering from the vestry, Agnes found Dr. Sheridan watching for her. He lifted his eyebrows, and Agnes nodded and smiled. So far, so good. Later on she would take her turn at getting the little darlings lined up for the processional. Today she was through until it came to the disrobing.

Agnes knelt for a minute of solemn prayer. Then she looked up the hymns. At the first note of "Oh, worship the King, all glorious above!" she rose with an eager personal interest. Here came the boys to whom she had ministered! After them, of course, the adult choir; but by that time Agnes was beginning to calm down.

For her the service reached its climax with the recessional, which happened to be a great favorite of hers anyhow. They did things beautifully here at St. Andrew's. Such perfection required repeated rehearsal and great nicety of timing. Yet as the choir swung into it, Agnes might have been hearing this good old hymn for the first time:

> O God, our help in ages past,
>   Our hope for years to come,
> Our shelter from the stormy blast,
>   And our eternal home.

So much they sang in position. Then with the first note of "Under the shadow of thy throne," the first marchers

147

stepped out of their stalls. They all proceeded across the front of the church. From the vestry came the concluding

O God, our help in ages past,
Our hope for years to come,
Be thou our guide while life shall last
And our eternal home. Amen.

Agnes knelt again. But this time her moment of private prayer was not only silent but wordless. Speech was not necessary when she felt so very close to God.

She and Dr. Sheridan had a chance for only a few words at the foot of the church steps before Eustace had her car in position; and of course Agnes could not keep the cars behind hers waiting. "See you this week," she said hastily; and with a strong pressure of her hand, he agreed.

After all that, reaching home was something of a comedown. Agnes was tired and a trifle rumpled, however; and by the time that she had freshened and changed, she found that emotion had sharpened her usual excellent appetite.

She had nothing planned for the afternoon; and by the time her roast chicken and apple pie had began to wear off, she found herself missing her Antioch prospect of Sully's weekly visit. Not missing it too acutely, of course; she had plenty of recent events to think over in quiet and at her leisure. But if she hadn't regretted anything left behind in her old home, this wouldn't be Marshfield at all. It would be Heaven.

It was still Marshfield, not Heaven, but Agnes was a little startled when Sully appeared upon the scene, life-size and taking his welcome for granted. His offering this time was a series of paperbacks unlike any he had ever before presented to Agnes: a pocket edition of *Roget's Thesaurus*, a dictionary, a cookbook, and an opus on how to achieve a successful marriage. Among them, these works ought to see a woman through almost anything; but Agnes found them of little immediate interest.

"Thank you kindly," she said. "These books are very informative. But they don't look as if they'd been picked out by the old Sully."

"They weren't. I'm a reformed character."

"Since when?"

"Since I shopped for these books when I changed trains, and realized that I didn't know which of the new whodunits you'd read."

"I haven't read any of them. *I* am a reformed character."

"You're prettier than ever. Or is it just that I'd forgotten how pretty you are?"

"The new blarney on top of the old malarkey! Wouldn't you like a drink, Sully?"

"I could be persuaded."

They were served, and he settled back. "Now tell me what you do with yourself in these fresh fields," he invited.

She told him about her enterprise with the Choir Guild. "I was a little bit doubtful when the rector suggested it. But so far I like it fine."

"You always steered away from organizations, I remember. But maybe it was just that you preferred to pick your own organization."

"It was Dr. Follansbee who picked—" began Agnes, and stopped short. Here they were again! This was just the same as saying, "When Miriam picked my organization for me, I did feel disinclined."

Sully caught it, and grinned. Avoiding his eye, Agnes

149

went on, "The last two Saturday evenings I've chanced a movie."

"Did Dr. Follansbee pick those for you, too?"

"Dr. Follansbee is a married man."

This time she really had put her foot in it. Sully guffawed. Agnes showed all her dimples. But as soon as he had got his breath back, she went on to explain, "I wouldn't have chanced going to a movie here in Marshfield. That would have been interpreted as dancing on Aunt Adelaide's grave. But I did allow myself to be talked into seeing the show in a neighboring town."

"Somebody talked you into it? I have a hated rival!"

"If you met him, you'd like him." Agnes had rallied. At her demurest, she went on, "I'm surprised you didn't go to see Miriam today."

"I'd no call to. I saw her yesterday."

"You what? I thought you worked Saturdays."

"I do. But I was showing a house in your neighborhood; and after the prospective tenants had driven themselves off, I dropped in at the Wainwright manse."

Agnes thought it over for a minute. This way he got them both in. But why would he want to get them both in, unless it was to observe and report?

"Then you've seen the new domestic?" she hazarded.

"Seen her and heard about her."

"The verdict is—?"

"I'd hate to eat any of her cooking even if I were invited to, which isn't likely."

"Miriam eats to live." Repeating the standard saying, Agnes sounded worried.

"She has taken in an old biddy who needs the job. Oh, a worthy individual! She wants to keep on working; that in

150

itself is praiseworthy. But she's past her work, and I don't know that she was ever very good. She must come cheap."

Agnes shot him a look. Miriam might be acting from mixed motives. Most people did, most times. Everybody did, sometimes. But this particular action manifested both the best and the worst in her.

"No, you ought not to go back and try to straighten up that mess," Sully mocked. "You're well out of it. Stay out."

"I can't very well do anything else just now. I have commitments here." Agnes glanced at Sully's empty glass. "Ready for a second, aren't you?"

"Aren't you?"

Both of them were. Agnes ordered it. Over the refill they met each other's eyes; both of them smiled and nodded.

Sully's mission was accomplished. Agnes found herself liking him better than ever. To be sure, she was no longer restricted to the Sullivan fare. Could that possibly have anything to do with it?

13.

AGAIN THAT WEEK, AGNES INVITED DR. FOLLANSBEE OVER FOR
tea. She wished to thank him for his suggestion that she
enter the Choir Guild and to ask him a few questions about
what lay ahead of her there. Incidentally, the occasion gave
her another chance to fill up on Sally Lunn. Once more her
weight was her own concern. (How brave the little mouse is,
when the cat isn't around!)

The Sally Lunn brought up the subject of hush puppies,
a Southern delicacy to which Rosa Lee Montgomery had
introduced Agnes one time when Miriam was away at a convention. They were so toothsome—and so fried! Agnes had
indulged in them afterward during Miriam's infrequent
absences. (No point to the little mouse's running into the
cat's jaws. Even a stupid mouse must know that much.)

152

Agnes learned that a committee of the Guild, changed monthly, attended the boys' rehearsals, which the choir-master, Walter Purdy, generally held separately from those of the grownups. He held that children had more respect for adults if they didn't see too much of their elders.

"That's one reason," said Agnes with a smile.

"Good as far as it goes. Doubtless there are others," Dr. Follansbee agreed.

"Children cannot sit still very long," remarked Agnes.

"Or keep going very long, either. At least, not in the same direction. Their span of attention is short."

"I wish I knew more about them." Her tone was wistful.

"You've taken the first long step toward learning."

"With your help, for which I'm very grateful."

"I'm enjoying it, too. So many people have no desire to learn. I have great sympathy with human frailty; but there are times when I get very tired of human stupidity."

"You ought to put that into a sermon," Agnes applauded.

Dr. Follansbee grinned appreciatively. "I'll do that very thing, and set the congregation wondering at whom I am preaching."

"Do they wonder whether you're preaching at them, or at which of their neighbors—?"

"I can only hope that I cause some soul-searching."

That sentence rang through Agnes's head after he left. There you had it! Hope was only the second of the virtues according to Christian doctrine. Yet every so often most of us had to fall back on the concept embodied in the beautiful old pagan myth, "Pandora's Box."

It had been a great favorite of Agnes's in her childhood. Late years she had thought of it too seldom. But she repeated it to herself now. It would stand a great deal of going over.

She put herself to sleep with it tonight. Or rather with half of it, for she began the story in the middle:

"Epimetheus had barely started for home when he knew that the box had been opened. Loosed on the world were war, famine, pestilence, disease: all the woes from which it had hitherto been free. This was Pandora's doing. His young wife Pandora, whom he had trusted with the great sacred chest. He had forbidden her to open it; and she had promised faithfully.

"When he reached home he trusted her once more. He asked her whether she had opened the box; and Pandora did not deny it.

" 'Did you let out all the spirits?' he asked. No, frightened as she had been, she had managed to close the chest before the last spirit escaped.

" 'Come, then,' he said. 'This time we will open it together.'

"Together they opened it; and there emerged from it that slim green-clad sprite who makes all the woes of the world endurable. Her name is Elpis, or as we say in English, Hope."

A lovely story, fraught with that inner truth which so far transcends fact. She must tell it to herself oftener.

Or had Agnes dragged it from the semi-oblivion in which it might much better have remained? For under its influence, the last image which flitted through her drowsing mind was not that of Dr. Follansbee, good kindly gentleman who had started this whole thing going for her. It was not that of Jerome Wainwright, with whom she had lived in contentment and trust until death did them part. It

154

was not even that of her father, who had once been the last thing in her waking thoughts.

It was that of the choirboy who couldn't sing. The steadfast friend, Dr. Hugh Sheridan, on whom Mrs. Wainwright had no designs and about whom she cherished no hopes. For once "the slim green-clad sprite" had deserted her. The fact that she had fallen violently in love with him was just her hard luck.

That week she made only a little progress with speaking to people in the street. But she began to get acquainted with her fellow members of the Guild. Nice women they appeared to be, intelligent and well-mannered. They could mention other members of the parish without disparaging them. In this way Agnes gained one or two bits of information; not important in themselves, to be sure, but they helped her to feel at home.

Then on Sunday she learned the names of several choir boys. Her first favorite was Roy Harris. "It's LeRoy really, but that 'Le' is sissy," he explained.

Agnes agreed with him sincerely. She had always felt the utmost sympathy for those unfortunate wights whose fond mammas had bestowed on them a monicker such as Claude or Percy, or worse still, one of those names like Marion or Vivian or Leslie, which are all very well for a little girl, but derogate a little boy's manhood.

Today she went into the vestry after the recessional, and succeeded in corralling three lads who would accept a lift home. Thus she made further progress in her design of getting acquainted. She also succeeded in avoiding Hugh Sheridan. Out of sight wasn't out of mind; far from it! Still, not seeing or speaking to him might help, if only slightly.

She had gone to the movies again last night with Tom

155

Jones. Not satisfied with that, he had suggested further encroachment. Sunday afternoon was a lonesome time for a man, he averred. Might he drive over and see her, if he promised not to stay too long?

"Stay for supper," Agnes invited. It was time she did something to repay his hospitality. That is, of course, if she expected to go on seeing him; and it didn't require extrasensory perception to tell her that Tom would be a hard man to lose.

She had a moment's misgiving after he had accepted. If Walter Sullivan again showed up, the three of them would constitute the proverbial crowd. But surely not even Sully would show up here in Marshfield two Sundays in succession. A trip like that was very different from his habitual "dropping in" at Antioch.

That is precisely what Sully did. He entered the Hammond mansion almost on Tom Jones's heels.

On being introduced, the two men greeted each other all too cordially. They both tried to wring the rival's hand off; they strove to give an impression that a hitherto barren life had been brought into flower and fruit by their meeting. Then they settled down and waited for the other fellow to leave.

Since Tom was staying for supper there was nothing Agnes could very well do except invite Sully, too. Agnes hadn't had so much fun in ages. When she was very young such a situation would have embarrassed her; indeed, it had happened more than once, with that very result. But now she delighted in seeing two grown-up, and for the most part intelligent, men behave like sophomores. It is to be feared that they enjoyed the meal more than the company.

Tom Jones drove Sully to his train. Not too tactfully, he

156

explained that this was no trouble, it was right on his way home. He left without having had two words alone with his hostess. Sully, for that matter, hadn't had one. Perhaps the encounter would teach him a lesson.

After their departure, Agnes caught the eye of a grinning Dora and shook her head. "Mr. Sullivan may have come over to talk business," she offered feebly.

Dora's smile widened. "If that was his idea, he can come back on a weekday."

"I'm sorry it made you extra trouble, and on a Sunday, too."

"That kind of trouble I'm always glad to take," said Dora. "It isn't as if I was young, and liked to go stravagering around the way the girls do."

" 'Stra—'?" The word was new to Agnes, but its meaning was plain enough. "Maybe not; but you might like to get some rest."

"I'm going to get some pretty soon. Some shut-eye, too. That is what a bed is for."

"Thank you for everything," said Agnes. "You're an uncommonly nice person, Dora."

"Thank *you*, Mrs. Wainwright," returned Dora. "The same thing goes for you."

On that cordial note, the evening closed.

Monday, Agnes looked up the three boys' telephone numbers and talked to their mothers. When she had explained the purpose of her call, LeRoy's mother was enthusiastic. "He has talked about you, Mrs. Wainwright. He says you are 'a good scout.' That's little-boy language; but it's high praise."

With her coöperation, the details of the expedition were settled and the hour on Saturday fixed. Mrs. Harris was the

157

sort that understood from the start. No wonder she had such a fine son.

Denny White's mother was reasonably cordial. She didn't see why Mrs. Wainwright should go to all that trouble, but . . . With her, too, Agnes arranged to talk to the boy himself at dinnertime.

Chance had arranged the mammas in descending order. Jock Clark's was cool; she sounded almost suspicious. At first, Agnes was minded not to urge her. Then she realized that her proposal was a little out of the ordinary, and Mrs. Clark might be a slow thinker.

Jock was a slow thinker too, as Agnes discovered at dinnertime. Roy said, "Oh, gee, yes! I'll be tickled to go." Denny's form of acceptance was, "That's peachy of you, Mrs. Wainwright." Jock hesitated until he was assured that Roy and Denny were coming.

When he finally answered, Agnes felt strangely relieved. Her party was not going to be haunted by the specter of a little boy left out.

Tom Jones called Agnes on Thursday. She was ready for him. She was going to the movies right here in Marshfield Saturday afternoon, she informed him; two shows in one day would be more than she could take.

"Did you say 'take'?" he teased. "Didn't you mean 'enjoy'?"

He was making the best of last Sunday's disappointment. When he spoke about coming over again this week, Agnes could do no less than say, "Yes, if you like."

"There's no chance that your Hibernian friend will show up, is there?"

"With Sully, there's a chance of anything. There's no certainty."

158

"The guy has staying power. I'll have to hand it to him."

"Did you expect him to rush off in the heat of the day without his blanket?"

Tom Jones chuckled. "When did I last hear that good old expression?"

"When did you first hear it? That's what interests me."

"Let's take that up on Sunday. All right?"

"All right with me. I'll be looking for you."

Her weekend was arranged for, then. All that Agnes had to do was go into details with Dora and give Eustace his orders. And, of course, wonder what would come unsettled. Something was certain to.

In a way, that was part of the fun. If your plans always went through without a hitch, that would grow monotonous. Distasteful, too, because in that unlikely event there would be nothing left for Hope-Elpis to do but crawl right back into Pandora's Box.

After this philosophical interlude, Agnes long-distanced Miriam. The old biddy answered the telephone, and reported that Miriam was out, "and I don't know when she'll be in."

"Thank you, I'll call again," said Agnes. "Will you please tell her that Mrs. Wainwright phoned?"

"*Mrs.* Wainwright? Mrs.—? Oh, to be sure, Mrs. Wainwright, I'll tell her."

Agnes wondered whether she would remember to. The poor old thing! Agnes experienced a fleeting sensation of guilt. Right now her own cup was running over almost too profusely.

On Saturday at the appointed hour Agnes picked up her guests, who had gathered at Mrs. Harris's to wait for her.

159

There was some squabbling as to which one was to sit beside Eustace in the front seat.

"The three of you will have to take turns," Agnes decreed.

That went down well enough with Roy and Jock; but doubting Dennis asked, "How can there be three turns?"

"One on the way to the movie, one on the way to my house for ice cream afterward, and one on the way home."

"Oh, are we going to have ice cream at your house?" asked Roy.

"That was my idea. Perhaps you have a better suggestion."

Roy beamed and shook his head. "Ice cream is ice cream anywhere."

Roy was—! He really was. Agnes would have hugged him on the spot, if she hadn't hesitated to embarrass him in front of his pals.

On their arrival at the movie theater, Eustace, obeying orders, parked the car nearby and brought up the end of the procession which entered. Agnes, heading the file, took a seat near the middle of a row. All three of the boys followed; Eustace took up his position on the aisle.

He enjoyed the movie almost as much as the little boys did, if not so noisily. Agnes would be the last person to discourage old loyalties; but she hoped that Eustace was beginning to find alleviations in working for a younger mistress.

"Ice cream" at the Hammond mansion included two kinds of cake and a wide variety of candy. All the boys ate with singular relish; there had been no meat and vegetables to take the edge off their appetites. When satiated, they strolled and looked, then came back for more.

Foremost in the fray was Jock. That poor child must have been held down at home. Agnes would never admire him

160

the way she admired Dennis the doubting. (Oh, sorry, of course his name was "Denny.") She would never love him the way she already loved Roy. But he was the one for whom she had sympathy. *Held down at home!* She would have liked to have him live with her for a while, so that she could spoil him: teach him the sweetness of having his own way! He couldn't have it all the time, of course; but to grow up without an occasional nibble at forbidden fruit was a barren prospect indeed.

Agnes took a small bite for herself when the boys were at length gorged and had been led upstairs to wash. A figurative bite, that is. As far as the actual "refreshments" went, she had eaten enough to keep her guests in countenance, and now rather wished that she hadn't.

She went to the telephone, called Antioch, and asked the operator to put her through to Walter Sullivan's office; she didn't know the number. His secretary answered; Mr. Sullivan wasn't in, but she thought she could locate him. Who was it calling, please? "Oh, yes, Mrs. Wainwright! Are you still over in Marshfield?"

Agnes was; but Mr. Sullivan mustn't put himself to any trouble on her account. She was leaving the house soon, and might be gone for the better part of an hour.

"It's no trouble, Mrs. Wainwright. I'm sure he'll be delighted to talk to you. Shall I ask him to call you this evening?"

"About seven, please," said Agnes. No sense in letting Sully know that she had the whole evening free; besides, it was her own choice.

She had already launched on her concluding speech when the secretary interrupted, "Just a minute, please! He's coming in right now."

161

So Agnes had to come plump out with her invitation. If Sully hadn't anything better to do tomorrow, would he like to come over here for supper?

"With you alone?" asked Sully.

"I expect Tom Jones, too. You and he got on so well before that I thought you'd like to see him again."

"You thought nothing of the kind," said Sully tartly. "You just want to let on that you have more than one string to your bow."

"Is that all the thanks I get for inviting you?"

"Oh, I suppose 'half a loaf . . .' "

"You aren't obliged to come, you know. Some other time . . ."

"That's enough along that line. It's darn sweet of you to ask me; but you might let me do my own refusing."

"Then you're coming?"

"You can count on me. I'll be looking forward to it."

She hung up just before the boys came clattering down the stairs. It must be many years since those walls had echoed to such a racket—if indeed they ever had. Agnes's mind came back to her duty as hostess; in the nick of time she remembered that at their age guests must always have something to take home from the party. Luckily, there was plenty of cake left; Dora wrapped generous pieces of both kinds in each package.

It was Jock's turn now to sit beside the driver; and Agnes saw to it that he was also the last to be delivered at home. She had accompanied each of the others to his door, not only as an act of courtesy, but for the fun to be got out of the scene. Mrs. Harris was as amused as Agnes herself at the account of a blissful afternoon and the burst of manners at the last minute. Mrs. White hoped that Denny hadn't

162

been "too greedy"; some greed she took for granted. But Jock, about to ring his own doorbell, looked up uneasily at his hostess.

Agnes understood. She kissed him lightly on the forehead; then she ran down the steps, calling over her shoulder, "See you tomorrow!" He had turned to look after her when the door opened; he never did get around to ringing the bell.

Eustace had remarked the incident, naturally. But on the way home, his one comment was, "That Roy, he's a humdinger. Born to be hanged, if ever a boy was." The omission was significant.

That evening, Agnes was both tired and strung up. After her pretense at dining, she had a hard time settling to anything. She wished—or almost wished—that she hadn't kept the evening free. Yet if she couldn't entertain herself once in a way, that spoke badly for her mental equipment.

She had planned to make this the first of several similar afternoons. She was committed to the undertaking, in fact; she couldn't favor three boys and then let the others down. But her heart sank at the prospect.

Then about the middle of the evening, while she was strolling restlessly from one room to another, all of a sudden she came on the reason for her depression. "I'm envious!" she said half-aloud. "I really should have had children of my own."

It was not too late yet; but she wasn't getting much of a start on the essential preliminaries. They could wait until later; in fact, they would pretty much have to. Tonight she'd much better relax and try not to think too far ahead.

She must invite Miriam over for a visit one of these days.

163

One of these days, before too long. That preoccupied lady might find herself too busy to come. But in that case, all she had to do was say so. Like Sully, let her do her own refusing. Anyhow, she would find herself unable to say, or pointedly to refrain from saying, that she hadn't been asked.

14.

Agnes's special three beamed at her on Sunday morning when she put the finishing touches to their toilets. Jock came back to say, "Won't you tie my tie for me again, Mrs. Wainwright? You did before; but it's sort of slipped." Actually, Jock! There was something so appealing in their turning to you for help. The time would come when a retied tie or a Saturday treat would no longer solve their problems. But the remembrance might linger.

Right now, the reputation was getting around. The three boys who were tapped for next Saturday's outing took a minute off to gloat over their companions. It wouldn't take too long to get around to the others; luckily for Agnes, the choir was half-adult.

That afternoon, Sully showed up early. He had a parcel of new novels in one hand and some expensive foreign magazines in the other.

"You took me rather by surprise yesterday," he apologized. "It wasn't until afterward that I realized how you were honoring me. This is the first time you've ever come right out and invited me."

His meekness wasn't any too convincing. Still, if he had made up his mind to behave, so much the better. Something different to read was a good idea, too. Agnes was beginning to get faintly tired, not so much of Stevenson himself as of all the furor that had been stirred up about him. It might be just a case of an over-zealous publisher; but when, late last night, Agnes had read, solemnly set forth in his *Collected Works,* the author's explanation of how he had come to write *The Master of Ballantrae,* for a fleeting instant she was guilty of the thought, *Suppose he hadn't? I should have made out somehow.*

Tom Jones had not been specifically warned in advance; but doubtless he had had his suspicions. This time neither of them overdid the so-nice-to-see-you-old-man stuff. In unison, they executed a series of deft conversational manoeuvres; at the same time they did full justice to the good cheer provided them.

This time Sully left a little early; the taxi which had brought him here called at a set hour. He was handing Tom Jones an advantage; but it was such an obvious advantage that it made Tom suspicious. It must have been against his better judgment; but the front door had barely closed on Sully when Tom growled, "You've known that fellow for a long time, haven't you?"

Agnes would have been put to it to answer that question

accurately. She simply could not remember meeting Sully. In a way it seemed as if he must always have been there; but she hadn't always lived in Antioch.

She smiled sweetly. "He's like a brother to me."

Tom eased a little. "You sure of that?"

"I can't be, quite. I never had a brother."

"What some man missed, not getting born into your family!" Tom had come to himself now. From an inner pocket of his topcoat he brought a small carefully wrapped package which he had destined for her until he found his adversary already on the scene.

Would he have presented it, Agnes wondered, if Sully hadn't taken himself off? A civilized code avoided bloodshed; but did it actually alter fundamental human emotions?

The next instant, she had forgotten their little comedy of manners. From its cerements emerged a vase about six inches tall, slender, shapely, perfect. Cameo Wedgwood, with the incredibly lovely legendary decorations standing out against a background of dark blue which verged faintly toward violet.

"Surely no one would ever dare to put a flower into that!" gasped Agnes.

"Better not! That flower would certainly blush unseen."

Agnes picked up the vase and sat turning it over in her hands. She listened to quite a lecture on cameo Wedgwood. It was still made, and sold widely; but they could no longer get that distinctive shade of blue even back there at the home pottery in England. They couldn't come by the clay. Those inimitable neoclassical designs were mostly the work of Flaxman; but which Flaxman was a question for scholars to argue about. There had been two John Flaxmans, father

167

and son; their work was much alike. Since they had had no idea that posterity would be interested, they had never bothered to differentiate.

"I don't see that it matters much, when all this beauty survives." Agnes looked up, started to smile in thanks, was suddenly grave again. "This is one thing the Hammond mansion didn't have."

"Has it now," Tom Jones corrected. "A small beginning, that is."

If he looked a little smug here for a minute, Agnes forgave him. He had just forgotten jealousy, and rivalry, and this thing called love, in his enthusiasm over something that really mattered.

She examined the beautiful small vase once more, then announced her conclusion. "It restores my faith in human nature."

"I didn't know you'd lost that faith."

"Not altogether. But it sometimes slips a little."

Finding the right place for this treasure might take a little time. It was still, in honor of its newness, standing on the mantel in the front parlor Tuesday afternoon when Dr. Sheridan telephoned. He had just completed a call in the next block; should he be in her way if he dropped in to see her for a few minutes?

"You're always welcome," she assured him. Then, lest that statement appear too general, she added, "Please come."

She had no time to dress in his honor. Luckily, Agnes made a point of regularly looking her best; in her mother's words, "I'm as nice as anybody who comes to see me." Anyhow, the color which mantled her cheeks and the added brightness in her eyes were adornment enough.

She reported to him on how she was getting along with

168

her boys. "Fine!" was his comment. "It's what I expected; but where boys are concerned, a person never can be quite certain."

"If you could, it might sort of spoil the fun." Agnes was again opening the door for Elpis-Hope; she changed the subject hastily. Taking down the Wedgwood vase from the mantel and handing it to him, she aired her new-found knowledge—and mentioned its source as an afterthought.

Dr. Sheridan offered no comment on Tom Jones; but after studying the vase long and carefully, he said, "To design things like this, or even to manufacture them! That would be a really satisfactory life; and in the end, a man would leave behind him something really worth-while."

"You sound almost envious."

"Not 'almost'! Quite!"

"But I should think a doctor, of all people, did the most wonderful work. Surely he is the one who can least be spared."

"Thank you for those kind words. Speaking for myself, I try to do my best. But in the end I lose out: my patients all die. Even those who survive me are going to die at the hands of another doctor."

" 'At the hands of—'? Isn't that a little severe?"

Dr. Sheridan relaxed, and grinned. "I didn't mean that the way it sounded. Please don't report me to the County Medical Society."

Dr. Sheridan had made a most uncharacteristic remark. There was more here than met the eye. But even if Agnes had felt free to ask questions, she wouldn't have known where to begin. Remembering the first duty of a hostess, she sat back and waited.

He returned the vase, and she set it back on the mantel.

169

She was now in a position to go on to the second duty of a hostess. "Would you like a drink?" she asked.

"Some other time. I hate to leave this pleasant place, but . . ."

"Come back whenever you're in the neighborhood and feel like it. For you, the latchstring is always out. Is that the way you say it, doctor?"

"That is the way I've always heard it said. It brings back pictures of a society which was more primitive, but certainly had its virtues. Right beside the stout front door was a hole. Through it the householder could poke out the end of a string. The select few might then enter at their convenience."

He got to his feet. "I'll try not to trespass on your hospitality."

Agnes said, "No question of trespass there." She managed to say it lightly. She rose, showed all her dimples, and realized that for once her passivity was working for rather than against her.

He smiled down at her; and this time it was a smile, not a grin. "There are various ways of routing unwelcome callers. I saw one exemplified in my neighborhood last summer. A very pretty girl lives right across the street from me. She is about nineteen, and has suitors aplenty. One evening, an unwelcome beau stopped in front of her house and honked his horn for her to come out and join him."

Agnes wrinkled her nose in distaste. Dr. Sheridan agreed, "Some of the younger set don't seem to know what a doorbell is for. Perhaps that was what my pretty neighbor didn't like. Anyhow, she ordered her four-year-old sister, 'Tell him I'm not home.' Angel Face obediently toddled out on the porch and hollered, 'She says she isn't home.' "

170

Agnes joined in his laughter. But a minute later she said rather sadly, "Do children have to be taught to lie?"

"They learn almost too easily. A white lie is a handy protection, however."

"So long as they don't lie to themselves?"

"That's a big subject. Let's not go into it right now."

"Right now" was just too short an interval. To prolong it a little, Mrs. Wainwright in person showed Dr. Sheridan to the front door.

She was doubly rewarded for her small courtesy. Not only did he wave her farewell from his car; he had barely started when, down the street, making right for her, came her favorite Imp of Satan, Roy Harris.

He had with him another boy, whom he promptly presented as "my fr'en', Dick Dickens. That is, his name is re'lly Stuart—or that's what his family think."

"Family names and playground names are often not the same," agreed Agnes, "just as the kind of dogs that appear in shows often have bench names which are different from their kennel names."

This piece of information was new to the boys. It required an amount of explanation which saw the three of them through removal of wraps and the guests' important choice between lemonade and hot chocolate. Wraps were disposed of, hands rinsed hastily. (More dirt came off on the towels than went down the drain.) Then cookies and apples were produced, followed presently by huge mugs of hot chocolate topped by marshmallows. Dora Dean raised her eyebrows inquiringly at Agnes, who controlled her shudder and ordered, "Hot tea for me, please, with lemon."

As soon as the sharp edge was off his appetite, Roy Harris explained, "I brought Dick along because I wanted him

171

to see for himself that there are some people who re'lly like children."

"Don't most people?" asked Agnes.

"Hah!" ejaculated Roy.

"Huh!" added Dick.

After a fresh onslaught on the food, Roy began again, " 'Wipe your feet before you come in the house!' 'If you're re'lly hungry, you can have a nice piece of bread-and-butter.' 'Certainly not; no dessert until you've cleaned up your plate.' 'Less noise there, please! I'm listening to the radio.' 'You may *not* have another comic program now; I want to watch the fights.' "

The mimicry was marvelous. Those admonitions may or may not have been heeded; but they were imitated to the life.

Agnes laughed and applauded. Then her sense of duty compelled her to put in a grownup's two cents' worth. "That's all very funny. But when we try to teach children to be less noisy and dirty and greedy, we do it for their own good."

"Hah!" said Tweedledum.

"Ho, ho!" boomed Tweedledee.

She hadn't fooled anybody. "Well, at least partly," Agnes amended.

"See?" Roy said to his friend, and Dick nodded gravely.

Mrs. Wainwright felt enormously flattered. Without much previous experience to guide her, she had somehow managed to come up to their high standards. She really did like children.

They were finally stoked up. "Shall we go into the back parlor and listen to records?" asked the hostess.

"That's one way to make us keep quiet," agreed Roy.

172

They started for the back parlor; but before they ever got out of the dining room Dick began to ask questions. Roy, in his character of Senior Guest, answered the first two or three. The answers were not any too accurate, but that didn't matter much. Dick barely listened, he was so eager to get on to the next point.

Roy gave up the part of cicerone, not from discouragement, but because something caught his eye and he too had to find out. By the time they were traversing the hall, Agnes was making the two of them take turns.

This lasted as far as the door of the front parlor; there Roy's inventiveness again took over. "This is sort of a processional," he decided. "Let's play church." Falling into solemn step, he began to sing through his nose, "Onward, Christian soldiers!"

As soon as they were fairly inside the room, however, he recast himself. "I'm Dr. Follansbee preaching. You sit there, Mrs. Wainwright, and be yourself. Dick, would you rather be choirmaster or— Oh, I forgot you don't belong! That's all right, though; you can simply be the stranger within our gates."

"In front of outsiders, let's not give St. Andrew's a black eye," Agnes warned. She didn't dare forbid Roy to play church; she had no answer for the inevitable, "Why not?"

The pseudo Dr. Follansbee told his auditors that here ended the First Lesson and here ended the Second Lesson. He went on, "I will now begin to preach."

He did so in dumb show, and devastatingly. Dr. Follansbee had one very unfortunate mannerism; every time he gestured with his right hand and arm, he must needs repeat the gesture with his left. Roy exaggerated the gestures into calisthenic exercises without ever losing the likeness.

173

Agnes covered her mouth with her hand, then realized, too late, that she might better have let him see her lips twitch.

Roy announced the subject of his next pantomime. "Here my mother sits." He made Mrs. Harris the picture of sweet attentiveness. "Here my father sits." Mr. Harris sat with drooping head and closed eyes; in an instant he began to snore. "Here Mrs. Wainwright sits." Agnes's hand went over her mouth, in Roy's imitation, to cover not a grin but a yawn.

The act was over, and about time. "Roy," said Agnes with mock solemnity, "do you know what the mamma monkey tells the baby monkey? She tells him, 'No boy shines.'"

That held Master Harris for as much as half a minute. Then he amended, "She tells him, 'No girl shines.'"

That delighted Dick so much that he began to repeat it verbatim. Then the two of them altered it to, "No boy-and-girl shines." Tiring at length of that, Roy essayed a higher flight, "She tells him, 'No Mrs. Wainwright shines.'"

This time Echo failed him; Dick went back to the "boy-and-girl shines." Agnes had to remind herself who it was started all this foolishness about "monkey shines."

When the clamor had died down a little, she suggested, "Perhaps we'd better let those records go till another day. I don't want your mothers to be sending out the Town Crier after you."

"What's that, the 'Town Crier'?" asked Dick.

This was Agnes's day for putting her foot in things. She explained, and that sent Roy off again. " 'Boy lost! Boy lost! Boy named Roy Harris. 'Nother boy lost! Boy named Dick Dickens. Let that one stay lost!'"

174

Of course poor Dick promptly started to holler, "I'm **not** the one who has to stay lost!"

Agnes squeezed his hand. "You're neither of you lost. That about the Town Crier is—" She had almost said "monkey business," but she caught herself in time. "That is something we'll talk over here, but not now."

"You mean you want me to come back, Mrs.—?"

"Yes, I do. I'm at home almost every afternoon along about half-past three. Every afternoon except Saturday, that is."

Her own use of the phrase "at home" recalled to Agnes the story she had heard from Dr. Sheridan. She told it now; but it did not get the reception she had expected. The boys saw nothing funny in such candor. Dick simply looked puzzled; Roy said, "That's all the sense a girl would have."

Agnes, going to the defense of her sex, pointed out, "I was a girl once myself."

"Did you have a big sister?" asked Roy.

"No. I was an only child."

"There, you see!"

What Mrs. Wainwright saw was that Roy liked to have the last word. Allowing him that might be the best way to get rid of him. Agnes moved toward the hall door while she was saying, "Thank you for coming, Roy, and for bringing Dick."

She helped them collect their paraphernalia. She would have liked to kiss them goodbye, but knew better than to attempt any such sissiness; she contented herself with shaking their rather grubby little paws.

Her forbearance was promptly rewarded. They were clattering down the front steps, and Agnes was still standing in

175

the doorway, when Roy said triumphantly, "There, you see!"

"She's a good egg, all right," Dick conceded.

The accolade! They had not only partaken of her bounty, they accepted her as one of themselves. Agnes realized that she was in a privileged position, much like that of an indulgent aunt. She could associate herself in their minds with treats and fun, while leaving discipline to parents and teachers—and, of course, choirmasters.

"Official spoiler to the children!" she said half-aloud.

In the front parlor, Dora Dean was already straightening the chairs. She caught Agnes's eye and shook her head. Then they both smiled.

"Such goings-on under Mr. Hammond's very nose!" Agnes agreed. "Yet I suppose he was once a little boy himself."

"He was before my day," Dora reminded Agnes. "Dr. Sheridan, now, must have been a proper little boy."

"By 'proper' I suppose you mean improper?"

"A little mischief, like most of 'em. If little boys behave, I always want to feel their foreheads for a fever."

"Little boys are not little girls," Agnes agreed.

"They are *not*. Will there be anything else now, Mrs. Wainwright?"

"Not now, thank you, Dora."

Dora withdrew, leaving Agnes to relive her afternoon. Through the later visit her mind moved back to the earlier. She crossed to the mantel, took down the Wedgwood vase, and stood caressing it.

Replacing it, she gave a little nod of satisfaction. Wedgwood and Flaxman and their likes led marvelous lives. So did doctors, in spite of Hugh Sheridan's discouraged talk.

176

But they weren't the only people who did anything worthwhile. Anybody who made a child happy was ranging himself on the side of the angels, and in bestowing got back more than he gave.

Roy thinks he invented me flashed through Agnes's head. In a sense, indeed, that was exactly what he had done. His Mrs. Wainwright, as he pictured her to himself, must be vastly different from the poor suffering sinner who stood in Agnes's shoes. He had given the lady something to live up to.

15.

AT THE GUILD MEETING THURSDAY MORNING, MRS. HARRIS said to Agnes, "I understand my young hopeful has gone to see you without waiting for an invitation."

"He has a standing invitation now."

"He also lugged along one of his pals?"

"He has been promoting me," Agnes acknowledged.

"Are you sure you don't mean 'exploiting'?"

"Quite sure. I could always let it be told that I'm not at home." This time, Agnes did not risk a repetition of Dr. Sheridan's story. In a gathering this size, there was too much danger of repercussions.

"But you've never had any children, Mrs. Wainwright," objected a stout complacent matron, Mrs. Mortimer. The

178

mother-of-the-Gracchi type that one: she plumed herself on the achievement of giving birth, as if that act had somehow endowed her with universal benevolence and complete understanding.

This was just the sort of thing that Agnes had been dreading in a gathering of women. But not all the members of the Choir Guild liked Mrs. Mortimer as much as she liked herself. Snappy little Mrs. Dundas, who generally listened much more than she talked, spoke up this time.

"That reminds me of something that once happened to me," she said. "Reminds me because it is so different."

This was a superb opening. Mrs. Dundas had everybody's attention. Now possessing the center of the stage, she proceeded to make good her position.

"It was some years ago," Mrs. Dundas began. "I was spending a few days alone in New York City; and on Sunday morning I attended eleven o'clock service at the great Cathedral of St. John the Unfinished."

"St. John the—?" Mrs. Harris got the point and began to laugh. For a minute she looked exactly like her son Roy.

"St. John's has a large boy choir," Mrs. Dundas went on. "A very fine one, if you like a boy choir. Personally, I don't care too much about them. Boys' voices are never true contraltos."

"They look awfully winning," said Mrs. White.

"That is just the point: their looks," Mrs. Dundas agreed. "Seated right next to me was another woman, also alone. She was seventy-five if she was a day, and just as nice as she could be.

"Well, the boys proceshed, and they sang the responses, and they sang the chants. Presently my neighbor could no longer contain her enthusiasm. She turned to me and said, 'Can't you just see what sweet little angels they are?' "

"Mary Dundas!" cried Mrs. White. "She didn't really—?"

"Hard to believe, isn't it, that anybody could live so long in this very varied world without finding out anything? Because even if you've no little boys of your own, the neighbors generally have plenty of that commodity."

The way that the ladies had come to her defense sent a warm glow to Agnes's heart. She had a wonderful sense of belonging.

An instant later, she found that she belonged almost too completely. Her lovely Mrs. Harris, her Roy's mother, turned to her to say, "The tickets won't come from the printer's until tomorrow. But we're giving our Fall Benefit Bridge; and I'd like you to play at one of my tables."

Agnes faltered that she was a very bad player. Mrs. Harris never even listened. She went on, "I realize that you're not well acquainted here yet, and can't be expected to make up a table of your own. But I've obligated myself for two; and I'd be delighted if you could help me out."

Against that approach Agnes had no proper defense. She couldn't say that out of deference for Aunt Adelaide's memory, she wasn't attending card parties that winter. Not when the prevalent topic at the meeting had been the fun little boys had at the Hammond mansion. She couldn't insist on buying tickets which she had no intention of using; that would be to flaunt the Hammond money in their faces. She temporized, "I'm not a good player; but I can always sit there and drop cards."

Afterward she realized that it was as good an answer as any she could have made. Agnes remembered enough of their old evening bridge club while Jerome was alive to be

180

aware that a bad player who acknowledged her defectiveness might be forgiven in the end. The dame (and it generally had been a woman) whose errors rankled was the bad player who thought that she was a good one.

With all due humility, Agnes bought the latest work by a noted authority on bridge, and studied it as earnestly as she might have studied her prayer book. But with considerably less profit. A session with her prayer book always left Mrs. Wainwright soothed and uplifted. The result of her present application was confusion and irritation. Helping along a worthy cause was doubtless fine; but this simply was not Agnes's idea of having fun.

Oh, for the strength of mind to have said "No!" Agnes had not left her old self behind when she came over here from Antioch.

With much trepidation, she had herself driven down to the guild hall on the appointed day. She would get through somehow, she supposed; and the coffee and cake would be doubly refreshing to a woman famished in spirit as well as in body.

She had wasted a good deal of worry (not for the first time in her life). All the aces and kings and queens in the deck flocked into her hand. Her erratic bidding might confuse her partner; it must have a similar effect on her opponents. She played several hands without disaster; and she did remember, when she was thrown into the defensive position, to lead the fourth from the highest of her longest or strongest suit.

Such luck could not last. It did not. For the final hands, Mrs. Wainwright found herself paired with Mrs. Mortimer. The mother-of-the-Gracchi looked as if she had lunched on coffin nails washed down with gall and vinegar; but for the first hand, which their opponents bid and made, she held her peace.

Then it was her deal. She sorted her cards, looked them over, and announced firmly, "Two no-trump."

Agnes scanned her own hand, swallowed hard, scanned it again. This time she had drawn from the other end of the deck. The highest card she held was a seven.

Her hesitation was enough for Old Gorgon Mortimer. Laying down the law with firmness and emphasis, she decreed, "My two no-trump means that you must name your best suit. You are required to keep the bidding open."

Agnes felt a pang of sympathy for the father of the Gracchi, be he ancient or contemporary. It was a three-card suit which was headed by the seven. Her four-card suit had the six for a topper. After a minute's further hesitation, she faltered, "Three diamonds."

Mrs. Mortimer promptly went to three no-trump. Second hand passed. So did Agnes, sure that this time she was doing the right thing. Fourth hand doubled. Mrs. Mortimer redoubled. Second hand led a low club; and Agnes's hand went down on the board.

For an instant, the Gracchi came near to being orphaned. Their mother was of a plethoric habit; and since her partner had simply followed the instructions so sharply given, there was nothing dear old Cornelia could do except hold her tongue.

She went down four tricks, doubled and redoubled. The very next hand, Agnes found herself holding all four aces, three kings, and a properly guarded queen. *"Three* no-trump," she said sweetly.

Everybody else passed. Agnes made a little slam, which

Good Old Infallible hadn't even tried to reach. Still, the overtricks added up rather neatly.

On the third hand, Mortimer & Co. set their opponents one trick. A poor revenge, but better than none at all. The fourth hand Agnes again played. She contracted for four spades, and made it.

Agnes downed her refreshments with real relish. The coffee and cake were passable, though nothing like as good as Dora Dean's. To Mrs. Wainwright, they tasted like nectar and ambrosia.

Thus fortified, she approached the president of the Guild and suggested, "We can use a little extra money, can't we?"

"I've yet to see the time when we couldn't. We've already filled our quota. But there's always the Bishop's Fund."

"With its insatiable maw," Agnes agreed. "Very well, then, a week from today I'm opening my house and providing the refreshments. The price of admission to outsiders will be one dollar; but any of today's company who care to attend may do so for fifty cents."

"Wonderful!" The president called the ladies to order and announced Mrs. Wainwright's most generous offer.

It found a good many immediate takers. Mrs. Gracchus hesitated. She was an inveterate bargain-hunter; her sort so often were. Offended pride struggled with avarice in her ample bosom. Avarice won.

"You are donating the prizes, Mrs. Wainwright?" she demanded.

"Yes, indeed!" said Agnes. She was carrying home first prize today: a pretty-enough travel clock which was doubtless the committee's booty from some badgered tradesman. But polite blackmail was no part of Agnes's scheme. No

183

server on committees she; while the money lasted, she proposed to pay her way.

She arrived home not merely with a trumpery clock, but with a most gratifying sense of accomplishment. She related to Dora Dean her triumph over Mrs. Mortimer: a double triumph, since The Old Redoubtable was thriftily tagging over here next week.

"Oh, her!" said Dora. That was all; but it was enough.

To say that Dora Dean entered into Agnes's plans for the bridge party is to give but a feeble idea of Dora's character and capacity. Actually, she took them over. Not only did she have to stand up for Mrs. Wainwright, her beloved Babe-in-the-Woods; Dora felt that the reputation of the Hammond mansion was at stake.

"Coffee and cake is all right at the guild hall," she decided. "Here at home we can offer both coffee and tea, and let them take their choice."

"We can also have cookies as well as cake," Agnes ventured.

"*And* sandwiches. Those frippery sandwiches women seem to set such store by."

"I think you're dreaming up something," Agnes charged. Then, smitten by sudden panic, "Where do we get the tables and chairs? And what do we do about prizes? I don't even know how many people are coming."

"Borrow tables and chairs from the guild hall. Eustace will see about having them carted up here for you. Buy more prizes than you think you'll need; you may want to give another party some day. You're going to use all new cards, too, aren't you? You can always lay by any extra packs; they don't eat anything."

The poor old Greeks used to have to go to Delphi when

184

they wished to consult an oracle. Besides, no sibyl of them all could possibly have baked a chocolate cake which rivaled Dora's.

Tom Jones showed up Sunday afternoon, uninvited but not unwelcome. His offering this time was a teapot of his own manufacture. Agnes, relaxing with him over glasses of Aunt Adelaide's wine, told him about her new undertaking.

"Fine!" he approved. "That's in the best Wedgwood tradition. Avail yourself of the old, but don't become a slave to it."

"Ah, the potter's craft!" Agnes ran a caressing hand over the new teapot.

"You're giving prizes, I suppose?"

"Have to. How else could I bribe them to play?"

"Use that teapot for a prize. I'll bring you a duplicate next week."

"Fine!" Agnes showed her dimples. "Did you say 'next week' or 'next time'?"

"It's the same thing, isn't it?"

She was neatly trapped; he had succeeded in pinning her down to a fixed date. Oh, well, if she decided later on that she wanted to ditch him, she could always find a way! Dora Dean could doubtless find some form of excuse a little more adroit than, "She says she isn't home."

"I'm trying for variety in the prizes," Agnes said. "I've already bought a bottle of cologne and half a dozen guest towels and two boxes of stationery: one notepaper and the other correspondence cards. Oh, yes, and a leather photograph frame! I mustn't forget that one."

"Your selection does you credit. Almost double credit," Tom proclaimed judicially. "Those bridge prizes not only have variety; they sound like things a woman might take home and use."

"Isn't that the big idea?"

"Is it? I've heard tell that there is such a thing as a perennial bridge prize. Something like one of these 'perpetual calendars.' "

"As if a person didn't have calendars enough sent around every year!" interjected Agnes.

"Exactly. Nobody ever used one of those perpetuals. They were taken home and saved to be used as prizes for the next big bridge party."

"But suppose the thing came back to the original donor!"

"That was a risk which the passers-on had to take."

Agnes shook her head. Now it was her turn to score. But she didn't wish to score too heavily. After all, Tom Jones had been helpful to her today. Into the bargain, she must acknowledge that she liked him.

She began rather slowly, "The source of your information is undoubtedly correct."

"Go on! Go on!" The words could not have been simpler; but Agnes could not be sure whether Tom Jones was gay or bitter.

"Her family name might well be as common as Jones."

"Or as uncommon as Wainwright. Agreed."

"Her given name I never have heard."

"It was Lucile. Still is, I suppose."

"You were—" Agnes had been about to say, "very fond of her, weren't you?" She checked herself in time, and substituted, "You were attracted by that name, naturally. It has a touch of old-fashioned romance."

"Is romance ever old-fashioned? What question did that old guy ask the Sphinx? You know, the one who is to

186

blame for all our modern perversions? You know, Eddie . . . Eddie . . ."

"Eddie Puss," Agnes supplied. "Spelled in Greek Oedipus. With your next glass of wine, would you like a sandwich?"

"Here's my hat, where's my hurry. No, thank you, Mrs. Wainwright. Better luck another time."

He accepted a second glass of wine, however, and sat staring moodily into its ruby depths. Agnes held her tongue. Was Tom Jones still carrying a torch for his lost Lucile, or was he merely nursing hurt pride? Not that his psychology need bother Agnes. He was good company once in a way; and his gifts were more than acceptable.

Not having to outstay Sully, Tom did not outstay his welcome. Thought of Sully reminded Agnes that the thronging concerns of the past few days had kept her from reporting to Miriam. It was too late to call her tonight. Perhaps, anyhow, it would be better to tell of results than of schemes.

It never occurred to Agnes that by her neglect she might be letting herself in for something. Anyhow, Miriam had kept her hands off about as long as she could endure it. She took it into her head to "run over" to Marshfield and pay her stepmother a surprise visit. It was simply somebody's bad luck that she selected that particular day for dropping in.

The bridge party was in full swing when she arrived. Agnes would have preferred not to play; but the eternal necessity for squaring up the tables forced it on her. To be sure, it might have been worse; one or two instead of three odd guests would have enforced cutting in, and the lady against whom the draw went would have had a fine opportunity for sulking.

Agnes was playing in the front parlor. At the stir of a late arrival, she looked up hopefully. This might mean a relief for her. Just as well it might mean a further complication, if the latecomer did not arrive alone. What she never for an instant expected was to see Miriam looming in the hall doorway.

Miriam, cloaked, booted, and spurred—or at least, that was the impression she gave. The guests had been relieved of their wraps, but according to guild hall custom had kept their hats on. That made Agnes's shining hair as conspicuous as the Helmet of Navarre, if not precisely in the same way. The apparel she coveted at the moment, however, was no headgear, real or legendary; it was the Mantle of Invisibility.

The hand had only two more tricks to go. Agnes nerved herself to play them. Then she made her excuses, advanced on Miriam, and greeted her cordially.

"I didn't know that I was walking in on anything," said Miriam stiffly.

"If I had had the slightest idea that you could spare the time, I'd have invited you over. Take my place now, won't you please? Here, let me have your coat."

"I haven't played in years," protested Miriam. "Not since the last time I came back from Europe; I always did play on shipboard."

"I'm sure you haven't forgotten how," wheedled Agnes.

"It may come back, if I give it time. All right if I stroll around and look on?"

It was decidedly all right. Miriam was introduced to the ladies at Agnes's and the neighboring tables. Then she

188

strolled into the back parlor. Agnes put her mind back on the game, which needed it. She wasn't having much luck today with her hands.

She made a creditable showing during that round. But when it ended, there came marching in from the back parlor Mrs. Mortimer, of all people.

Her presence at the next table was enough to throw Agnes off her game, if she had ever been on it. Still, the shifts might not—they surely would not—

But they did. Agnes sat there at the same table as if she had been anchored. And inevitably, with the frightful inevitability of advancing years or oncoming night, Mrs. Mortimer moved up. With the fateful certainty of death and taxes, she became Agnes's partner.

Agnes shouldn't have done it, of course; she was the hostess. But she was also a Costen and a Wainwright, and, by implication if not by blood tie, a Hammond. She was certainly not a poor relation of a Gracchus-by-marriage.

"It's nice to be playing with you again, Mrs. Mortimer," she said sweetly. "It's only fair to warn you that I've been holding pretty poor cards this afternoon."

"There is so much in the way a hand is played," boomed Mrs. Mortimer. Her steady march up-country was due to sagacity, not luck; the inference was plain. Of course, too, a good partner helped considerably.

"Indeed there is," Agnes agreed. "That's why I've decided on a response which I intend to use from now on. If my partner opens the bidding with two no-trump, and second hand passes—"

She paused to let that sink in. Then she resumed, "And I hold a bust hand, a hand without a possible trick in it, I intend to pass."

189

There was a soft gasp behind Agnes, then a snicker. She turned to look up into Miriam's face. Miriam was startled as well as amused. She hadn't known that Ladybird had it in her.

"Beginners always think they know everything about the game," Mrs. Mortimer thundered.

After that she felt better. Agnes didn't grudge her her retort. Right here and now, she didn't grudge anybody anything.

16.

When the paying guests started for their wraps, Agnes went in search of Miriam. She found her stepdaughter leafing through the expert-on-bridge; apparently she intended to linger for a few private words with her hostess.

"I'd love it if you could stay overnight," Agnes said. "I'm afraid I won't be able to offer you much to eat except leftover party food. But it will give us a chance for a good visit."

"It's kind of you to invite me, Ladybird. But Mrs. Cummings expects me."

Fortunately, there were no auditors when that nickname came tumbling out. Agnes could afford to overlook it. Besides, Miriam was quite evidently waiting to be teased; that in itself was a novelty.

191

"You can telephone," Agnes pointed out, and showed her a nearby extension.

"You are tempting me," said Miriam. After only a little further urging, she called long-distance.

She got through almost at once; but she couldn't seem to make "the old biddy" understand. Such stupidity was embarrassing, even at second hand. Hastily, Agnes bethought herself of her duties as hostess.

When she had sped the last of the parting guests, she went in search of Dora Dean. "Miss Wainwright is spending the night," she said. "Will you have the guestroom next to mine made ready, please?"

"I'll send one of the girls right up," Dora promised. "It won't take more than a few minutes."

"I have a new toothbrush for her," Agnes went on. "I always buy them three at a time; it saves bother. She carries a pocket comb. But about night clothes I'm a little bit puzzled. She prefers pajamas."

"There are some among Mrs. Hammond's things. She bought them a year or so after Mr. Hammond died. She used to take them with her sometimes when she traveled."

Agnes was slightly startled. Pajamas somehow didn't seem in character. But how much did she really know about Aunt Adelaide's character?

"I haven't even started to go over her things," Agnes apologized. "It's the sort of job that's just too easy to postpone."

"It brings back . . . memories." Dora swallowed hard. "What will you be wanting for dinner, ma'am?"

"I told Miss Wainwright not to expect anything except what was left over from the party."

"That ought to suit her fine. She sure tied into it this

afternoon, the girls told me. Acted like she was half-starved."

"That's a tribute to the excellence of your cooking." Agnes spoke smoothly enough; but she couldn't quite keep her face straight. If Rosa Lee Montgomery had overheard Dora's statement, her comments would have been more pithy than polite. Perhaps Agnes ought not to encourage servants to speak out. But in that case, think what she would have missed!

Agnes went back to her guest, and detailed the arrangements made for Miss Wainwright's comfort. "I'm afraid I'm putting you and Dora to a lot of trouble," Miriam deprecated. But obviously she was delighted at having so much fuss made over her.

Agnes thought of offering a bottle of Aunt Adelaide's good wine. She decided against it. Miriam was on her best behavior right now; no sense in rubbing in the fact that so many of the good things which might have been hers had fallen to Agnes instead.

Dora thoughtfully put a preface to the second edition. No doubt the soup came out of cans; but knowing just which cans to open and combine, and which touch of added seasoning would set the whole thing off—that was an art in itself. Miriam quoted those hackneyed lines from *Lucile* about civilized man's inability to live without cooks. Just for an instant, Agnes's mind strayed to Tom Jones and his Lucile. But that subject would keep. More immediate interest centered in Miriam's implication that the old biddy's feats in the kitchen were, to put it mildly, uncivilized.

They spent the evening listening to records. They retired early; it had been a large day for both of them. Agnes's last waking thought was that either Miriam had changed greatly or she had misjudged her stepdaughter.

Neither conjecture was correct. It became apparent at the breakfast table that Miriam had got out of the wrong side of the guestroom bed.

She began by tiding into Agnes about keeping so many servants. She didn't even call her stepmother "Ladybird"; she called her "you."

"It's perfectly absurd for you to keep three women and a man just to wait on one woman," began her tirade. When Agnes ventured that a big place like this entailed a lot of work, Miriam brushed aside that consideration with a curt, "Nonsense! They spend most of their time waiting on one another."

"They enable me to entertain," Agnes insisted.

"If yesterday's shindig was a fair specimen, that's not much of an achievement. You have a lot of cackling women in here wasting an afternoon and eating their heads off, on the pretext that you are raising money for some worthy cause. If the good of the cause was what you had at heart, you might better have given it the money to begin with."

"More coffee?" suggested Agnes.

"I haven't finished my first cup. Coffee-drinking is just a habit, anyhow. The way you put sugar and cream in yours makes a bad habit worse. You are taking on weight; and you haven't the will power to deny yourself things that you must know are doing you harm."

"Surely I'm the best judge of what may be doing me harm."

"Surely you're no judge at all. If you were, I wouldn't have to talk to you like this."

The duty was self-imposed. Moreover, Miriam was one of those select souls who enjoy doing their duty. They

194

know what the other fellow's duty is, too. Better than he knows it himself. Far better!

Miriam succeeded to a limited extent; she spoiled Agnes's breakfast for her. The fact that the servants she denounced might overhear her remarks and put their own interpretation on such never seemed to occur to the belligerent Miss Wainwright.

She finally did take herself off. Agnes's feeble "Come again" was followed by the unspoken rider, *when you can't stay so long.* She had pressed Miriam into staying. What she got served her right, in a sense. But it seemed a severe penalty for the exercise of a little hospitality.

That very afternoon, Hugh Sheridan phoned and came over. This time Agnes's agitation was not on his account, and did not subside when he reached the Hammond mansion.

He perceived her upset, of course; and to her offer of a glass of wine he responded, "I'd like it. You look as if you needed it."

"I think I'm coming down with something," Agnes parried.

He laid his hand on her forehead for an instant; then briefly he took her pulse. Old-fashioned methods of diagnosis these; that gave Agnes her cue for a casual remark. Her pulse was going much too fast; but his professional touch on her wrist was not responsible.

"I didn't know doctors still did things like that," she remarked. "I thought that nowadays they ordered X-rays and electrocardiograms and laboratory tests."

"We can always do that if we want to keep the patient amused." He grinned. "Or run up the bills. When I was a little boy, a good old family doctor always wanted to look

195

at a person's tongue. One time when my mother was the patient, I was near the door when Dr. Brown was leaving. He said, 'How are you today, Hugh?' Right away I stuck out my tongue at him.''

"Do you want to see mine?"

"I'd rather listen to it."

The wine arrived. As soon as the two of them were alone again, Dr. Sheridan lifted his glass to Agnes. After the first sip he said, "You're not sick. Other people have their troubles, too. Want to tell Papa?"

Agnes remembered that you could put a thing in a general way, naming no names. "A hypothetical question," Jerome used to call it.

She nodded. "If a person treats you like God's gift one day, and like dirt the next, what does it show?"

"I'd say offhand, it shows he's of a divided mind, but much interested in you."

"Oh, this isn't a he! It's a she."

"You get on better with men than with women, don't you?"

"Oh, not here in Marshfield!" said Agnes hastily.

Too hastily. Dr. Sheridan must have had his suspicions before; she had now confirmed them.

He smiled, but he preserved the incognito. "The lady may be unhappy, somewhere deep underneath."

"She may be. She seems very sure of herself."

"So sure that she wants to do your thinking for you?"

"Have you been listening to gossip, doctor?"

"I know a born boss when I see one. The general manager type. It's not uncommon."

"At least she used to be consistent. If she sometimes went

196

too far, perhaps it was as much my fault as hers. I ought not
to have given in so easily."

"Do you always insist on sharing the blame?"

Agnes dimpled. "My mother used to tell me that I would
say a good word for the Devil himself." She and Miriam had
thrashed the subject out, too.

"Well, wouldn't you?"

"Certainly! It must be awful to be condemned to spend
eternity in Hell torturing all those poor souls."

"To you, the Devil is only folklore?"

"Well, I've never met a person in whom there wasn't
some good. So if the Devil did exist—I'm afraid I'm getting
in pretty deep. I sound confused."

She felt better, anyhow. Dr. Sheridan had not only listened to her problem; he had contrived to administer a pat
on the back. There for a minute or two Agnes and he had
been very close.

As close as they might ever get. But the very measure of
what she had missed revealed to Agnes how much she had.

They sat there in an understanding silence which they
were both loath to break. It was only when Agnes reached
for the decanter that he shook his head and set down his
empty glass. "No, thank you. I'd like to stay longer. But
by the time I get so old that I can do as I please, I'll be so
old that nothing pleases me."

"With you, that time will never come."

This time it was Agnes who had administered the pat on
the back. He appreciated it, too. The afternoon had more
than made up for the morning; and that was an affair which
took some doing.

At the Guild meeting Thursday morning, there were
echoes of Agnes's party. "A great success," Mrs. Dundas

197

summed up. "It put our official benefit bridge quite in the shade."

"Oh, I wouldn't say that!" Agnes disclaimed modestly. "Surely there's room for both."

"Peaceful coexistence?" asked Mrs. Harris.

"Exactly!" Agnes agreed. "Those words mean something, when they don't come out of the mouth of a politician."

This gave Mrs. Mortimer her opening. "They mean the same in themselves, no matter who uses them."

Mrs. Harris murmured approval. But her eyes caught Agnes's, and one of the lids descended ever so slightly. Roy's mother, all right. That half-wink alone was enough to assure Agnes that she hadn't dreamed her original choirboy.

She had further proof that afternoon. "Dick" Dickens appeared at her house and announced, with just a shade of anxiety, "Roy said I was to meet him here, if it was all right with you, Mrs.—"

"Indeed it is all right with me. Come in and make yourself at home, Dick."

His hesitancy over her name might arise from trouble with the word itself. Then again, it might mean that he was still uncertain of his welcome. She thought of asking him to call her "Aunt Agnes," and decided against it. With a considerably younger boy it might have worked. There too, it might not have. It was one of those things which grown people dream up when they might be more suitably occupied.

Dick had already deposited his wraps and his schoolbooks in the hall. He glanced toward the front parlor, grinned, and said, "Roy is funny, isn't he?"

"Very. I'm just as well pleased, though, that he isn't twins."

198

"Two like Roy? Oh, now you're the one that's funny, Mrs.—!"

"Wainwright," suggested Agnes.

It worked. He repeated carefully, "Mrs. Wainwright."

They were laughing together when there was a second ring at the doorbell. Roy walked in on them, and glanced eagerly from one to the other. Then his face fell. He must have sent Dick on in advance just so that he and Agnes could become better acquainted. But the Harris strategy had worked almost too well. If Mrs. Wainwright should like Dick better than she did him—!

"We were waiting for you," said Agnes quickly. "Now the party can begin."

"What party?" Roy demanded. But he cheered up at once.

The refreshments were ordered. "The boys will have time to wash while I'm making the cocoa," Dora Dean hinted broadly.

"Oh, gee, do we have to wash?" blurted Dick. Somebody was always taking the joy out of life.

Roy was undaunted, however. He began to pantomime cleansing, decorous enough at first, but soon lapsing into licking fingers and then wiping his face with his sticky fingers. For the sake of grown-up honor, Agnes had to fetch a wet washcloth and a towel and do a job of sorts on the two of them. But Roy was a hard child to discipline, even if Agnes had had more practice. Sternness amounts to very little when you have already laughed.

He had initiative, too, and a talent for getting on with people. When he and Dick had stoked up, Roy suddenly demanded, "Do you know any stories, Mrs. Wainwright?"

199

"Lots of them," Agnes assured him. What was the varmint up to now?

"The same ones I know?"

"Such as—?" This wasn't holding up her end. Agnes changed the sentence to, "Such as *Robinson Crusoe* and *Ali Baba* and *Aladdin*."

"Want to play one of them now?" Bless his little heart, he was including her! "Not *Robinson Crusoe*. Dick and I can play that when we're by ourselves." They could; and there wasn't much doubt as to which one would play the part of Man Friday.

"In *Aladdin*, I could be the Princess Balroubadour," Agnes suggested. She could be Aladdin's mother. Neither of these ladies was any too bright; but the narrator of the *Arabian Nights* tended to underplay the women—and for good reasons of her own.

"Fine!" Dick accepted in both their names. "I begin, then." He got to his feet, and in a voice seething with duplicity addressed Roy. "Are you little Aladdin, the son of Mustapha the tailor?"

In a shrill childish treble, Roy replied, "My father's name was Mustapha, but he is dead."

They were off to a flying start. As the Widow Mustapha, Agnes had a tendency to foul her lines; but they promptly set her right and rushed ahead. She was one of them now; but they must indulge a newcomer. The Princess Balroubadour had nothing much to do except stalk across the stage. Dick was the most active performer, being not only the villain of the piece but the Slave of the Lamp. Roy was the center of things, however; and why not? He was stage manager as well as leading man.

They ran through the thing in grand style—and in record

200

time. The boys had a second round of refreshments. Then they and their hostess moved of one accord to the wraps and the schoolbooks.

At the front door, Dick fell a little behind his friend. Almost pleadingly he said, "You didn't tell me about the Town Crier."

"I will next time," Agnes promised. "All right, Roy?"

"Sure," said Roy. "And next time we'll play *Ali Baba*."

"Hooray!" shouted Dick. "I'm Cassim Baba, the wicked brother. I say, 'Open wheat' and 'Open oats' and 'Open rye' and 'Open barley.' "

"But you can't think of 'Open sesame,' " taunted Ali Baba.

They were still rehearsing when they went off down the street. Agnes remembered that Cassim Baba was a bad man because he stole from his own brother. Ali Baba was a good man; he stole only from the Forty Thieves.

It had been a very happy session; and it presaged others. The afterglow lasted until well along in the evening. Then it didn't exactly fade; but it receded far enough to make room for that preoccupation of hers. "That" preoccupation: the one about Miriam.

Agnes would have liked a child of her own; but that did not seem to be in the cards for her. In a way it didn't make too much difference, now that she had little boys underfoot most of the time anyhow. In another way, it made all the difference. She would have dearly loved to be the mother of a little boy; little boys were such a strange mixture of angel and gutter pup. Or a little girl whom she could indulge to her heart's content. A little girl who would eventually grow up and marry and make Agnes a proud grandmother.

Being a grandmother was the crowning achievement of a successful life. Agnes was two steps away from that; and

201

even if she eventually made it, that would take a long time as well as several batches of good luck.

But there was a much shorter route to the same end— or almost the same end. If Miriam married, Agnes might become a grandmother in a few short years.

Marriage and motherhood might make a great difference in Miriam. Might? They surely would. Miriam would make an excellent if exacting wife and mother; and Agnes would be a grandmother by brevet while she was still a young woman.

She could give Miriam's children a little needed spoiling, too. There would be every excuse for that. She wouldn't mind too much if *they* called her "Ladybird." In her new-found dignity, however, perhaps Agnes might have some say-so as to what she was to be called.

Grandmother. Grandma. Gram. Gammie. The names tuned in together like a set of chimes. While she was telling herself stories, too, she must not forget that American children were brought up with their mothers' families. Even if Mrs. Wainwright were not the only grandmother, she would be the favored one.

But wishes were not horses. Not only was there nothing Agnes could do to set Miriam's feet on the bridal path; she could not fairly imagine it. Men simply do not propose to a marble statue of Pallas Athena or Diana the Huntress.

As for espousing a handful of worthy causes, and loving and cherishing a woman in the intervals between her service on committees—! A man might be tricked into it. But Miriam was no tricker. Apparently, too, she was satisfied with the life that she had chosen. She couldn't be expected to sacrifice it in order to fulfil her stepmother's daydreams.

Miriam might well run for Congress one of these days.

202

Come, this was better! If Agnes were still living outside the congressional district—

No "if" about it. While Agnes was making up the story, she might as well make up a good one.

Here goes! Miss Miriam Wainwright is running for Congress on a platform of "Law and Order." She proposes to give jobs to all the worthy old biddies who need them. This will not only cut down the relief rolls; it will cut public payrolls. This in turn will lower taxes.

So far, so good. The work wouldn't be well done. But Agnes remembered that Jerome had more than once let it be known as his opinion that public work was usually not well done anyhow.

A wealthy relative upstate was contributing to Miss Wainwright's campaign fund. Miriam was running as a Republican, no doubt. "When it comes to paying my taxes, even voting Republican doesn't help" flashed through Agnes's mind. Could she claim as an income tax deduction the money she contributed to Miriam's campaign fund? Agnes must remember to ask Mr. Kent about that.

Here for a moment Agnes half-believed in her own fable. It was nonsense, perhaps; but it had an underlying plausibility. Miriam was the perfect Madam Chairman; there was no point to confining her talents to the town where she happened to have been born.

And where her stepmother had inherited the family home. Agnes came down out of the clouds very abruptly. Painting a rosy future was all very well until you reached the point where you believed in it yourself. That way madness lay.

Agnes deserted the future and began to relive the immediate past. " 'My father's name was Mustapha, but he is dead.' 'Alas, poor Mustapha! I was your father's brother.' 'I

203

never knew my father had a brother.' 'I have been away a long time, Aladdin. But I have come back to make you all rich.' "

All this may never have happened; in a literal sense, it hadn't. But so many generations had loved it and believed in it that in its own way it was true.

Recalling this afternoon's play-acting, Agnes felt warm and relaxed. It seemed to her that, sometimes at least, there was enough happiness to go around. Even Cassim Baba must have gloated when he supposed his cheating had been successful. His impersonator had a fat part. The climax of the drama came when Cassim Baba could remember everything except the one thing important.

No wonder generation after generation had doted on the *Arabian Nights*. The moral to one of its tales, if moral there was, got lost in the interest of the story.

17.

Agnes's series of Saturday parties for her choirboys drew to its end. She might repeat it in January, when things again began to lag. There were two strong reasons against doing so immediately: a custom tends to stale, and she had thought of an interesting variation. The two faces of the same medal, possibly.

She was confronted now with Thanksgiving, a holiday which would give Dora Dean full scope for her art. It seemed to have stolen up on Agnes. But since it did not, like Easter, shift its position in the calendar, she must have had the usual warning. Time went so fast here in Marshfield.

She consulted Dora, who promptly declared for a one

o'clock dinner. On Sunday, Agnes invited Tom and Sully
to that jollification. Oh, not in front of each other! She went
to the movies with Tom Saturday night. Sunday afternoon
she waylaid Sully while Tom was explaining to Dora Dean
that although he had the utmost respect for her professional
know-how, he still felt that there were two schools of thought
as to when, and whether, vegetables should be mixed.

Tom Jones had accepted with thanks. Sully said, "I was
just waiting to be asked."

"If I had known that—" threatened Agnes.

"Yes, what?"

"I suppose I should have asked you anyhow. I'm used
to you."

"That's the whole trouble," muttered Sully.

Agnes gave him a sharp look. She hoped he wasn't getting
any silly ideas.

"Is that fellow coming too?" demanded Sully.

"You surely don't expect to dine tête-à-tête on Thanksgiving?"

"Hardly. I was just wondering whether there will be
drumsticks enough to go around."

Agnes wasn't quite sure herself. There was one point
here on which she still had to make up her mind.

"I am inviting Miriam," she stated.

"Naturally, Ladybird."

Agnes ignored the insult. "You may ride over with her
if you like; but you will not be required to escort her.
Miriam comes and goes independently."

Sully chuckled. "Agnes, I declare I cannot make you out.
Sometimes I think you're a poor sweet little put-upon
simpleton. Other times I think you're the smartest person
anywhere around."

206

"I'm neither the one nor the other. But I'm grateful for your interest."

"It would suit you just fine if I married Miriam, wouldn't it?"

The shot told; but Agnes recovered herself in an instant. "Get rid of you? I'd be stuck with you both for the rest of my natural life."

This was even funnier. "Gave yourself away that time, didn't you?"

Agnes finally boiled over. "Walter Sullivan, if you were only three years old—"

Hesitating to say what she would have done under those circumstances, Agnes heard a polite cough from the doorway. It was Tom Jones. There was no telling how long he had been standing there.

"You two talk to each other for a few minutes," Agnes commanded. "I want to see whether I can get through to Miriam in Antioch."

She couldn't. But by the time she rejoined them she had simmered down. Sully was all right in his way. He had simply come too close to the mark when he talked about marrying Miriam.

Not that it was anything but talk. Sully cherished his freedom as only a chronic bachelor can. And what made him think that Miriam would have him, anyhow?

Quite unbidden came the thought, *Sully must have been cute when he was three years old. He wouldn't make a bad father, either.* Sharply, she chided herself, *But Heaven help any poor woman who married him.*

She got through to Miriam the next day. Miriam would be delighted to come for Thanksgiving. She would have to leave in good season, however; early, indeed.

Was Miss Wainwright just a shade remorseful for an occurrence which neither of them had forgotten, though they had both tried to? Or was she merely reminding her stepmother that she was talking to a busy and important person?

"It's a long way to come for a slice of turkey," Agnes soothed.

"Not too long a way to come to see you, Ladybird." Oh, yes, she said it! Whenever Agnes began to feel compunction —and she often had occasion to feel it—out came that atrocious nickname. Nickname? It was an epithet!

Thanksgiving Day was not primarily a turkey-eating day, much as Agnes liked her turkey and looked forward to tasting it as set forth by Dora Dean. She was thinking of that when, in a magazine which turned up in the back parlor, Agnes read a rather frayed clipping.

It must have meant a great deal to Mrs. Hammond. Or no, don't bother about that, Hammond heiress! What does it mean to you right now?

Agnes blinked, cleared her throat, and read aloud to that keenly interested audience, Mrs. Wainwright:

Holidays

Every day is Thanksgiving Day
   If you have a thankful heart;
Every day is New Year's Day
   If used for a fresh start.

Every day is Christmas Day
   To a spirit filled with joy;
Every day as it comes to us
   Is a brand new glistening toy.

208

It was signed "Gwendolyn Seeley." The name was strange to Agnes. But whoever Gwendolyn Seeley was or had been, she must have experienced many of the common vicissitudes of life. Probably she had had her share of private troubles, too: had seen her loved ones leave her; had seen dear ambitions disappointed; had felt at times that the struggle was not worth continuing.

Yet she had not only continued it; from the bitterness she had managed to distil a brew that was sweet, and—to Agnes at least—just a little heady. It had gone to Aunt Adelaide's heart, too; else why she had kept it by her all these years during which it yellowed and almost wore to tatters?

"Kept it by her." But had she? Perhaps she had simply laid it aside and forgotten it. Agnes glanced impulsively at the magazine in which she had found the waif, and discovered to her relief that that particular number was less than a year old. Gwendolyn Seeley's message had been cherished for a long time; it had just reached its second mark.

The message moved Mrs. Wainwright to action, indeed. She telephoned Dr. Sheridan and invited him to come for Thanksgiving dinner. When she learned what served her right, that he had already accepted an invitation (he told her whose; he was not "pleading a previous engagement"), Agnes said, "Then can't you join us for supper? Just come in any time that you feel like picking the bones of a turkey."

"Indeed I will! I not only enjoy cold turkey—I believe I almost prefer it to hot! I have a smug feeling that I may be helping somebody to avoid the deadly aftermath, turkey hash."

"There might be such a thing as turkey soup, too," Agnes

209

conjectured. "Let's not talk about things like that, however. It's out of the spirit of the season."

During the next two days, she talked briefly to both Mr. Kent and Mr. Estabrook. Both of them brought up the subject of Thanksgiving dinner. If they had intended to invite Agnes to be "the stranger that is within thy gates," they should have done the calling, and called sooner.

How neatly both the lawyer and the banker had "saved their credit and their bacon, too!" To be sure, Jerome Wainwright had never made his home an annex to his office. A doctor's wife was different.

Or a clergyman's, Agnes added hastily. Dr. Follansbee had announced that on Thanksgiving morning there would be Holy Communion at eight, then no further services. "But during the afternoon, Mrs. Follansbee and I will be at home to all members of the parish and other friends who may care to call. Thanksgiving is a family holiday, and a friendly one." Mrs. Follansbee wasn't completely wedded to her husband's job, however; she never came near the Choir Guild. A smart woman, to settle things on her own terms.

Agnes did not go near either the church or the rectory on that fine day there at the end of autumn. She had her hands full right here at home.

She had planned to decorate her table with a fruit centerpiece, and had laid in supplies accordingly. Then on Wednesday evening, there was handed in an elaborate and rather stiff floral centerpiece with an accompanying note: "Dear Ladybird, I am ordering this by letter, and can only hope that my instructions will be carried out intelligently. I am looking forward to the occasion. Devotedly yours, Miriam."

210

A nice piece of attention on Miriam's part, no doubt. The only trouble was, Miriam never had learned the difference between attention and interference.

About an hour later arrived Sully's telegraphed flowers. Tom Jones's came Thursday morning. The same messenger delivered Dr. Sheridan's sheaf of chrysanthemums and greenery.

An embarrassment of riches, thought Agnes. Aloud to Dora she remarked, "This gives me almost too much to be thankful for."

"Do you want to look over the vases again, Mrs. Wainwright?" suggested Dora.

Agnes did so, and found her head clearing. The important thing was to play no favorites. She was grateful to them all; and today, least of all days in the world, did she wish to hurt anybody's feelings.

"It's a big house!" she said slowly. "Yes, and it's my house!"

She set Miriam's offering on the sideboard in the dining room, and flanked it with two vases containing Sully's flowers. Tom Jones's tribute was suitably distributed about the sitting room, with a preface set forth in the front hall. Dr. Sheridan's gift was almost evenly distributed between the front and back parlors. It was equitable. It was decorative. It gave Agnes full freedom to go back to her original plan.

On a large silver platter she laid a small pumpkin. To the principal points of the compass she allotted four grapefruits. Then on a bed of greenery she laid out oranges and lemons and apples, interspersed with bananas. These were crowned with Malaga and Tokay grapes, artfully accented by a few bunches of good old Concords.

211

A bunch of these last Agnes appropriated and devoured. She was surely entitled to this much after breakfasting on coffee and toast and then wrestling with a complicated problem.

When it came to planning the table setting of which this was to be the focus, Agnes found herself compelled to outline the plan and then entrust most of the details to Dora Dean. The resources of the establishment were so vast, and the heiress knew so little about them! Miriam and those pajamas of Aunt Adelaide's: those pajamas may have been the shirt of Nessus! The books and the records might have belonged to anybody, though they were clear indications of Mrs. Hammond's taste. But there were inner recesses into which Agnes hesitated to intrude. Hesitated, almost as if she feared to.

The table was finally set for the four of them. Four was too few to be set off against all that grandeur. Yet considering the mixed character of the company, perhaps it was just as well that they would have a good deal of space between them. Too late to worry about that now! The arrangements were complete, even to a decision that this time Agnes would herself compound the two martinis which should sharpen, not dull, the party's appetite for the great feast. Agnes went upstairs, with just about time enough for a quick shower and the donning of gala raiment.

At the last minute, she realized that she had not left quite time enough. There was always that forgotten but important detail: that little extra on which everything depended: that hole in the dike through which would seep enough moisture, not perhaps to inundate the district, but certainly to dampen the spirits of the entire assembly.

Agnes dashed down to Dora, interrupted her at a high

212

moment of her culinary art, and demanded that she find
Eustace and send him down to the station to meet incoming
trains from New York. "I don't know which one they'll be
on," she continued breathlessly. "Miss Wainwright and Mr.
Sullivan, that is. I don't even know that they are coming
on the same train. But if he doesn't mind an indefinite
wait—"

"That's all right, Mrs. Wainwright," Dora interrupted.
She could stand the floundering no longer; besides, she
had more important business to get on with. "Eustace left
almost half an hour ago. He said if no guests of yours were
on the next train, he could always give a lift to somebody
else's."

Agnes, disheveled though she was, turned radiant. "Oh,
thank you, Dora! Thank you and Eustace both. It's a good
thing I have the two of you to do my thinking for me. It's
an exercise in which I haven't had enough practice."

Her mind was much relieved, even if her time was
shortened. Agnes dressed, made up (just a little bit more
than she would have a year ago), and descended the stairs
at the moment when the second maid was admitting the first
guest.

Who turned out to be Tom Jones. Not only did he arrive
here under his own power, and park his car as if he had
parked it here before. He brought in a fairly large Thermos
bottle, made as if to hand it to the maid, then presented it
to his hostess.

"It's a trifling present," he explained. "A jugful of
Martinis made according to my own special recipe. If your
other guests don't care for them, you may save them or
throw them out. But you may decide that they are, on the
whole, not too bad to serve."

213

"In other words, you don't trust women barkeeps?"

"I trust them the way I do women drivers. They are fine; they are adorable; but I think the rough work of life should be left to the stern sex—so-called."

"Very well. Thank you, Tom," said Agnes. "We will have the cocktails here in the front parlor, I think. I'll see about chilled glasses. Unless, of course, you brought those with you. You didn't? Oh, well, after all I am the hostess! Now, wouldn't you like to rest your hat and coat?"

Very vivacious, though she looked demure enough in a "basic black" dress and a small string of pearls which had belonged to her mother. But Mrs. Wainwright sobered suddenly when the next ring at the bell heralded the guests from Antioch.

Miriam too was on her best behavior; and Miriam's natural stiffness was regularly more than a match for Agnes's. Tom's cocktails were exactly what the situation called for. If Agnes had attempted to mix under present circumstances, as she had so rashly planned to do, her right hand would certainly not have known what her left hand was trying to do.

Alcohol thawed the ice. It threatened to congeal again for one dreadful moment after they entered the dining room and Miriam discovered that her offering had been relegated to a subordinate position.

This time, Agnes thought fast. "Miriam dear," she purred, "I can't think how you knew what would exactly complement the centerpiece I had planned. Do you have second sight?"

Miriam swallowed hard. Then, with matching sweetness, she replied, "There was no magic in it. I remember our many Thanksgivings back home in Antioch, Ladybird."

214

Sully snickered audibly, and no wonder. Miriam had certainly won the catfight.

Agnes paid him for that snicker, though she didn't blame him. "Will you carve, Tom?" she asked. "You know all about such things."

She had planned the invitation; she didn't realize just how pat it would be right now. Tom picked up the cue as well as the carving things. "Is that a compliment or a rebuke?" he demanded.

"It's a simple request from your hostess," said Agnes, very much in her element now. "Miriam prefers dark meat; cut hers off the thigh, please. I don't know about you, Sully. Are you past the drumstick age?"

"Past my first childhood, and not yet quite into my second," said Sully promptly. "I like both dark and light meat. Don't be stingy with that lovely brown skin on either. Do we get stuffing now or later?"

It was the real old-fashioned Thanksgiving dinner, even to two pieces of pie for dessert. The guests weren't asked whether they preferred pumpkin or apple, either. They were served both.

When they finally rose from the table, Sully remarked, "I don't know which is indicated, a walk or a siesta."

"Guests may have their choice," Agnes answered sweetly, "or if they want both, they may have them in either order."

"Oh, come on now!" drawled Sully. "At least give us a hint."

With all the dignity that she could muster, Agnes led the way into the front parlor. While she was doing so, memory came to her aid. At the end of the long Stevenson shelf, apparently tucked there to keep the *Complete Works* in a compact line, was a small volume entitled *Drawing-Room*

215

Games and Amusements. It might give her some hints; or in itself it might provide a few minutes' diversion.

It did better than that. Agnes began to read it aloud to the assembled company; but over the first sentence of the preface she choked, and Sully had to take the book from her and edify the hearers with the words, "To the harassed hostess pondering wearily with herself how to amuse her guests this book is dedicated."

He was only halfway down the page when his veracity was questioned. He had just enunciated, "But tact should, of course, be exercised in the choice. When you invite the Archbishop of Canterbury to dinner it would be a mistake to ask him to play 'Muggins.'"

"That's what it says," Tom Jones confirmed. "But mightn't the original mistake lie in asking the Archbishop of Canterbury to dinner?"

He honorably handed the book back to Sully, who finished the preface, read the index to *Writing Games,* and then allowed Tom to instruct the company on how to play *Consequences.*

Miriam had her turn after that, then Agnes. But they didn't play *Consequences* or any other writing game. They were too eager to get on to the *Talking Games.*

Agnes took advantage of one prolonged burst of hilarity to glance into the dining room. The cranberry- and gravy-stained cloth had been removed, and replaced by a clean length of white damask as large and almost as heavy. A second-best set of dishes was stacked at one end of the table, the supper silver laid out. Dishes of nuts and raisins balanced one another around the centerpiece, a special supper feature which was a surprise to Mrs. Wainwright.

The picture of an *un*harassed hostess, she rejoined her

216

guests before they had a chance to miss her. Agnes still believed in the words of the poem,

> Every day is Thanksgiving Day
> If you have a thankful heart.

But about the official holiday itself, there was still something noteworthy and heart-warming.

As soon as the dinner dishes were finished, the two maids had taken off. One of them was due back at seven, the other not until bedtime. Agnes decided to keep an ear out for the doorbell. Only to help Dora, of course. Of course!

Agnes had Dr. Sheridan to herself for a minute in the hall, received his cordial greeting, watched his face light up at the sound of the hilarity which followed the directions for *The Cook Who Does Not Like Peas*. "Reminds me of your—er—incumbent, Miriam," Sully commented. "Maybe that's why she doesn't know how to cook peas."

"An uncle of mine once said that his wife couldn't boil water without burning it," Tom added pensively. "Bread and cheese and kisses were all right at first, maybe, but not after the honeymoon was over."

Agnes explained about the entertainment book. Then she introduced him into the middle of the riot. "Dr. Sheridan has come to help us pick the turkey bones."

"Don't let me stop the fun," protested Dr. Sheridan. "I'm early."

They received him cordially and assured him of his turn at the book. What Agnes could not account for was the look of relief that crossed Miriam's face when she saw Dr. Sheridan.

She understood it a little later, when she saw that in

shifting to make room for the newcomer Miriam had edged closer to Sully, and at the next surrender of the book still closer. That was all right with Agnes. She liked having men around.

She had a pretty good selection of them here today, too. She was either lucky or discriminating, or both. It was not against the laws of Nature for a woman to be both. Agnes Costen Wainwright might be such a woman, at least here and now.

Here and now was enough for one riding on a wave of exaltation. Let Dull Care wait until tomorrow. Dull Care—and turkey soup! Fear, and remorse, and cranberries the third time in succession! For by that time, today would be safely bestowed where nobody could take it from her.

18.

ACTUALLY, FRIDAY WAS NOT A COMEDOWN; IT WAS SIMPLY the day after the party. Agnes demolished her Thanksgiving centerpiece; the fruit went into the refrigerator, and began to make a piecemeal appearance at breakfast. The pumpkin turned into tarts for Sunday dinner (and supper). Agnes worked over the floral offerings for two or three days, salvaging and rearranging; on Monday, she felt that she was justified in making a clean sweep.

On Monday, too, her Christmas plans, which had been magnificent but vague, began to take substantial shape. Agnes's moods veered sharply. She ought not to have undertaken so much. Still, most of her plans were a secret as yet; it wasn't too late to draw back. Draw back, indeed! When she had no one on whom to blame her weakness? This was the chance of a lifetime to make people happy: to show them, and herself as well, what Mrs. Wainwright could do, not only on her own behalf, but as steward of the Hammond money.

First and foremost, naturally, came the children. All her choirboys must be treated alike; but they must be TREATED, in capital letters. Then there was the matter of Christmas cards: a compound of enjoyment and annoyance in varying proportions. Agnes put in a large order for engraved cards, tried to remember her old list, began a supplemental new one.

Her gift list last year had included Miriam, Rosa Lee Montgomery, a half-jocular tie for Sully, and for Aunt Adelaide a book that had once belonged to Grandfather Costen. Now here came Dora Dean, for whom she could surely find something sensible and suitable; the maids, who would appreciate gift certificates; Eustace, who might like money in one of those trick cards which came for the purpose; Tom Jones, who deserved a tie and a half—and perhaps Dr. Sheridan. Doctors got some dreadful offerings from their female patients. Agnes might think of some really original offering. She might fall back on the conventional handkerchiefs, tie, socks (she could surely guess his size). Or she might just send him one of her cards with a special handwritten message. Best not go too far.

It would be fun to reassemble her Thanksgiving party for Christmas. Dangerous, though; it was inviting anticlimax. Better think that over. Sound out Sully and Tom. Lay herself open to a hint from Miriam. Consider half-hidden resources; she was unlikely to stumble again on such richness as that book of games which the Archbishop of Canterbury should not be invited to play.

Agnes scribbled a few memoranda. She felt very business-like while she was doing so. On rereading them the next day, she felt committed. That was all right, too. But she'd better get on with the job.

She set the date for a big Saturday afternoon party here at the house, and invited all her choirboys verbally. Then she telephoned their mothers. Next she began memo'ing in earnest. Refreshments; gifts; games; tree. She planned to make this a real party. Her very inexperience might help her. It left her with a free hand.

There is no such thing as a free hand; she was destined to learn that soon enough. Led by Roy and his faithful Denny, her urchins began to inquire, "Mrs. Wainwright, can we have rough-house?"

Agnes was uncertain what they meant; but on general principles she answered, "No." If they felt that they had to ask permission in advance, it must be something pretty bad.

Not a particle daunted, they kept on asking. Agnes was driven to consult Tom Jones about terminology.

Tom grinned, "English translation, 'Are you going to wet-blanket us?' Keep right on saying 'No,' since that's what you began by saying. It won't make a particle of difference anyhow."

Agnes felt easier. They were not "sweet little angels"; but if kept amused, they should be fairly tractable. A bored boy was a bad boy. They didn't come to parties in order to be bored. They got enough of that from authoritative sources.

She remembered the paper caps that came in crackers. The dining room could be festooned with paper chains,

221

too. How about a grab bag? Or its variation, a Jack Horner pie? Or both? Careful, Agnes, pull up somewhere! There are other holidays coming.

On the score of refreshments, too, Agnes's original plan tended to go overboard. Ice cream, cake, candy: fine! But unless these delicacies were preceded by something solid, the little guests might be sorry they came. Frankfurters, hamburgers, fried chicken, buttered rolls. Then for drinks, hot chocolate and cold Cokes.

Agnes indulged her fancies, then returned to earth. The paper chains would never do in the Hammond dining room. Holly could be used, naturally, and pine branches. She would have liked a Christmas tree in the back parlor; but she mustn't challenge comparison with the Sunday School tree or their trees at home. Poinsettias instead, and two small orange trees. (She had to send out of town for them.)

A grab bag, yes. Before that, let them draw numbers to see which one should have first chance at the bag. Then, to avoid hurt feelings, bring in a second grab bag and let them draw in the reverse order. This was an original stroke. Agnes wondered how many people had thought of it before.

Refreshments. Here Agnes consulted Dora Dean, as well as her own common sense. They decided on two enormous platters of sandwiches, one chicken, the other half jelly and half peanut butter. Hot chocolate and cold Cokes: that stood. So, of course, did the ice cream, two frosted cakes, and a great deal of candy. The paper crackers which you pulled in order to release party caps she ordered from New York.

Agnes thought about asking two or three mothers in to help her, but decided against it. With the entire crew of boys expected, it wouldn't do to play favorites among the

222

mothers. Eustace might better take over again. He would enjoy both the job and his bonus.

He did. He also helped with the clearing up afterward. Agnes's plans worked out beautifully, to a point. But she had failed to allow for the extracurricular activities. As soon as the first pangs of hunger had been satisfied, it became a popular pastime to snatch at the other fellow's paper cap. The flimsy headgear was soon reduced to tatters. The litter settled impartially on the table and the floor.

The young gentlemen returned to the great business of eating. When they were full to repletion, a sudden calmness descended. But it didn't last. The more active spirits came out of their coma in four or five minutes; those who would have liked a little longer rest were pestered into activity.

The grab bag gifts then became ammunition. Some of the tenderer spirits would have liked to keep theirs. In a few cases they succeeded; here, too, interest soon lagged. But not until Mr. Hammond was looking down from his frame at a scene of carnage such as had never before disfigured that front parlor.

One of the more anxious mothers telephoned. Agnes put her off. But when a second call came through and then a third, Agnes began, with some help from Eustace and Dora, to marshal the procession toward washing up and wraps, and what souvenirs were left to take home with them.

Dora had again provided wrapped pieces of cake; this time there were also bags for candy. Agnes reached the front door in time to take a look at the weather, which was pleasant enough so that the boys might all be allowed to walk home. The hour was still early, the streets light enough, the parents on the alert. You must not overprotect boys, those "sweet little angels." You'd get no thanks if you tried to.

223

They made their jerky little speeches of thanks. They started home in groups of two and three: irregular groups, impatient of the laggard, then doing their very best to make him lag again.

Mrs. Wainwright's original three were the last to leave. Poor Jock Clark's face lighted with a smile of which Agnes would not have supposed him capable. "May I come back some other time?" he whispered.

Denny White mimicked, "Are you little Aladdin, the son of Mustapha the tailor?" He was out of hearing before Agnes had a chance to pick up her cue.

That left Roy Harris, the one and only Roy. When he lifted his face toward hers there at the very last minute (he hadn't far to lift it; he had grown an inch in the last month), Agnes choked over the words, "Come again! Come again— soon."

Roy nodded, but he stipulated, "Next time, can we have rough-house?"

"Certainly!" said Agnes.

She understood now what the question meant. While she was helping to restore things to order—that is, keeping an eye on the work but staying out of the way of people who were busy with their allotted tasks—she planned next year's Christmas party.

She would hire a hall. Preferably not the guild hall; the Masons must have something to let in this town, or if not the Masons, some other lodge. She would have rented furnishings in. The paper chains would go up this time. There would be confetti to throw, and serpentine paper. Agnes would get a man in to help Eustace clear up.

It wasn't until after she was in bed that night that Agnes realized how much she was taking for granted. She was planning for "next year" right where she was now, and under very much the same circumstances.

No harm in that! A lovely plan was a fine thing in itself, whether or not it ever came to fulfilment. This one might be upset in any one of several ways.

This year's further plans were a different story. Their fruition lay right ahead of her.

Her Christmas cards were mailed, a large batch of them. Agnes resolved that she would make no last-minute corrections or omissions. As she might have foreseen, there went a large paving block in the road which led to the nether regions. This year there were many more unexpected cards than had ever fallen to her lot before; not to answer them would have been unforgivable. She was a newcomer in Marshfield; she could not afford to let anybody think that she was putting on airs.

Agnes opened the cards on their arrival. Incoming gifts were scrupulously laid aside to await the official moment. Outgoing gifts to Antioch, except Miriam's pearl pin and Sully's necktie, were mailed early. Rosa Lee Montgomery had been taken care of with a gift certificate. Eustace was dispatched on the afternoon of the twenty-third with the local gifts: uniform jackknives for all Agnes's choirboys, home-baked fruitcakes for the boys' mothers, a basket of Dora Dean's preserves for Dr. and Mrs. Follansbee. Mr. Kent and Mr. Estabrook had been put off with cards. Dr. Sheridan's gift-wrapped ties joined Tom's in the front parlor.

The Thanksgiving party would reassemble on The Day itself. But for Christmas Eve, Agnes had planned a small domestic celebration, to be followed by attendance at the midnight service. She had been somewhat startled when

225

Dr. Follansbee announced that service, less by its celebration than by the fact that on Christmas morning there would be eight o'clock and nine o'clock Communion, but no service of any kind after that. The tradition was that the Babe of Bethlehem had actually been born on Christmas Eve. But there were other traditions, often contradictory. It boiled down to a question of which one was going to be violated.

Mrs. Wainwright's choirboys would be kept up late Christmas Eve. But they would not be on duty at all on Christmas Day. That way, the thing made sense. If you were a little open-minded and patient, a good many innovations did make sense.

Eustace set the tree up in the back parlor on the afternoon of the twenty-fourth. Behind closed doors, Agnes trimmed it. The tree was only six feet tall, but very full and symmetrical. She used three strings of lights, two boxes of colored balls, a dozen miniature stockings made of red net and filled with hard candy, a dozen candy canes. The edibles would eventually go to visiting boys; but the tree in its pristine newness must not be revealed to anybody until the proper time tomorrow.

When she had closed the massive double doors of the back parlor, Agnes felt very important, very much pleased with herself. She was Santa Claus's little assistant. She was also the whole entertainment committee rolled into one. No doubt she was being a bit childish; but no one was in a position to reprove her for her folly.

The two maids had been allowed to leave early in the afternoon, with permission to stay out until the middle of the evening. Dora served Agnes with the Christmas Eve meal which was traditional in the Costen family: oyster stew and coleslaw, followed by the first Christmas cookies of the season. Then Agnes secluded herself in the back parlor and played all Aunt Adelaide's records of Christmas carols.

She had everything back in order by eleven; she had turned out the lights and opened one of the doors when she caught sight of Dora just entering the front parlor on the way to call her. They really had plenty of time. Mrs. Wainwright motioned her cook-housekeeper to a seat and began to declaim

'Twas the night before Christmas, and all through the house . . .

Dora listened as if she had never heard it before. But wasn't that the very best of Christmas? It was very old, but very new. It was an ordained festival, both sacred and secular. It had been here since before any of us could remember. Yet in a sense, every time that Christmas came to us, the Babe of Bethlehem was born anew.

"Thank you, Mrs. Wainwright," Dora said when the recital concluded.

"Thank *you,* Dora," Agnes countered. "Everything is proceeding according to plan, isn't it? That is—I mean—I hadn't planned to speak my piece to you."

"I've never enjoyed it more," said Dora simply.

She was ready and waiting. Agnes changed her clothes; the two of them took their places in the car in ample time. The ladies were side by side in the old Hammond pew; Eustace had parked the car nearby and taken his place at the rear of the church well before the voluntaries ended.

The decorations were simple and lovely. They were so unobtrusive, indeed, that Agnes scarcely noticed them,

227

though she would have been pained by their absence. The choirboys, in their red cassocks, *did* look almost like "sweet little angels." The music went on and on. Every time that the service reached a climax, a respite soon followed. Then in its turn came an even higher climax.

Agnes had not only lost all track of time; she had lost all sense of personal identity. Then, of course, it had to happen: that inevitable something which occurs to remind us mortals that, however heavenly the moment and the surroundings may appear, we are still earthbound.

Agnes had knelt once more, feeling something slip to the floor beside her. Even in her moment of devotion, she realized that she must retrieve her purse. Still on her knees, she reached out for it.

The article resisted; but Agnes tugged the harder. It came off in her hand so suddenly that she sat back in the Hammond pew much harder than she had intended to, and stared in shocked incredulity.

For this wasn't her purse at all. Her purse was still lying on the floor at her feet. In her white-gloved hand she held the shoe which she had snatched from the foot of the woman kneeling in front of her.

Agnes thrust the shoe back toward its owner so hastily that she forgot all about her purse, which Dora Dean restored to her while they were returning down the aisle. Apparently she had been the only witness of the contretemps. Even at the height of her chagrin, Agnes remembered to be thankful that a doctor must keep more or less regular hours.

Dora would never in the world give her Mrs. Wainwright away. As for Agnes's telling on herself, there wasn't a chance in the world of that. Even a poor little simpleton like Agnes had a paltry something left to think with.

228

By the time that the warm kind house had received them, the Hammond heiress's embarrassment, exaltation, and confusion were all bogging down into simple weariness. She did remember to say, "Thank you, Dora," when a second installment of Christmas cookies was placed on her bedside table. She snuggled into the bedclothes. She remembered her childish resolve to stay awake this year and catch Santa Claus in the act. Inevitably, the next thing that she knew it was Christmas morning.

The next thing she knew, sure enough, it *was* Christmas morning! She was waking up. She hadn't caught Santa Claus. But she had the whole long lovely day ahead of her.

Immediately after breakfast, Agnes began work on the dining-table centerpiece. On the big silver platter she laid a groundwork of evergreen. A small jar in the middle supported other sprigs of evergreen and a few perfect twigs of holly. Other holly lay flat in radiating spikes, with twisted red ribbons to mark the boundaries. Here and there was the relief of mistletoe. Agnes had dallied with the idea of hanging it in doorways according to the time-honored custom; any man who caught a woman under the mistletoe was entitled to kiss her. But on considering the expected company, she decided to use the Druids' parasite in a strictly neutral position.

Once that masterpiece was completed and placed, Agnes devoted most of her time to keeping out of the way of her hired help. She changed her clothes presently, cast a final glance over her arrangements, and sat down in the front parlor to await the arrival of her guests.

They were due about noon. Tom Jones arrived first, presented his gift, inquired whether she wanted to open it now or wait. Agnes decided to open it now; her curiosity had

229

been aroused by the small size of the package. After all, she could rewrap it if necessary.

It was a cameo Wedgwood brooch, set in a plain but very strong mounting: against a light blue background, the Graces were laving the hoofs of a winged horse.

"Lovely, lovely!" gasped Agnes. "But surely nobody would ever dare to wear it?"

"It might distract attention from the wearer," Tom conceded. "But as a conversation piece, it will serve. You simply pick it up when there comes a lull."

Agnes laid the brooch, huddled in its wrappings but not retied, on the mantel. "Miriam and Sully are spending the night," she explained. "So don't go trying to outstay him this time."

"And don't try to guess which is keeping an eye on the other. Very well, I won't," Tom promised with artificial meekness.

Miriam and Sully arrived soon after that. They were greeted and established. Then ensued a lag. Agnes wondered whether to assemble the servants and inaugurate the opening of the presents or wait a few minutes longer for Dr. Sheridan.

She had almost decided on the latter, when he telephoned. He had been delayed, but would be along soon. They were not to wait for him.

Agnes didn't wait, precisely. But she allowed things to drag a trifle. The present-opening was all set but hadn't actually begun when Dr. Sheridan appeared, immaculate, smiling, and only a trifle deprecatory.

"Kid with a sliver in his foot," he explained. "Wouldn't have been ten minutes' work if the mother herself hadn't had a terrible fear of doctors. First she messed the injury up,

230

making it three times as bad as it had been. When she finally called me and I took over, she began to wring her hands and shriek, 'Oh, doctor! Don't hurt him!' I suppose I needn't go on."

"Do!" said Agnes. "That is, of course, so long as you don't give any names." But he shook his head.

He hadn't forgotten his gift to Agnes, an armful of new long-playing records. She received other tributes. Guests and servants examined and thanked and bore away. The tree was revealed and admired. Agnes provided the ingredients, but invited Sully to mix the cocktails.

It was only ten minutes past the appointed hour when they all filed into the dining room. Dora had roasted a suckling pig with an apple in its mouth. A German dish, surely. But it was followed by an English plum pudding blazing in brandy.

Agnes was pouring the coffee—unmistakably American coffee—when she took it into her head to tell of last night's mishap at the church. "You never!" gasped Tom Jones.

"She did. She couldn't make that up," said Sully.

Dr. Sheridan summed up, "I thought I had heard something before. My mistake! How I wish I had been there!"

Only Miriam said nothing. Agnes, coming to her senses rather tardily, hoped that Miriam would continue to say nothing.

They played a paper game from the Thanksgiving Day book, but found it a little too much like homework. They re-examined their own presents and one another's. Agnes suggested supper, was met with groans, brought in servings of lemon ice which were well received.

Handing Dr. Sheridan his portion, she whispered, "Don't

231

you want to call that poor kid's house and talk to his father? He has a father, I suppose."

Dr. Sheridan did just that, received an equivocal answer, excused himself soon after. He had enjoyed his holiday, Agnes felt sure. But that strange shadow which lurked constantly at the back of his mind had again obtruded.

It was his private shadow, anyhow. But Mrs. Wainwright had called that case to his attention. Now she wished she hadn't.

Tom Jones took himself off a few minutes later. Briefly, he tried the brooch at her throat, at her waist, on her shoulder. Then he laid it back on the mantel, shook his head, and said, "I'm sorry for you, gentle Agnes. The debris around the place— Oh, I said that, you didn't! I wouldn't call her debris, exactly. Maybe she is a legacy. Maybe you inherited her. Maybe here's my hat."

"You had an overcoat, too, didn't you?" Agnes suggested. "It's a cold night."

"It's been a lovely day. Exit Tom Jones. Right?"

"Right. But don't stay away."

"Try and make me!"

Once more the front door closed on a departing guest. Agnes turned back to the scene of the revelry. The maids were due soon, after their short afternoon recess. Agnes left word that the clearing-up could wait until tomorrow. She invited Miriam and Sully to join her across the hall.

They were barely seated when Agnes yawned. She would have liked to change to something loose, gloat over her new possessions, read for a time, raid the refrigerator presently. All that would have to be shared, or wait for another evening. She was still the hostess.

232

"Another Christmas passing into history," she philosophized.

But Miriam was in no mood for relaxation. "That story of yours about what happened in church last night—" she began to fume.

"Tell it not in Gath, publish it not in Askelon," Agnes cut in. "You might keep quiet about it in Antioch, Long Island, too. That's another gossipy burg."

"I know enough to do that without being told," snapped Miriam. "You're welcome to your own ideas of what is amusing. But it's high time you stopped traipsing around with nobody but a servant to keep you company. It isn't dignified, and it isn't suitable."

"That's right," agreed Sully with a broad grin. "What the little woman needs is a husband to keep her in order."

Miriam flushed and bit her lip. She shouldn't have gone so far in the presence of a third person. This particular third person was one whose good opinion she valued. This was not the only time she had done her best to forfeit it; but this time she had gone out of her way to be offensive.

"I promise not to do it again," said Agnes in a tone of mock solemnity. "I'm too lazy to learn a new game out of Aunt Adelaide's book. But how about having a go at good old Twenty Questions?"

"Refresh my memory, if you'll be so good," said Sully. "It's a long time since I played those nursery games; and I haven't any children in whom I can renew my youth."

Whether he was genuinely forgetful or was simply being considerate didn't make too much difference. Miriam had a chance to get her breath back.

She had the sense not to apologize. But for the rest of the evening she was strangely subdued.

233

"Ladybird" (thus addressed only two or three times) had paid in advance for the interval of peace. True; but people didn't always get what they paid for. That held good in Marshfield, just as it did in Antioch, Long Island. Presumably it happened that way at Antioch in Syria, too, and had happened in ancient Askelon and Gath. It was always gratifying when you got your money's worth.

The two whose turn it was not took turns asking, "Is it animal, mineral, or vegetable?" When this intellectual pastime palled, they all had supper. It was reasonably early when they separated for the night. Agnes's bedtime book remained for once unopened, her plate of cookies untouched. She fell asleep murmuring

> Every day is Christmas Day
> To a spirit filled with joy.

There were times, she feared, when she didn't half appreciate her blessings. It would pay her, some time soon, to stop and count up.

19.

HER HOUSE GUESTS LEFT SOON AFTER A LATE AND LEISURELY breakfast. The festive rooms were by that time in perfect order: a rather empty order, if you stopped to think about it.

But Agnes hadn't much time to be lonesome. In the middle of the morning, Roy and Dick arrived, announcing themselves as "Cassim Baba's brother" and "the son of Mustapha the tailor."

They admired her tree. They partook liberally of Christmas cookies. They informed her that the Sunday school Christmas party hadn't been half as much fun as hers. Then they invited her to "come see" their trees.

Here the agreement split for the first time. Both the

235

young comrades began to holler, "Mine first! Mine first!"

It would never do to play favorites; and although Agnes was a shade the fonder of Roy, that was not Dick's fault. Roy had taken a shine to her initially, and had opened up a whole new life to the Widow Wainwright. If it hadn't been for him, neither of the boys would have been here today.

Agnes had recourse to a stratagem which might well have been in use before our ancestors came down from the trees: she made a game of it. "We'll draw for it," she announced.

They applauded that idea. They waited while she went across the hall, found a magazine, and tore two strips from the margin of a page devoted principally to advertising. They inspected the strips. They watched while she turned her back and concealed in her fist all but two ends which, thus ambushed, looked exactly alike.

She was apparently just on the verge of success when Roy piped up, "We ought to draw first to see which one draws first when it comes to settling the question."

He was a smart boy. Dick grinned and said, "Oh, go ahead and win! You will anyhow."

"I declare, Dick, I believed you are sprouting wings," Agnes approved. "Want me to feel and find out?" They had taken the decision very neatly out of her hands.

Before they left the house, Agnes gave each of them a candy cane and a net stocking from her tree. Roy grinned impishly. "I wondered when you were going to come across with those. Oh, thanks for my knife!"

"Mine, too," chimed Dick.

The delay in their politeness was not to be held against them. The boys had been too much interested to remember earlier.

The three of them set off on foot. They met other parties bound on similar errands. It appeared to be a day of open house in Marshfield. It was a day for children to exhibit their gains. If grown people too indulged in a little showing off, oh well! Surely once a year gloating might be allowed to pass itself off as gratitude.

Sully telephoned his Christmas thanks and groaned over his prospects for New Year's Eve. "Everybody thinks a bachelor should be available for unlimited whoopee. My annual chance to join the great society of people who later wish they hadn't."

"You make me realize how fortunate I am," said Agnes smugly. "I plan to celebrate with a quiet drink right here at home."

She stuck to her virtuous intention even when Tom Jones tried to tease her out of it. He didn't believe her, to begin with; and when she evaded his bait of a lovely little country tavern where he could pass her off as his long-lost sister, or if she'd prefer a noisier jollier place there were plenty of those, Agnes scored with him as being hard to get. That, or playing it, which was perhaps even better.

She found Dr. Sheridan waiting for her Sunday morning when she came home from church. He had just stopped in to say hello, he explained. He was on his way home from a tough case. "I'm going to snatch a nap while I can. The end of the holiday season always brings me a rush of business. They call it 'a virus' nowadays. In my youth it was 'the flu,' in my father's day 'grippe.' By any name at all it's achy and sneezy."

"I notice there's always a lot of it around in January," Agnes agreed. "I suppose the bad weather has something to do with it."

"Late hours and too much to eat and drink help, too. But I can't do my patients' thinking for them."

"Do you ever wish you could?"

"*Do* I?" He groaned; then he grinned. "Years ago, I called for a young colleague and waited in his outer office while he was interviewing his last patient of the afternoon. All at once I heard him holler, 'The whole trouble with you is that you're a complete damn fool!' It was, I have no doubt. But a doctor isn't supposed to talk that way to his patients."

"Your friend had reached the breaking point?"

"He had, and he was beginning to realize that he wasn't well suited to private practice. He's a pathologist now: deals with diseases, not with people."

Dr. Sheridan made his little speech about "the fine Christmas you gave me." Yes, the flu was once more going around. He answered her question about the child with the problem mama. He stayed a bare quarter of an hour; but in that length of time she learned something about a doctor's life in general, if not about this particular doctor's.

This was all very well. Everything was all very well. Yet on New Year's Eve, when she followed her cherished plan, Agnes was unaccountably depressed. She donned her fluffiest housecoat. She re-examined her Christmas gifts and distributed the hoard. She installed two new calendars. Yet as she strolled from room to room, the house seemed empty. Empty and echoing: a place of whispers and of shadows.

She was—yes, she was lonely. She burst into a storm of noisy sobs. It endured only briefly; but it cleared the air for her. Agnes was ashamed of her spasm of self-pity. Alone of her own choice, she ought to be able to endure her own society.

She had the quiet drink at home; and it tasted good. The

238

bells were ringing, the whistles blowing. Hope sprang afresh. Was she forgetting her dear elf Elpis? Agnes would better get back into the spirit of the season.

She had a second drink and a small sandwich. According to the calendar, the Eve had ended now and the Year was under way. But according to Agnes, an eve never ended until she went to sleep. She turned out all the downstairs lights in the front part of the house: her part. She took a third drink upstairs with her. It was barely tasted when she dozed off.

Agnes had got through the session, and that was that. All the same, she was well enough pleased when, at noon on New Year's Day, she answered the telephone, and Tom Jones teased, "How's your hang-over?"

She went a little farther than she had intended, indeed. She agreed to meeting him in New York for a weekend this very January. It gave her something to look forward to. Not Mr. Jones's society so much; she could have that any time, and for the taking. But New York as she had never seen it before: under escort, not under guidance.

As it turned out, she did not have too much escort, even. She actually enjoyed a taste of New York on her own.

She had phoned to warn Sully that she wouldn't be at home this coming Sunday. He hadn't come over this past Sunday or she could have told him to his face. She might have let him take his chance; she wasn't accountable to him for her arrangements. But she was a trifle piqued at being taken for granted.

"I hadn't thought that far ahead," said Sully. "Here it is only Tuesday. Kind of you to call me, though."

Now he was deliberately being provoking. In her silkiest

tones, Agnes informed him, "If you care to come over any-how, Dora will give you something to eat."

Sully retorted, "Didn't you ever go to school? Or don't they teach the classics any more? I used to be told that 'The gift without the giver is bare.' "

" 'Who gives himself with his alms feeds three.' I remember that much. But the connection is a little hard to trace."

"Not for me, Ladybird," he mimicked. "Do you want this trip kept a dark secret?"

"The news will get out afterward."

"But you don't want anybody forbidding the banns?"

"I'm not—" Agnes began, and checked herself. "Oh, have it your own way! What do you want me to bring you from New York?"

"Not a necktie. I haven't got used to my Christmas ones yet."

"Grow a beard to hide them," advised Agnes. "Goodbye for now; I'll be seeing you again one of these days."

"So long, Mary! Don't forget to come back home."

"In the words of another poet! Isn't education wonderful?" jibed Agnes, and hung up. Sully was an amusing soul, say on Sundays and legal holidays. A woman must know how to take him, to be sure. When Agnes was the woman concerned, he was to be taken in small doses.

That was Tuesday, as he had reminded her. Directly after breakfast Wednesday morning, Agnes took a train for New York. She left with Dora Dean the name of the hotel where she had reserved a suite. "Call me about this time in the morning if anything comes up."

"Nothing will," Dora assured her. "Still, it's just as well to be prepared."

"That's right. An emergency foreseen ceases to be an emer-

240

gency. If Dr. Sheridan calls, you may tell him where I am. With anybody else, just say I'm expected back some time Monday."

He doesn't know you're leaving? Dora was too respectful to ask the question in so many words. It would have implied that there was some deep reason behind this particular reticence.

There wasn't, of course. Dr. Sheridan always telephoned before he came to see her. In common courtesy, Agnes must leave a message for him. He might not call while she was away. He might be too busy or too tired. Or—he just might not call.

Agnes thrust the thought of him resolutely out of mind. She wasn't making this trip in order to give herself more space to pine in. Mariana, while she stayed in the moated grange, was at least not putting herself to a lot of additional expense.

Mrs. Wainwright's hotel suite bore not the remotest resemblance to a grange; and the nearest to a moat that she could see from her seventeenth-story windows was the sparkling and busy East River. She called room service and put in her order. Over a late and leisurely lunch, she glanced at early editions of the afternoon newspapers. Did Mariana have to eat what was set before her? Did the grange take in any newspapers, or even magazines? The books in the library would be moldy as well as out of date. Poor Mariana! No wonder she was reduced to hoping against hope!

The thought of the grange library gave Agnes a bright idea: why not take home books as presents? For the maids, shilling shockers. (She was yet to learn that each of those commodities now spoiled a five dollar bill.) For Dora Dean, the latest in cookbooks, to be presented with a little speech

241

about carrying coals to Newcastle. For Eustace—oh, she'd find something for Eustace! The volumes for her choirboys she'd have gift-wrapped and mailed to them; that would give them a lot more fun. Sully rated the latest compendium of four-letter words which was passing itself off as a novel. For Dr. Sheridan and the rector she would like a good novel each—if good novels were still published. Nothing for Tom Jones, to be sure. With him she hoped to live an interesting chapter.

Agnes wrote out her list and laid it aside. Then she showered and changed, and set out for a stroll unplanned, unsupervised, and totally aimless.

Nobody knows where I am! she thought exultantly. *Nobody on earth!* She had achieved a height of independence which a year ago she would have deemed impossible.

Her ebullience presently subsided. Floating on clouds was all very well for a time; if protracted, it amounted to nothing but a waste of opportunity. Agnes set her course westward, Fifth Avenue'd for a time, began again to occidentalize. She reached Broadway just as the lights were coming on.

It wasn't until the second man had tried to pick her up that Agnes realized that perhaps an unescorted woman was better off indoors—or at least with a destination to hurry to. Mrs. Wainwright was a highly respectable widow. If she didn't look all that respectable, so much the better. But she flagged down a taxi and had herself driven back to her hotel. After a brief nap, she changed clothes again, dined demurely in a quiet corner of the dining room, and spent the evening at a small place across the street where they showed foreign movies. It had been a varied day, at least; it was her own choice that it hadn't turned out spicier.

242

On Thursday morning, Agnes wrote a note to Rosa Lee Montgomery, for whom she had a street address but no phone number. She would like to see her, if Rosa Lee could come over to the hotel. Ask for room 1707 when she telephoned.

All that hotel stationery was a temptation. Agnes might write a note to Miriam. It would get her stepdaughter off her conscience. If she spaced it out properly, she could manage the show of communication without giving anything away.

Agnes took a fresh sheet, dated it, and began, "Dear Miriam." But that was as far as she got. She found it impossible to go on.

"Here I am in New York all by myself, and enjoying it," was not only rude; it was also a half-truth. Tom Jones was due to arrive tomorrow. "Wish you were here" was an obvious lie, when she hadn't even notified Miriam of the trip, much less invited her. "I have booked a hotel suite for my stay" sounded like a reproach.

The stationery was a temptation? Nothing of the kind! It was a reminder. A reminder of duty, accepted, resented, doing its best to have its way with her. Yet it was to escape duty that she had come here. This was a party of pleasure. What point was there in spoiling her own enjoyment?

Agnes tore the sheet of paper in two, dropped the lower half into the wastebasket, shredded the date line and the "Dear Miriam." Then she made sure she had her charge plate and a considerable sum of money with her, and sallied out on a shopping expedition.

An unsupervised expedition! While giving herself a loose rein, Agnes actually picked better than she used to. She indulged her own taste, and that for the benefit of a possible audience. Possible, probable, likely. She hadn't had so

243

much fun since the first time her mother let her pick out a hat for herself.

One outfit in particular was expensive, and perhaps extravagant. If Agnes never made another such trip, she was unlikely ever to wear it again. It would scarcely do in Marshfield or Antioch; but it would be just right in New York under certain circumstances.

The circumstances occurred sooner than Mrs. Wainwright had expected them to. Agnes had bought an "evening suit": a simply-cut skirt and jacket of light blue crepe, the collar of the jacket trimmed with blue ostrich. She bought two Juliet caps in a matching shade, one of the same material as the suit, one of satin. To these she added a hat.

The rest of the duds would be sent. But Agnes loved the hat so much that she carried it home with her.

"Home" being, of course, that hotel suite. There, in front of a full-length mirror, Agnes tried on the hat. It was the same shade of blue, but it was unmistakably a hat, not a cap of any kind. It fitted Agnes's head exactly. It had a tiny veil. It was too perfect to be true. Yet it was true. It was an ideal hat, but it was a real hat. It showed that such things could be.

Agnes had dinner alone in her sitting room. After she had finished, she turned on television, wearied of it, turned it off. The rest of the evening she sat at the windows and watched the ships come and go on the East River.

Ships, which bulked so large in story and song. "When my ship comes in." My ship, freighted with my future. Agnes's ship might come in any day now. What would it bring her?

Rosa Lee appeared the next morning; she was heralded only by a phone call that Miss Montgomery was downstairs. Agnes got room service at once, and ordered coffee and sandwiches. Agnes had barely finished breakfast; her guest, too, might not be hungry. But in a temporary as well as a permanent home, the demands of hospitality must be met.

Rosa Lee was all smiles at the sight of her Mrs. Wainwright. Her own news was brief but satisfactory: she was cooking in a small restaurant now, and liked it. If she tired of the job, she could go back to housework. "Or get married. But," she wound up philosophically, "if I'm going to do housework anyway, I'd sooner be paid for doing it."

Agnes poured a second cup of ceremonial coffee. Leaving hers untasted, she took the new hat from its wrappings. Her other purchases arrived at that moment, so she displayed them all; but the hat took Rosa Lee's eye just as it had taken Agnes's. Agnes modeled it, and Rosa Lee exclaimed, "I declare, Miss Agnes, that's pretty enough for a bride. It will do just right for you to get married in."

"If I planned to get married, which I don't," Agnes disclaimed; but she could feel her color rising. The idea was all very well in the abstract: the blue hat with its wisp of veil would be just right for a second marriage, or for a home or parsonage wedding, or for a bride who was not too young. Any or all of these conditions Agnes could fulfil; but scarcely in the absence of a groom.

"Mr. Sully still around?" pressed Rosa Lee.

"Yes, in a manner of speaking. But he isn't likely to be much longer."

"Only way you'll get rid of him—" Rosa Lee gestured toward the hat.

"On the contrary, Rosa Lee, I can marry him off to somebody else."

"Marry off that old bachelor bird, somebody got to put salt on his tail."

245

The two of them laughed together. The talk shifted to general topics; soon after, Rosa Lee took her leave.

Tom Jones arrived early that afternoon; he was staying at an hotel a block from Agnes's. That not only salved the proprieties; it gave Agnes a good chance to send him home should the need arise.

Agnes had been enjoying herself, not waiting for him. Yet she was unfeignedly glad to see him. Tom was Johnny-on-the-spot; but he made himself extremely useful.

He accompanied her on her trip to the bookstore, he made one or two indecorous suggestions about selections, but on the whole he behaved himself well enough. He also went along when Agnes bought a large selection of household delicacies to vary the local Marshfield provisioning for the rest of the winter. This time, Tom paid the bill; and Agnes was grateful for the attention. It was nice for a change to have a man fork over; that was one thing the critters were good for.

For the rest, Tom Jones not only paid the piper; he called the tune. That first Friday evening he took her to dinner down in Greenwich Village, and after that to a gay little resurrection called *The Threepenny Opera*. It was "Off Broadway" all right; but nobody wanted to go to Moscow. Least of all Agnes and Tom, who strolled around the neighborhood until they began to get chilly, then found a small Italian place for a generous serving of spaghetti and some excellent red wine.

Agnes had done well enough on this first occasion in the same old basic black and string of pearls. To the Saturday matinee on Broadway she again wore the old reliable. But before dinner she went back to her hotel and changed. Now she wore the new "evening suit" with the matching Juliet

246

cap. It served her for dinner, a very lavish "On Broadway" musical, and a night club appearance afterward.

Sunday afternoon they went for what Tom called "a pick-me-up stroll." It restored Agnes to complete consciousness; indeed, it nerved her to a pitch of unsabbatical daring. After a simple quiet dinner at Tom's hotel, they went back to hers while she changed. This time Agnes wore the blue evening suit without any cap whatever; her glistening hair was completely unadorned.

It was a Sunday night to be remembered. Agnes was floating on clouds. It was a shared enchantment, too.

They took no thought for the morrow. But postpone it as they might—and did—the morrow caught up with them. On what to them was Monday morning, though that was not the story the clock would have told, Agnes and Tom did their separate packing and checking and embarked on their joint journey home.

It had been a halcyon interlude. By its nature, it could not recur. It was nothing to build on. But one thing would survive as long as memory lasted. There on Sunday evening, when Tom Jones had led her into a night club which she had read about many times in the newspapers, Agnes Wainwright, uncapped and uncrowned though she was, had felt herself a Fairy Princess. It was just like stepping into a storybook.

20.

Tom Jones rode on to Rosemount. Eustace was waiting for Mrs. Wainwright at the station in Marshfield. At the Hammond mansion, Dora and the maids formed a welcoming committee. It was a very pleasant ending to a highly successful trip. Agnes had no reason in the world to feel let down.

She didn't feel that way. Of course she didn't. Agnes drew a long breath, and addressed herself to the business in hand.

Her bags had gone upstairs; only a package of books remained. From it she extracted the four that were designed for present company. They were duly unwrapped and admired. Agnes ordered a light dinner; glanced over a list of phone calls—church ladies only; she went to her room,

248

unpacked, freshened and changed. Once more she tried on her blue hat. Then she put it away very carefully, as if she might not see it again for a long time.

She was downstairs again when the phone rang. It was only Tom Jones assuring himself of her safe arrival; yet her heart leaped up at the sound of his voice. Somehow it made her feel that their excursion was not really over.

"We'll do it again some day, I hope," he wound up. That was a definite hope, and quite feasible. With the usual finger-crossing against unkind chance, it gave her something to look forward to.

Agnes had barely hung up when the phone rang a second time. It was Dr. Sheridan. Was it too late for him to stop by briefly? He was just leaving his office, and the sight of a healthy face would do him all the good in the world.

"Not so healthy at that," said Agnes crisply. "I got back this afternoon from a week's whirl in the Big Burg, and I'm a good deal the worse for wear."

"I didn't know you'd been away. Serves me right for not keeping better track of my friends."

He sounded contrite; but Agnes could not refrain from heaping coals of fire. "Do come over," she urged. "Come as fast as you can get here."

She had a cocktail waiting for him. But the real coal of fire was the book which she had brought him from New York: the very latest in art books, imported, expensive, and not too readily to be come by. It showed that she had been thinking of him during those days when he had forgotten her.

He began to turn the pages slowly, scrutinizing each plate as he came to it. "They do such beautiful reproduction

249

nowadays," he pronounced, "it's almost as much fun to look through the books as to visit the galleries."

"And not nearly so fatiguing," Agnes added. "A really conscientious gallery-goer must get into quite a state."

"A conscientious gallery-goer? I supposed the artist was the one who put everything he had into a picture, and the viewer merely viewed, with full liberty to leave when he had had enough."

"That was my idea, too. I never could see the sense in making a task out of what should be a pleasure."

"If we could only make a pleasure out of what might be considered a task! We try, of course. We sometimes succeed. But not often enough. Not nearly often enough!"

A brief silence fell. They were getting in deeper than either of them cared to go. Then Dr. Sheridan finished his drink resolutely. (That might be a reflection on Agnes's barkeeping. Time enough later to find out about that.) He lifted the book, hefted it, grinned at her. "You picked this for me with your own fair hands. It's a good thing you didn't have to carry it in them."

"Maybe I could if I had to. But what are porters and chauffeurs for?"

"Maybe they wonder what employers are for. But let's not go into that now. It's been a lovely interview. It is a lovely gift. You shouldn't have brought it to me. But you would, you being you."

He had turned the phrase neatly enough. It wasn't the cocktail only. Agnes proved that to herself by downing a second one.

Three books remained from the package: Miriam's, Sully's, and the joint gift for Dr. and Mrs. Follansbee. The homecoming was just as good as the trip had been. If she had a few little tasks left over, so much the better. They would serve as reminders.

The week went by cheerfully enough. She sent Eustace to the rectory with Dr. Follansbee's book, and mailed theirs to Miriam and Sully. Agnes wrote notes to both of them, announcing that the book was on its way. To Miriam, she went on to say, "I bought this book for you on a recent trip to New York. It was enjoyable, but I'm glad to be home." The word to Sully was, "I've broken the news to Miss Wainwright, so you're safe enough there. Better let *her* tell *you* that I've been in New York, though. You don't want her to get the idea that you've been holding out on her."

All the choirboys received their books, and returned thanks in various ways: by word of mouth, over the telephone, and in two cases—doubtless under parental pressure —in stiffly-worded notes. Thursday's meeting was a real joy; several members of the Guild told her that they had missed her, and the Mother of the Gracchi grunted what might have been confirmation.

That afternoon, Tom telephoned again. She went to a Saturday night movie with him, and invited him over for Sunday dinner. His star was decidedly in the ascendant. He was good company as well as a good escort. Agnes was never heartbroken when he left; but there were times when she really missed him.

Not being royalty, Agnes could not very well propose to him. But if and when Tom Jones got around to popping the question, there was a fair chance of his getting an affirmative answer. He knew his way around, and would never discredit her in the eyes of her friends. He might be a good father. He could live with her in the Hammond mansion and commute; being the owner, he made his own hours at the factory.

251

Such a match would get him away from memories of Lucile; it would rid Agnes of the threat of Miriam. Dr. Sheridan could be the honored friend of them both.

That last was a parenthetical consideration, of course. But it did carry some weight. About as much, on the "for" side, as would balance the "against" consideration that to change her name from Wainwright to Jones would be an awful comedown. Even hyphenating in the English style wouldn't help that one: "Wainwright-Jones" was downright ridiculous. She would carry a certain image forever at her heart; but that was no reason why she shouldn't do her best to make a nice fellow decently happy.

Thus matters stood on Monday, a week after Mrs. Wainwright and Mr. Jones had returned from their New York safari. But late that afternoon, Sully telephoned. He had not put in an appearance on Sunday; Agnes had wondered in passing whether he was sulking in his tent. But he wasn't the sulking type; good salesmen never are.

He began by thanking her for the book that she had sent him: it was a current best seller, "so popular, Agnes, and so dirty!" He went on to invite himself over for luncheon tomorrow. He was taking the day off, and wished to consult her on a matter of importance.

"To you or to me?" asked Agnes, startled by his unwonted seriousness.

"To both of us, I hope. We'll have to find that out, however."

"Oh, all right!" Agnes agreed. "Let me know which train you're coming on, and I'll have Eustace meet it."

She was not as nonchalant as she tried to sound. All evening she wondered uneasily what fool notion Sully had taken into his head. Surely he wasn't thinking of—?

He was thinking of just that. He did scant justice to the excellent meal that Dora had prepared. He talked much less than usual; what remarks he did utter were generalities which failed to glitter. Then, in the front parlor, he began to do sentry-go. After a few minutes of that, he let her have it. He managed a grin at his own nervousness; but beads of perspiration stood out on his forehead.

"Why, but Sully," faltered Agnes, "I never supposed you felt that way about me."

"I never knew it myself until you walked out on us. Your absence makes Antioch 'one with Nineveh and Tyre.' "

"Bless me, you *are* educated!" Agnes felt the feebleness of the jest; but between pity and embarrassment, it was the best that she could do.

"I'm not so much, maybe," Sully went on. "But if you married me you could come back to your own home, and stop being custodian of the Hammond Museum."

"I could do that anyhow, if it happened to suit me."

"You wouldn't want to go back under guardianship; you know that as well as I do. But if you marry me, I'll find Miriam a nice apartment with an adjacent garage. All by her independent self, she can live out of tin cans and cracker boxes to her heart's content. We could have her over for Sunday dinner sometimes, just so long as we didn't make a habit out of it."

"You make it sound like a good idea. All the same, I'm not having any, Sully."

"The name is Walter," he said stiffly.

Agnes met his eye, held it for a long minute, then shook her head. "Not to me," she said quietly.

Sully took his defeat with no very good grace. "If it's that

253

cup-and-saucer stiff you're thinking about, you're making a great mistake," he growled.

"Must it be somebody else?"

"You mean I'm simply unacceptable?"

"I mean nothing of the sort. If you're going to put words into my mouth, please make them kinder words."

"The one kind word that I would like to hear you are denying me." Sully smiled forlornly.

Agnes's heart was torn with pity for him. But pity was not love. It got people into almost as many scrapes, perhaps. But there was less excuse for those scrapes; even easygoing Agnes knew enough to avoid them.

Poor old Sully! He left as soon as her car could be called for him; but the thought of him was not so easily to be dismissed. Agnes was very fond of Sully. The fact that she didn't choose to marry him was nothing against him. Agnes couldn't marry all the men she was fond of; that would be not only against the law in present-day America, but highly impractical. But if Sully had finally wearied of his bachelor existence, that in itself was something gained. The loneliest and most forlorn creature on earth was a bachelor stricken in years.

Agnes could do something for Sully besides marry him herself. She was not a matchmaker; or, at least up to now, she had not been. But was there any valid reason why she shouldn't be? She had tried her hand at a lot of different things lately. She'd every right to try her hand at one more, if she went about it with a little discretion.

Miriam had "Ladybird" on her mind. But, to some extent, the reverse was true, too. To Agnes, it seemed high time that the tables were turned. If instead of turning they stuck fast, that might teach Nosey Nettie (next-of-kin to Meddlesome

254

Mattie) that there were times when her services were not required.

Wednesday's mail brought Agnes a singularly stiff note from Miriam. She began bravely enough, "Dear Ladybird, It was most kind of you to remember me while you were in New York." But after the usual cant phrases of thanks, emphasizing, "I haven't had time to read it yet, but I'm sure I shall enjoy it when I get around to it," came a paragraph of a different tenor. "Nothing much that has happened here lately would be of general interest. I am busier than ever; but this is no place to go into my doings. If you need anything that I can get for you, please let me know. Affectionately yours . . ."

It was Miss Wainwright's own way of telling her stepmother to go to hell. Relations between them were so strained that any change might be an improvement.

Agnes remembered the little boy who was too kind, and too intelligent, to draw lots. Grown people might well profit by such an example. Out of the richness of her own life, erratic by some standards but extremely enjoyable to Mrs. Wainwright herself, she decided to have a try at this novel undertaking.

One point was clear to her right at the beginning. She would have to begin with Sully.

She wrote him a note that very afternoon: "Dear Sully, Please give me credit for not having said on a recent occasion, 'This is so sudden!' I didn't offer to be a sister to you either, did I? Never having been anybody's sister, I wouldn't have much idea of how to go about the job. But I still think a great deal of you. When we have been through a 'cooling-off period,' I'd like to see you again. Pending that happy day, won't you at least indicate that I have not altogether curdled the milk of human kindness for you?"

Sully wrote back, "Thank you for your letter. I see that I've underestimated your cleverness. Why should blue eyes and dimples make anybody think that a woman is guileless? Blue eyes are merely a matter of pigmentation, and a dimple is a muscular defect. But thank you anyhow."

That was a reply, but it was no answer. It egged her on. Agnes Wainwright was going to see Walter Sullivan happy, if she had to break his neck in order to do so. The difficulty was in getting started.

She consulted Dr. Sheridan about her perplexity. She took care to name no names. That salved Agnes's conscience; it also obscured the issue. Still, just talking to somebody might help her get the thing straight in her own mind.

"If a man and woman, both single and in the prime of life, are made for each other, but don't seem to realize that they are—" she paused for breath, "—how do you bring them together?"

" 'You' meaning you, Mrs. Wainwright?"

" 'You' meaning 'me,' yes, sir."

"It sounds risky. You might run into a *Courtship of Miles Standish* situation."

"Oh, he has already—" Agnes checked herself. She hoped she didn't look as silly as she felt.

"It's hard to give advice in the dark." Dr. Sheridan wasn't taking her seriously. On the whole, that was a relief.

"Well, I suppose I'd better wait and see." Agnes shrugged.

"That might be sound policy. Anyhow, it's good news that you aren't walking out on us."

The subject dropped of its own weight.

With Tom Jones, the situation was different. He had been

256

established for months as a regular visitor, while Dr. Sheridan was merely an occasional. When Tom missed Sully for the third successive Sunday, he inquired, "What's become of your sidekick?"

"My sidekick?"

"He certainly isn't *mine*. That Sullivan person who was in the habit of taking the trip over from the home town every week, in the hope that you would smile on him."

"He's broken himself of the habit."

"I can see that. But wasn't his mind made up for him?"

"He suggested another arrangement. When it didn't suit me, he decided that I needed snubbing."

"Bear up, bear up!" urged Tom. For a minute there he looked unbearably smug. He had found out what he wanted to know. Much good might it do him! Agnes wasn't thinking about him; she was going ahead with her project.

She called Miriam, heard her news, worked around to asking whether she had seen Sully lately. "Why, yes!" said Miriam, surprised. "Haven't you?"

"Not too lately. I think he's getting tired of me."

"Oh, I wouldn't say that!" Miriam remembered her manners, but her voice had risen a note. "He was over a week ago Sunday, but he didn't stay long. This past Sunday he was going into New York, he told me."

"Busy, like all the rest of us! You must make time for me soon. I haven't seen you in weeks." But Agnes was careful to cut off the conversation before Miriam could get around to plans for remedying that omission.

She called Sully then, and invited him over. "I'd like a little visit with you. It needn't be on Sunday."

"Sunday is still sacred to the potter who pots teapots?"

257

"That line is good enough for a Mother Goose rhyme! Come for luncheon or dinner any weekday."

They agreed on a date. Sully refused to have Eustace meet his train, however; a taxi would do for him. He was being a little bit defensive; and all the better if he was. It showed that he wasn't getting his hopes up again.

They lunched simply this time. Agnes gave him his coffee in the sitting room. When he had refused a second cup, then changed his mind and accepted it, he stirred the sugar in, and waited.

"I've been thinking things over, and I've found what to my mind is the perfect answer," Agnes said sweetly, and paused.

"For you and me? You're not suggesting that you'll be a sister to me after all?"

"I'm not, but I'd like you in the family. What should you say to becoming my stepson-in-law?"

It took a minute for that to sink in. Then Sully said simply, "Good God!"

"Startles you, does it? But it's a fine idea."

" 'Startles' isn't the word. It doesn't just scare the pants off me; it has me stark naked under a boiling shower."

"Oh, come on, Sully! You know you admire her."

"I may admire Westminster Abbey. But that isn't the same as saying I want to get into bed with it."

"There's more to marriage than the thing you keep harping on."

"More, and worse. 'All cats are gray at night.' But in the evening, or across the breakfast table—" He closed his eyes and shuddered dramatically. The essential male in him was flattered, though the rational man was taken aback.

"She's been in love with you for a long time," Agnes

pleaded, "though she's too proud to admit it even to herself."

"Who told *you* she has, if she doesn't know it herself?"

"The oracle at Delphi. You know it, too, if you'll just stop and think."

"I'm not thinking about all the women who may be in love with me. Luckily for me, it isn't Leap Year."

"She'll make you a good wife, too, if you take a firm stand in the beginning."

"Says you!" he derided.

"No, I mean it. Don't ask, 'Do you want steak or chops, Miriam?' Say, 'You'll eat chops and you'll like them.' If you don't care for the cook, fire her and tell Miriam to get another one."

"*Taming of the Shrew* stuff, eh?"

"Tell her not to buy you any neckties; you prefer to trust your own bad taste. Announce that you prefer the home of your choice; you'll rent out the Wainwright house for me."

"Ouch! That's a hot one."

"Say that when you work evenings you'll have just a small meal at dinnertime and a good supper later."

"That's when I won't have to fire the cook. She'll quit."

"Miriam can see about your supper for you. You can help her afterward with the dishes."

"There I have it, cut and dried. All this from you, gentle Agnes!"

"I'm giving you the benefit of my experience."

"You're giving yourself the lion's share and the hyena's too. You hope to get rid of us both by the same fell stroke."

She changed the subject then, and gave her counsel time to sink in. Sully stayed for another hour. Either he wasn't

259

so much repelled as he pretended, or he preferred any sort of talk so long as he could linger in her company.

He relented so far as to let her order the car to take him to the station. Then at the last moment, he turned to her and put out his hand. He gave Agnes's a firm grip, then dropped it and turned away. Over his shoulder he said, "This is all very well. But she must realize that she's second choice."

Agnes could scarcely believe her ears. He might be only fooling. He might not realize the full implication of his words. Yet he had certainly said "second choice." And how could Miriam be that, unless he got around to choosing her?

21.

Lent was upon her before she knew it. On Shrove Tuesday, Agnes ate the traditional pancakes, and wondered why in English it was still called "Shrove." That implied confessing and being forgiven, "shriven." Penance must have come in somewhere along the line. But nowadays the epithet was singularly inaccurate.

"Mardi Gras" was much better: "Fat Tuesday." Agnes had found out in her inquisitive childhood that during the Middle Ages people actually fasted during Lent. Poor creatures, there along toward the end of winter they were undoubtedly hungry most of the time anyhow; if they could make some spiritual profit out of dire physical need, so much the better for them.

261

They gave themselves a final fling before they entered on the season of abstinence. Every particle of fat they had left— some of it they must have hoarded for the occasion—was thrown into some sort of vast conglomeration with the flour or meal or whatever it was, and the whole stirred up together and baked. People gorged themselves for once. More power to them!

Agnes loved the Penitential Office for Ash Wednesday. She loved the Litany, too, and the so-called "Spanish Litany." Fish was always a treat to her. Even if she had believed in mortification, the season gave her little chance to practice it.

Agnes supposed that she really ought to give up something for Lent. In her childhood, the practice had not been encouraged. Papa had told her that there would be time enough for such things later on. Once Agnes had overheard her mother half sobbing, "You are so right, dear! We've deprived her of enough already. Poor little only child!" Then her father comforted, "Hush, darling, hush! It isn't your fault. Hush, do you understand? We'll make it up to her somehow."

Agnes, advancing into her teens, had decided to give up candy for Lent. She had kept her vow, at a cost of inner turmoil and occasional outer writhing which only people who remember their own teens can realize. The first year, when she reached her goal, she was spent but satisfied. She had kept her promise to herself.

But later, doubt set in. She had accomplished what she set out to do. She was rewarded almost too bountifully to suit her. The candy Agnes ate on Easter Sunday tasted better than even candy had any right to taste. Was there any merit in going without when that simply gave you more time to look ahead to repossessing?

As a married woman, Agnes had continued to give up candy during Lent. With Jerome, it had passed for one of the little woman's pretty whims. After his death, the Widow Wainwright had simply postponed the question. Not only did Miriam frown on "Popish observances"; Agnes had found herself involved in a year-round penance of keeping her opinions to herself.

Rather hastily, Agnes decided to give up desserts during Lent. "Oh, Mrs. Wainwright!" Dora Dean said reproachfully. "Not for every day in Lent, surely? I have a devil's food cake cooling. But if you'd rather I didn't ice it until tomorrow, you have only to say the word."

It was a nice point: a very fine point altogether. It would serve no purpose, heavenly or mundane, to hurt Dora's feelings. Besides, if the boss forewent desserts, was that binding on the help as well? Or were they to regard themselves as a lower order of beings, and go ahead and indulge anyhow?

"Which icing were you planning on making, Dora?" asked Agnes serenely.

"Caramel nut is a good one, Mrs. Wainwright. I use pecans in that one. Cocoanut fudge is all right, too. Personally, on that dark chocolate cake I like a white frosting piled on real thick. That's the one I was planning on. But I can always change."

"Don't," advised Agnes. "Or at least, make only the one small alteration. Before you ice the rest of the cake, cut me out one little sliver and serve it to me as is. You can do that, can't you?"

263

"I can, of course. I will, if you say so." Dora looked puzzled, almost displeased.

Then suddenly her face cleared. "You're right, Mrs. Wainwright. It's so very simple! I should have known that without your telling me: cake as good as my devil's food doesn't need an icing. I'll serve it the way it is, and use those frostings some other time on a plain white cake."

"Thank you, Dora," said Agnes simply. "That will be very nice, I'm sure."

There was nothing else she could say. But renunciation seemed not to be so easily achieved, except perhaps in a monastery, where everybody abode by the same rules. Agnes didn't smoke, so she couldn't very well give up smoking. What little she drank was almost always in company, and she couldn't very well abstain in front of guests without enforcing abstention on her guests.

Renunciation was a negative virtue anyhow. Wouldn't it be more praiseworthy, as well as more practical, to do something which she did not particularly care about doing, but really ought to?

Agnes had no craving to visit the old homestead in Antioch. But she was a property-owner there. It was still her voting residence. To stay away as consistently as she was doing might leave a wrong impression: "Now that she inherited all that money upstate, she thinks she's too good for us." A duty visit needn't last longer than overnight. It would be that much off her mind.

Yet here, too, the question was not completely one-sided. The place in Antioch belonged to Agnes, just as it had ever since Jerome willed it to her. Yet Miriam had been in charge of the establishment for months. If Agnes went over there now, wouldn't it seem as if she came to inspect Miriam's housekeeping? Even if she didn't make the trip for that specific purpose, she could scarcely help noticing.

There was an even stronger reason for staying away: until that matter of Walter Sullivan came to a head (if it ever did!), Mrs. Wainwright must certainly be careful to keep hands off.

Ten days into the Lenten season, Sully showed up for a Sunday visit. He was quieter than his wont, and he left before Tom Jones did. Agnes, walking to the front door with him, invited, "Come again, Sully."

"Come again when I can't stay so long?" asked Sully with a touch of bitterness.

"You said that, not I; and I don't think it was altogether a kind thing to say."

"Not altogether kind? It was an abominable remark. Can you forgive me, Agnes?"

"I can. I do."

"Then I really may come again?"

"Come next week, if you like."

He studied her face for a long minute. Then he gave a little shrug—of resignation or of hopelessness; they were much the same.

"I'll come," he said quietly. "I don't care how often she changes her name, there is only one Agnes Costen."

"Just as well there is." Agnes not only gave him her hand, she pressed his. She had never liked him quite so much as at this moment when they agreed to disagree.

Agnes was naturally prone to look on the cheerful side of things. She fell asleep that night thinking how sweet her choirboys were in their Lenten attitudes and music. The Easter party which she gave for them would be something. They earned it all the more because they were for the most part preoccupied with their own interests and concerns, which they managed much better than Agnes could have managed those concerns for the little—"angels."

In the darkest part of the night, Agnes wakened suddenly, sat up, turned on the light. Something had disturbed her. She reached for her glass of water, sipped, set it back. Then, and then only, did she realize that her plate of cookies remained untouched on her bedside table.

Her renunciation had made itself. It might be a minor renunciation; but it was *there*. Agnes was grateful for it.

Next morning, she began her list of Easter cards and Easter presents. There would be guests for Easter dinner, she hoped. Agnes wondered what Dora Dean's idea of the mainstay would be. That was one subject on which Mrs. Wainwright had differed perpetually from Rosa Lee Montgomery. Rosa Lee had been all for making it ham. Agnes had held out for lamb. Spring lamb: the paschal lamb.

She had obtained it, too. But it wasn't the best thing that Rosa Lee cooked. They didn't eat much lamb in the South.

One thing, Agnes decided, she would do for herself during Lent. With needed assistance, of course; but the responsibility was Mrs. Wainwright's. She would go through Aunt Adelaide's clothing and personal possessions and arrange for their disposition.

It was an unwelcome task at best. But it was the least Agnes could do to honor Aunt Adelaide's memory.

Or no, that was not a good way to put it. It was something Agnes could do in Aunt Adelaide's service. If it hadn't been for Aunt Adelaide, Agnes would still be wishing that her own Sunday breakfast, eaten under her own roof and at her own table, might taste the way Sunday breakfasts used to taste under her parents' roof, when popovers were a treat, not a sin.

Agnes asked Dora to save a little time soon in order to help her with a difficult task. Dora answered with eyes downcast. Whether that was to conceal a gleam of mirth at Mrs. Wainwright's delay in getting around to the obvious or a secret triumph at having arranged things on her own terms and so well in advance didn't make any difference to Agnes.

She asserted her authority as best she could. "You know where most of the clothing should go, Dora. Anything you want for yourself or anybody else, you are more than welcome to. The only items I would like to retain for the present are a few casual garments for a few difficult guests."

That was easy for Dora. "A guest is a guest."

Agnes nodded. "It's a large house, and has a reputation for hospitality. Thank you, Dora. I get along better with Mrs. Hammond's books than I ever did with my own. Her set of Stevenson is something which still occupies me. What bothers me is some of her intimate personal possessions."

They went upstairs together then, and had a reasonably quiet session sorting out and disposing of Aunt Adelaide's gold-backed brushes and combs, some incredible fans, a vinaigrette, a sweet miniature which had been either cherished or overlooked: even Dora Dean was not certain which. She could not identify it.

But then came two photographs, not framed or in albums, as so many others were. One was of Aunt Adelaide as a young woman: more mature than the painting in the back parlor showed her, but very much in the prime of life. The picture showed only her head and shoulders; it was large and obviously expensive, and every detail was rendered with great fidelity.

267

A beautiful woman, exquisitely dressed: poised, proud, aloof. Yet the expression was faintly wistful. In the eyes of the world, young Mrs. Hammond had had everything. Perhaps she had had everything that one woman could have. It had been her misfortune to realize that even in the luckiest life there is some inner lack. An inescapable sadness lies forever at the heart of things.

There was a penciled date in the corner of the mat. A little mental arithmetic informed Agnes that the picture had been taken about four years after Mr. Hammond died. His widow had kept this picture close at hand for a long long time. It was the only hint of the tentative that Agnes had detected in her otherwise decisive character.

The other picture was almost as large, but an entirely different class as to both subject and workmanship. The supreme effort of a small-town photographer, it showed at full length a woman in fancy dress. Small-town "fancy dress," belonging to no age or country that the beholder could discern: trailing panniered skirt, sleeves made in tiers of puffs, a lace ruff, buttons, beads, embroidery, everything that an ambitious and not particularly skillful dressmaker could pile upon the one costume.

The wearer was plump and pretty, and beaming with self-satisfaction. Obviously, to her this turnout was a triumph. The accessories to all this elegance were an ostrich-feather fan, a small brocade bag, long dangling earrings, and a pair of very substantial serviceable spectacles.

This photograph was labeled "Cousin Mary Fitch." The reason why no definite disposition had been made of it was easy to guess. Cousin Mary Fitch had been proud of the picture, or she wouldn't have bestowed it on her wealthy and important relative. It must have been a difficult gift to acknowledge. Common politeness would have forbidden Aunt Adelaide to inquire, "Why in thunder didn't you take off your glasses?" She was probably fond of her amiable if silly relative. She was forced to keep the picture against the day when Cousin Mary Fitch might come visiting. But it was nothing that Mrs. Hammond could frame or insert in an album for the irreverent to make fun of. Some people simply had no sense of the ridiculous.

Agnes showed this picture to Dora Dean. "Oh, yes!" said Dora. "She came to see Mrs. Hammond twice after I started to work for her. Cousin Mary was married three times. Outlived all three husbands."

"Three husbands!" echoed Agnes. "Mrs. Hammond never even got around to a second."

"People wondered a good deal about that. It couldn't have been from lack of chances."

"Cousin Mary must have been easier to satisfy." Agnes hesitated a moment, mulling over this point. "After all, who is there for a woman like Mrs. Hammond to marry?"

"A woman like Mrs. Wainwright—" Dora suggested slyly.

"Isn't brilliant, has no head for business, has never been much of a traveler," Agnes finished for her. "I've sometimes thought maybe that was what Aunt Adelaide had in mind when she planned to get me away from Antioch and—and things."

"I wouldn't know, Mrs. Wainwright. She was doing the best she could for all of us."

"We'll do the best we can for other people, too, won't we? Mrs. Hammond took a liking to me. So—"

"It isn't hard to see why she did that, Mrs. Wainwright."

"I'm easy to get along with, I guess. Maybe a little too

269

easy sometimes. I haven't much backbone. That's enough about me for the present. I'm going to put Cousin Mary Fitch's picture right back where I found it. It's a real puzzler. But I'm taking Aunt Adelaide's down to the back parlor with me. You'll see about everything else in here, won't you, Dora?"

Agnes had barely finished propping Aunt Adelaide's photograph up when Dr. Sheridan rang up. Agnes invited him over, of course. She not only showed him this photograph, which he had probably never seen before; she asked him about Cousin Mary Fitch.

"I may have met the lady," he acknowledged. "Under which of her aliases, I wouldn't know."

He had met her, Agnes felt sure; her guilelessness must have amused him. She excused herself and fetched the picture from upstairs. "Aliases," indeed! He too had recognized that whiff of the ridiculous.

He glanced at the picture, tried to suppress his grin, and nodded. "She was Mrs. Pomeroy when I was called in to prescribe for her sore throat. She wasn't in disguise then."

"She and Mrs. Hammond were cousins?"

"I believe they were related somehow. First cousins do not usually lay emphasis on the title."

"They didn't inherit their brains from the same side of the family. There! I said that; you didn't. I suppose she is dead by this time?"

"She sent you no message at the time of Mrs. Hammond's funeral?"

"I can't be certain. I've dealt with so many strange names since I've been living here."

"She was Mrs. Pomeroy—my records would show when. They would also show where she lived at that time. But it might take quite a while to run down the information; my files are not cross-indexed."

"It isn't all that important. If I had business enough of my own to attend to, I wouldn't take the same interest in other people's."

Agnes hadn't found out a great deal; but Dr. Sheridan had given her something to think over. Also one more reason for wondering why this particular Lenten season appeared to be turning itself into a prolonged Thanksgiving for Agnes Costen Wainwright.

To keep herself from getting too vainglorious—or too superstitious—Agnes long-distanced Miriam that same evening. She invited her stepdaughter to come over some time soon, to stay as long or as short a time as suited her. "You know you're always welcome here, Miriam; but it doesn't do any harm to tell you so, does it?"

"Doesn't do any harm, no." Miriam made no attempt to keep the scorn out of her tone.

"Then I may expect you—when?"

"Not for some time. Thank you just the same, Ladybird; but I don't believe you realize quite how busy I am."

"Suppose you call me whenever you have a free moment. I'm always glad to hear from you. You may reverse the charges if you find it more convenient to call from an outside station."

Agnes hung up, and tried—without much success—to feel ashamed of herself. She hadn't intended it that way; but this time she was the one who had, in the traditional phrase, saved her credit and her bacon too.

That very next Sunday, Walter Sullivan put in an appearance. He looked better; he was obviously glad to be here. Agnes was delighted to see him. He had come in no penitential spirit. All the better that he hadn't! Life was too short to be spent in moping.

It was too short anyhow. But that could wait. Agnes's immediate concern was with her guests. With just a shade of apprehension, she wondered how Sully was going to take Tom Jones.

Tom appeared to be the least of Sully's concerns. Sully was intensely interested in his dinner, as well he might be; Dora was surpassing herself. Not that she needed to; she simply enjoyed doing so.

The three of them were dawdling over their dessert when Tom Jones left the table to look up a disputed reference. Sully started to push his plate aside, took one more forkful of lemon meringue pie, and put it down untasted.

"I declare," he said, "the flavor still lingers on the palate. But the palate itself is beginning to be a little bit dulled."

Agnes made no attempt to lift her own fork. "We try not to send people away from here hungry."

"How do they ever manage to get away from here? That's the real question." Sully managed what amounted almost to a full breath. "I'd like to stay here right along. Maybe I could manage it somehow. Maybe Dora Dean is the one I really should marry."

"If she'd have you!" snapped Agnes. "When you re-build this place into apartments, Sully, remember to ask Dora whether she wishes hers to be for herself alone or for herself and Mr. Dora Dean."

"When? If and when!" With an abrupt and totally unexpected gesture, Sully raised Agnes's hand to his lips.

The two of them were again staring at their dessert plates when Tom Jones came back with the reference he had been seeking. He laid it carefully on the table, opened it at the

272

place he had marked with his finger, glanced up to be sure that he had his audience's attention.

He had, after a fashion. But it was a very small audience. In that short interval, Sully had managed to escape them.

Was "escape" quite the right word? He had taken his departure, anyhow. Agnes was both relieved and remorseful to find him gone. But she would have to say this for Sully: he had managed an extraordinarily graceful exit.

22.

It never pays to brag, even to oneself. Agnes supposed that she had staved off Miriam very neatly. Mrs. Wainwright had acted with unwonted sagacity; she patted herself on the back for her achievement.

Then on Thursday of Passion Week, when she returned from her Guild meeting with nothing on her mind except the consciousness of a pleasant duty done and the soothing prospect of luncheon, she found Miriam waiting for her. Yes, and furious at being kept waiting, though her arrival had not been heralded by either letter or phone call.

"My dear, if I had known you were coming—" Agnes faltered. That innocent remark made things worse; it accused Miriam of lack of consideration for her hostess.

"I didn't know it myself," snapped Miriam. "I had the most extraordinary session last night with Walter Sullivan."

"Sit down and tell me about it," Agnes invited feebly. She herself sank into a chair, wished that she had taken off her coat.

But Miriam continued her pacing. "He had called me in the morning and invited me out for dinner. It was rather short notice; but with as old a friend as that, I didn't see why I should stand on ceremony."

Agnes murmured assentingly. She lacked initiative even to ring and order herself a glass of water, though she was frightfully thirsty. She wished she had been almost anywhere rather than here.

It wasn't the place she objected to, of course. It was the emotional situation. Yet who had brought that about? Agnes Costen Wainwright and nobody else. The fruit of one's own folly is bitter eating. That it was seasoned with good intentions didn't help a bit. In fact, it seemed to curdle the mess further.

"He took me to a small place in the country," Miriam went on. "It was clean and quiet. I rather enjoyed their broiled chicken. Ladybird, are you listening to me?"

Agnes was indeed listening. Her perturbation began to give way to interest. Could it be—? Was it—? She had only to hold her horses and she would find out. Her stepdaughter was, for once, on the verge of disclosure.

"During dinner, Sully didn't talk as much as usual," Miriam swept on. "I didn't attach any importance to that. Even he must run out of wind some time, I thought. But afterward, when he was driving along through the country, he began to act queer."

"As if he had something on his mind?" asked Agnes.

Miriam whirled on her. "He says that he asked your permission to marry me. That's one of his jokes, I suppose. But did you know he was going to propose?"

Agnes nodded. "I gave him, not my permission, of course, but my blessing."

"That will do to tell," said Miriam bitterly.

"Don't be unreasonable," urged Agnes. "Girls do get married, you know. It happens right along."

"Not to me!" Miriam managed a faint smile. "I like Sully. But Ladybird, I always thought it was you he came to see."

"He came in search of a home from home, like any other sensible bachelor. It's high time he had a home of his own, however."

"If that's what he had in mind, he made a mistake in proposing to *me*. I'm not a born homemaker."

"Nobody is. But you can learn. You're smart enough."

"But Ladybird, if I should marry him—I'm not planning to, but if I should—where would we live?"

Come, this was better. This was getting down to cases.

"Not with his mother-in-law, I'm sure," said Agnes dryly.

"His moth—? You? There, Ladybird! You see how impossible the whole idea is."

"I may be dense; but I don't see anything of the kind."

"But Ladybird, if we actually did decide to do such a thing, what would become of you?"

She had said "we." Now was the time to strike. Agnes drew a long breath and let fly. "If you would stop calling me by that absurd nickname, perhaps I might try to explain."

" 'Absurd'? But Ladybird, I thought you liked it!"

Madam Chairman reduced to repeating, "But Ladybird"! Agnes's tone became kinder when she said, "You never

276

asked. I wasn't asked, either, when they dubbed me 'Agnes.' But that *is* my name; and names are meant to be called by."

"You never said—" faltered Miriam, then rallied far enough to assert, "I thought it suited you. It sounds so pretty—and so gentle."

"No, I never said. Your keeping it up was as much my fault as it was yours. Suppose we forget about it and start all over."

"Suppose we do." Miriam still couldn't bring herself to the point of reform. She had had a most upsetting twenty-four hours; her preconceived ideas were toppling one after another.

"So far so good. But here's a more important point." Agnes really had the bit in her teeth now. "I feel guilty because I have two houses and you haven't any. But I can deed the Wainwright homestead to you."

"I couldn't take it," snapped Miriam. "Father willed it to you."

"You've always resented his doing so."

A slow painful flush crept from Miriam's severely tailored collar to the edge of her coiffure. She actually had a lock of hair out of place; that showed how deeply this crisis was affecting her.

"That was only natural," Agnes temporized. "But I think you might realize that a stepmother has no bed of roses."

"You married the family, didn't you?" Miriam's color began to recede. "I've been a pig. I see that now. But I'm very sorry. Truly I am."

"Sorry—" Mrs. Wainwright prodded.

"Sorry, Agnes." Miriam made ample amends.

"Spoken like a gentleman," Agnes applauded. "All right,

then, for the present I'll keep the Wainwright house. But I'll will it to you, naturally."

"You'll outlive me. See if you don't."

"It's possible. In that case, I'll arrange to have the Wainwright place descend to your oldest unmarried daughter."

Miriam's color changed again. But this time it was not with the flush of chagrin; it was with a blush of maidenly embarrassment. For the first time in Agnes's experience of her, she looked adorably girlish.

"Sully is getting a bargain," Agnes said impulsively. "I hope he appreciates it."

"I haven't accepted him yet," Miriam demurred.

"You won't be cheating yourself," Agnes swept on. "Let Sully select your first little home for you. Take along with you from your father's house anything that you like. Later, you can always change."

"You are so much nicer to me than I deserve." Miriam rose to leave. Agnes hesitated on the brink of an invitation to stay and lunch here, but decided against it. For once in her life, she was going to let well enough alone.

"Take it out on Sully," Agnes advised. "I mean it in this way: marriages are made in Heaven. Or at least, that is what we are told. But our own experience teaches us that they have to be fulfilled here on Earth. So put your brains to work on your marriage. Here endeth the sermon."

"Thank you, Ag—Agnes. Thank you more than I can say." Miriam kissed Mrs. Wainwright hastily on both cheeks; then she ran out of the house. She did not wait for Eustace to be summoned; she did not send for a taxi. The walk to the station might do her good.

Agnes plodded upstairs, freshened, was torn for a moment between her desire for a nap and her craving for a

278

meal. Hunger soon won. After she had eaten, she could relax. She still didn't believe in her luck. But maybe one of these days she might manage to deserve it.

Palm Sunday was always to Agnes a day of suspense. Ahead lay the deep vale of Good Friday, followed by the sharp rise to Easter. The temporary triumph symbolized by the palms had never quite satisfied her.

This year she also had her private reasons for uneasiness. She confided them to Tom Jones when he put in his customary appearance. "So you see I have my fingers crossed," she wound up. "I want them both to be happy. I want it quite terribly. I think I've made them see things my way; but there's always the chance of a slip-up."

"Don't be impatient," urged Tom. "Miriam probably has her heart set on being a June bride. My first wife—"

"Your *what*?" interrupted Agnes.

He looked a little sheepish, but he explained coolly enough, "Lucile, the woman I was once married to. I've mentioned her before, haven't I?"

"Not quite in the same terms, I think. What about her?"

"She was a June bride. Kept me waiting all that time, though it had started when I kissed her under the mistletoe."

Agnes felt a pang of pity. He must have been so happy there at one time. The death of happiness was a thing that nobody bargained for; yet it happened all too often.

Tom sensed her emotion and pressed his advantage. "She had too much sense to go on living with me. But I've improved a lot since then."

"Do you expect me to take your word for that?" chided Agnes.

"You can see for yourself that right now I'm not so bad."

She could indeed. Also, whoever got married then—or

279

didn't—Mrs. Wainwright had another birthday coming up in June. She had years enough ahead of her, doubtless. But she was getting too old to cry for the moon.

That very evening, something was settled. Tom had just glanced at his watch and announced that if it wouldn't bore her too frightfully he'd like to stay another hour or so, and Agnes was on the point of a jesting reply, when the phone rang.

It was Sully. He led off with, "Hello, ma-in-law! I want you to be the first to congratulate me."

Agnes caught her breath; the very relief was something of a shock. But after an instant, she came back, "I congratulate myself. I feel that I'm not losing a daughter. I'm gaining a son."

"I've a hunch that has been said before. Not to me, however. You'll have to help my ignorance. Do you think Tiffany's is a good place to shop for engagement rings?"

"They probably stock 'em. But it's no place to go if you're bargain-hunting."

"Bargain-hunting?" echoed Sully. "Do you think I'd pinch pennies at a time like this?"

"Ma-in-laws always think the worst, don't they?"

"They have a bad reputation; but some of them manage to live it down."

"All right, you've been funny enough for about long enough. Seriously, Walter, you're doing a very wise thing; and you'll never regret it. Where are you speaking from, by the way?"

"From your house in Antioch. The Wainwright homestead. Miriam's girlhood home."

"Fine! Then will you please put Miriam on the wire?"

280

The dialogue between Miriam and Agnes was short and a little stiff. They were both afraid of saying too much.

But before Agnes had time to terminate the talk, Sully came to the telephone again, "I'd like to come over and talk to you one of these days," he said.

"It's always a pleasure to see you, Walter. Just let me know in advance, and I'm sure I can suit your time."

"What do you think I'm doing now? And will you please can that 'Walter' stuff?"

There it was again! There was no sense in her trying to act dignified; people just did not take Agnes seriously.

"All right, Sully," she conceded. "Holy Week is crowded; but if what you want to see me about is important, I'll get you in somehow."

"It's not all that pressing. I'll call you again later. Or you can always call me at my office and reverse the charges."

"How much of your time do you spend waiting around your office and hoping that business will come in?"

"You've never worked in an office, have you, Agnes? Never even for a week?"

"Ma-in-law might better stop acting like the Grand Inquisitor, in other words? You're right, Sully, absolutely right. Get in touch with me again later. Your news has made me very very happy."

"I'm not exactly blue myself. Shall I give your love to Miriam?"

"Please do. And keep a sliver of it for my new son."

Agnes rang off and turned to Tom. "Just like that!" she informed him.

" 'Just like that!' Like what? It struck me he was damned long-winded."

"You're not the strong silent type yourself, Tom Jones."

281

"Maybe not. But he's wasted most of my precious last half hour for me."

"Wasted it for *you*? I suppose when you're here I have no right to talk over the telephone?"

"Sure not," Tom agreed cheerfully. "Just take the handset off the hook; then the other party will get the busy signal."

There was no sense in trying to argue with him, even if Agnes hadn't been too happy to argue. Anyhow, why was she always expecting things to make sense? She should have learned better a long time ago.

"All right, get on your way," she said. "I suppose I'll invite the young people over a week from today. If you care to join us, good. We'll have the paschal lamb, of course."

"You enjoy ritualistic eating, don't you?" asked Tom dryly.

"I enjoy *eating*." It was out before Agnes realized a rather startling implication: in all these months of Dora Dean's cooking, she had gained not more than two or three pounds. There was no great fun in overeating when no self-appointed censor was at hand to frown on the procedure.

Was she going to enjoy that freedom all the rest of her life? The prospect made Agnes a little dizzy. She might forge other fetters for herself later on. But for the present, oh joy! oh bliss! She could not only eat cookies in bed every evening, she could raid the refrigerator in the middle of the night, and then again along toward morning. There was no one who had either the authority or the opportunity to stop her.

During Holy Week, however, Agnes had no time for mundane indulgence, even if she had had the desire for it. She had to dispatch presents to all her choirboys: three handker-

282

chiefs apiece, which she had ordered by mail from New York. How much longer they would remain hers was a question; they would cease to be boys only too soon. But right here and now they were what they were, and they made her very happy.

They all sent her cards. She received a great many other Easter cards, too, and sent out a whole flock of them. She telephoned Sully and Miriam separately, and invited them both to come out to Marshfield for the Easter weekend. She invited Tom Jones for Easter Day itself.

Then, after a short period of indecision, she invited Dr. Sheridan. She had hesitated to put him into the awkward position of fifth wheel at a family party; but she reassured herself that the particular quartet of Miriam and Agnes, Sully and Tom, was not yet a family party. Indeed, there was no certainty that it ever would be.

Sully presently called back to say that if all went well, he hoped to drive Miriam over Saturday, and hoped Agnes saw nothing against the plan. On the contrary, Agnes approved of it. Sully was already beginning to act on her advice; a few more such moves and he would be off on the right foot.

Agnes planned the Easter dinner and the Easter decorations. She decided to wear the blue hat for Easter, and a suit which, although it had been bought before her nightclubbing costume, was a novelty to her Marshfield circle. For the three-hour service on Good Friday she would wear black, of course. Unforgettable three-hour service, with its memorable Seven Last Words. How she had missed that all during the years she had lived in Antioch!

She would like to show Miriam some special attention: something unostentatious, and suitable for the season.

283

Agnes did a little brain-racking, with the usual result: she couldn't think of anything.

But then, after she had ceased to agitate herself (for the idea was apparently a good one, but she was not openly committed to it), the answer came to Agnes. In the middle of Friday evening she remembered seeing somewhere among Aunt Adelaide's possessions an old-fashioned "gift-book" which should be just what the occasion called for.

It was half white and gold, half yellow cloth, most elaborately printed and illustrated; the Resurrection was set forth repeatedly and in detail. The text was the good old standby hymn, *Come, ye faithful, raise the strain*. It was inscribed, "Happy Easter, dear Adelaide, from your loving husband Herbert," and dated early in their married life.

She had kept it all these years, and the volume must have had lovely associations for Aunt Adelaide. Agnes, turning the pages in a mood of pleasant melancholy, came at length to the end, and gave a start of surprise. For there, pasted inside the back cover, was a poem which had been clipped from some magazine of bygone days. Agnes read

Easter for Us All

Christ is risen at Eastertide,
But not the weary, heartsick man,
Not the one whom God forsook!
Let me tell you if I can.

Christ who comes again today
Is once more a little child,
God and man, but nonetheless
"Gentle Jesus, meek and mild."

284

To Agnes's way of thinking it was very sweet and touching, and it evoked long-ago memories of the bedtime prayer which English children are taught at a stage when Americans would be learning, *Now I lay me down to sleep.* But her eye had leaped to the signature. There it was printed for anybody to see, *Gwendolyn Seeley Davidson.*

That was the name of the woman who had written the Thanksgiving Day poem which Agnes had taken to her heart. But apparently by the time the Easter poem was printed, the author had taken to herself a husband.

They must have been very happy together, those two. Indeed, indeed they must. In passing on this book to the bride-to-be, Agnes would be not only handing on a keepsake but bestowing an omen. From the gracious shades, Mrs. Davidson would be doing something to cheer and benefit the living.

Blinking away the tears, Mrs. Wainwright went in search of a pen.

23.

It was the best Easter ever. Agnes hated to see it draw to an end. Yet it left her with something to look forward to. When her house guests took their departure in the middle of Monday morning, Miriam asked with that new-found humility which became her so well, "May I come again some time soon and talk my plans over with you?"

Sully beamed on the tableau from behind his fiancée's back. Then his right eyelid descended ever so slightly; with his lips he shaped the word "Thursday."

They both wanted to see her; and they wanted to see her separately. If this sort of thing kept on after they were married, Agnes would be compelled to discourage it. But right now she felt flattered to have them turn to her for encouragement and counsel.

286

Their advance billing was so good that their respective shows might not live up to it. To ward off possible disappointment as well as because the Spring outdoors beguiled her, Mrs. Wainwright spent a good deal of the next two days out of doors.

Aunt Adelaide's tulips were superb. There were varieties here which Agnes had never even seen; and in the sort of winters they had here upstate, there wasn't too much danger that the bulbs would winter-kill. There were flowering bushes, too, including three kinds of lilacs; Agnes was enough of a botanist to be able to identify even the rare Persian. The forsythia, cheerful harbinger of spring, had already lost its lovely yellow blossoms and was putting forth delicate green leaves. Other low-growing shrubs, planted in ranks, had taken over the task of blossoming.

Farther back, there were currant bushes, and raspberries. There was a strawberry bed and an asparagus bed. So much of what she saw here brought back Agnes Costen's childhood. Lamb would again be the official dinner on the Fourth of July; but by that time asparagus would have yielded its sway to green peas. The asparagus, instead of being cut every day, would be allowed to grow. At midsummer, the lovely feathery plants would wave in the wind. When red berries appeared in the fall, some of the plants could be harvested and taken indoors. They made beautiful bouquets.

Would Agnes be here to see them? She devoutly hoped so.

There was space for a small kitchen garden and a small annual flower garden. At the front of the house, clematis and wisteria climbed their trellises. The smooth lawn was kept in shape by a power mower. Like the car, it was not the

287

latest model; but, again like the car, it recognized the driver's hand when Eustace took over.

How the place must have changed over the years! It dated back to the days when household help, indoors and out, was cheap and plentiful. Then mechanization had come along. Yet the machines still needed somebody to run them. The human element could never be disregarded. At the Hammond mansion it never had been. That much was evident.

Agnes returned from her Thursday-morning Guild meeting in excellent spirits. The Easter octave was still on. The festival atmosphere was due to prevail some time longer. With the advance of the season, too, she might be able to entertain her choirboys out of doors. Later on, she might even venture on an old-fashioned garden party.

Would that be restoring a precedent or shattering one? Should she make it "For the benefit of . . ." or allow it to stand as a simple act of hospitality? She could find out about that from Dora Dean. Or, as a matter of fact, from Dr. Follansbee. Ranking Dr. Follansbee second to Dora, even in her own mind, tickled Agnes. She was still showing her dimples when Walter Sullivan walked in on her.

"Had your lunch yet, ma-in-law?" he inquired.

"Not yet. Won't you join me, son-in-law?"

"I was hoping for an invitation."

"Hoping"? How long had it been since Agnes thought of her green-clad sprite? Had she been just too happy to think?

A person could be that happy. That could occur, undoubtedly. If it didn't occur too often, that was probably just as well. A single taste of the milk of Paradise was a memorable experience. But to indulge in it right along might spoil one's taste for lesser brews.

Sully had not come simply to pass the time of day. Or to eat Dora's cooking, though he did it ample justice. Yet it wasn't until he had declined a second helping of dessert that he began to come down to cases. Grinning from ear to ear, he drawled, "I've found you an excellent customer for the Wainwright homestead in Antioch, gentle Agnes."

Agnes did not sound a particle gentle when she snapped, "A customer? I haven't even made up my mind to put it on the market."

"You're no longer living there. You don't collect any rent from those premises. Taxes go on and on."

Agnes got her breath back. "Without a doubt, Walter Sullivan, the stage lost its greatest ornament when you decided to go into business. But I suppose you prefer to eat every day."

"I have certain prejudices. Who hasn't?"

Agnes's dimples had escaped from her control when she conceded, "All right, go ahead and spring it. You and your customer!"

"On this sale I will not even charge any commission," Sully assured her. "The customer I was speaking of is a character known to fame as Walter Sullivan."

The dimples vanished suddenly; for an instant, Agnes's face was devoid of expression. Then, as full consciousness returned, she held out her arm and ordered, "Pinch me, Sully, so that I can be sure I'm not dreaming. Or no! On second thoughts, don't pinch me. You would enjoy that altogether too much."

"Isn't that the perfect plan?"

"It seems so to me, Sully. It sounds altogether too good to be true."

"Might I suggest an alteration, Agnes? Instead of saying

289

'altogether too good to be true,' why don't you say 'almost too good'?"

"I stand corrected," said Agnes. "After a slight pause, while I try to get my bearings back, will you please go into particulars about this remarkable offer?"

He was proposing to allow Miriam to go ahead and live in her childhood home, but only as Mrs. Walter Sullivan. There would be no question of bequeathing the property. Early errors would be blotted out, early jealousies forgotten. It could work out. It might well work out.

Agnes braced herself for the next step. "The idea is good, Sully. So far, I have nothing much to say against it. But now is the time to go into particulars. How much does your wonderful customer offer to pay for the Wainwright property?"

His offer sounded fair enough. Agnes could see no real drawbacks to its acceptance. But she informed him that she would talk it over with Mr. Kent and possibly Mr. Estabrook, and let him know.

For the first time during the interview, Sully betrayed a flash of temper. "You have become altogether an upstate New Yorker," he informed her.

That naturally delivered him into Agnes's hands. She said suavely, "I find that the climate here agrees with me."

"I'm glad something does." The words were surly enough; but Sully was again grinning. "Do you want to call me when you finally decide to talk business?"

"It's your turn again," Agnes said coolly. "You're the one who has an office telephone and a secretary. I've enjoyed this interview vastly. Let me hear from you before too long."

His offer was, of course, the perfect answer to the problem: as neat as anything in higher mathematics. It tied up

290

all the loose ends. It meant a definite break with her past; but wasn't that what she had been desiring all these many moons? It left her free to go ahead with her new life. One after another, Agnes dealt with her misgivings; or rather, she tried to formulate them so clearly that she could deal with them in an intelligent fashion. She simply could not rid herself of a lurking uneasiness.

In the end, she gave in and called Sully, "Does Miriam know about this extraordinary offer?" she inquired.

"You should know better than to ask that."

"Maybe so. But I am asking."

"She does not. The time may come when I decide to talk over my business affairs with her. But right now her job is to be a good little fiancée and not ask questions."

Agnes giggled. "I believe you're beginning to enjoy the game for its own sake."

"If I am, that's nothing which need send you running to Mr. Kent and that other geezer."

"Mr. Estabrook," Agnes supplied. "Are you proposing to pay spot cash?"

"Certainly not. You've lived a sheltered life; but even you should know that nowadays every respectable American home has a mortgage on it."

"Oh, is that the catch?"

"On the other hand, it's the clincher."

Agnes's head was beginning to spin. "Will you put this into writing, please?"

"I'll be glad to. Talking over the phone is all right up to a certain point; but one's memory is only too apt to play tricks."

"Sully, there are times when what you say almost makes sense."

291

"Thank you for the compliment, dear. Its guarded nature makes me think you mean it."

Agnes closed the conversation by saying, "An innocent mistake is still a mistake. Under some circumstances it might well provoke a disaster." She was being sententious. That was a good rehearsal for her new part. Mothers-in-law were supposed to lay down the law, weren't they?

Sully's letter arrived two days later. He named what seemed to Agnes a fair figure, and offered her an alternative on terms. He could raise the mortgage money through a bank, or she could hold the mortgage herself. There were advantages to either course.

There might be; but Agnes did not feel obliged to review them. So long as she was making a break with her former home, she preferred a clean break.

That same afternoon, Miriam telephoned to ask when she might come over and spend the night with Agnes. There were so many things she would like to talk over.

There might also be some things she wanted to find out. That was all right, too. There never was any harm in asking.

Agnes set the date, spoke to Dora, then remembered to list her future engagements and consider possible conflicts. Her organization duties could be dealt with if need arose; they never had meant to her what Miriam's had amounted to in Miriam's own eyes. Miriam appeared to be putting them second to her personal interests right now. That might be either a gain or a loss; it depended on who did the judging.

Agnes's personal plans were easy enough to sum up. She could deal with her choirboys any time, or turn them over to Dora or to Eustace. As for *that* Tom Jones, this was her chance to show him a beautiful big sign lettered KEEP OFF THE GRASS.

She telephoned him, got through to him instantly (as she always seemed to with Tom), and announced, "My step-daughter is coming over Tuesday to spend the night with me."

"Fine!" said Tom cordially. "Whose idea was it in the first place?"

"Hers, of course. Miriam knows that she is always welcome here."

"I am not. Not at present, that is. Wasn't that what you called up to tell me?"

Agnes tried to sound stern. "You may qualify as a mind reader. I don't."

"It's a good thing you don't. If you were to read what is in my mind now—! All right, we won't go into that. Miriam and her victim are clearing the way for you and me. Give her my best regards."

There were times when Tom and Sully sounded so much alike that Agnes could scarcely tell which from t'other. Not that it made any vast difference, now that she had cleared the way for whatever it was that Miriam wanted to ask her.

That was a question on which conjecture was unprofit-able. Agnes gave it up. She went out into the grounds, wandered around the whole place, speculated on what it would be like to do a little active gardening herself.

So far, she had never tried it. But that wasn't the same thing as saying that she couldn't try it. She might even succeed. Whether she succeeded or failed, she might enjoy the endeavor.

There was Hope for an instant returning to meet her. In gratitude for the encounter, Agnes promised herself that if

293

she in person couldn't help Eustace, she would try to clear the way for somebody who could.

Miriam duly appeared at the appointed moment. She rearranged her assigned guestroom and suggested a short stroll through the grounds before the two of them had anything to eat "—or drink." Agnes was beginning to wonder whether it was just one more of their destined squabbles when Miriam said suddenly, "Where would you feel more comfortable, Lady Agnes? Out here or indoors?"

Lady Agnes was not a bad compromise. Mrs. Wainwright hesitated for only a fraction of time. Then she said quietly, "Indoors, thank you, Miriam. I would like a small glass of chilled wine. What would you like '—to drink'?"

Miriam expressed no preference. But when the glass of wine appeared before her, she took a gingerly sip at it, then a second, and finally a third swallow.

"The truth is, Agnes," she blurted out (and now there was no equivocation about *Lady Agnes*), "I don't know what to do about Sully. He wants to give me an engagement ring. I don't want to hurt his feelings; but I feel that I am not the diamond solitaire type."

"No, you're not," Agnes agreed heartily. "Don't think that because you're marrying him you have to make yourself over in some imagined image. An image probably distorted anyhow."

"I would like a wedding ring that might cover everything. They have them now, don't they? Wedding rings set with precious stones all the way around? Rings that would go well with all the rest of me?"

"Indeed they do! Tell Sully that that is what you'd really like: what would look well on you, and feel well. Then when it comes to the more intimate garments for your trous-

294

seau, stick to pajamas, Miriam. But sometimes indulge yourself in a negligee which is a little bit negligent."

There was a slight pause while Miriam took that one in. Then Agnes, much to her own amazement, kept the upper hand which she had almost unwittingly assumed. "You're getting a good man. In small things as well as in large, see that you do your best to deserve him."

"My prayerful best!" Miriam tried to take a light tone, but her lips trembled.

"This is not a betrayal of confidence," Agnes went on. "Your man ought to be grateful to me for telling you. It will spare his blushes." She fetched Sully's letter and gave it to Miriam to read.

Miriam went through it at a fair clip first, then a second time more slowly. After that she challenged, "You put him up to this!"

"I did nothing of the kind. He thought it up all out of his own little head."

"But—but I never thought that Sully—"

"He surprised me, too," Agnes acknowledged. "And I dare say himself."

Miriam was characteristically concerned about the fly in the ointment. But this time she had to hunt for it.

"Agnes," she finally brought out, "are you sure you really want to sell?"

"You don't see anybody putting a pistol to my head, do you?"

"It was where you came as a bride," argued Miriam.

"It was your childhood home, to which you will return as a bride."

"Are you sure you want to continue living here in Marshfield?"

"For the foreseeable future, yes. Does that expression mean much, Miriam, 'foreseeable future'? I read it in the newspapers every now and then. But a man who could actually foresee the future could, in the words of the old song, 'break the bank at Monte Carlo.' "

"Break the stock market, too." Miriam began to relax. "I've never done anything to deserve so much happiness. But if it comes my way, I'd better seize it. Such things do not happen twice in a lifetime."

"It isn't physically impossible," Agnes agreed. "But it's extremely unlikely."

Miriam's attention drew to a sharp focus. "You've changed so much since you've been living here, La—that is, Agnes."

"Not altogether for the worse, I hope?"

Miriam laughed aloud. "There is an instance in point. You never used to ask those trick questions. Something like, 'Have you left off beating your wife?' "

"Something different from it, too. I don't restrict myself to questions which must be answered 'Yes' or 'No.' "

Miriam went back to the letter and read it a third time. Then she asked quietly, "Which of Sully's offers are you going to accept? Or would you prefer not to say?"

"They both seem fair enough. I haven't yet made up my mind."

She had, actually. Agnes was going to bid Sully finance the mortgage through the bank. When you made a break, it was best to have the break as clean as possible.

"You are coming over to see me again soon, aren't you?" Miriam's tone was not exactly humble; but for Miriam, it was a real comedown.

"Indeed I am! A great many details remain to be settled.

296

More of that later. But there is one thing I'd better tell you right now, Miriam."

"Only one?" Miriam jested. But she looked uneasy.

"One will be all you need to take in right now. Even before you actually begin to settle in at your new home, which is also your old home, you will need really competent help."

"Help around the house?"

"That's what we are talking about, isn't it?"

"Incompetent help—" faltered Miriam.

"Is no help at all. It's a hindrance. When a husband comes home from the office, he is entitled to expect comfort and companionship. 'Comfort' of course includes a good dinner properly cooked."

"Well, yes," Miriam agreed. Her tone betrayed a certain hostility. All along she had been waiting for the catch. Now it was visibly confronting her.

"Rosa Lee Montgomery—" began Agnes, and paused.

Miriam fell into the trap. Her lips tightened in the old, all-too-familiar way. "Yes?" she encouraged. If you could call it "encouragement," in the tone of voice she used.

"Rosa Lee Montgomery may know somebody who will fill the bill for you," Agnes finished serenely.

She had scored. She enjoyed her brief moment of triumph. She, Agnes Costen Wainwright, had asserted herself over her stepdaughter, Miriam Wainwright, and made it stick.

It was just as well that Agnes did enjoy herself. And savor her triumph to the full. This was the last happy hour that gentle Agnes was to know for some time to come.

24.

Rosa Lee Montgomery did indeed know somebody who "might try working for Miss Miriam"; but she sounded so dubious that Agnes hastened to reassure her, "It won't be just Miss Miriam, really. I'm going to be over there myself for a time; then after I move out, Mr. Sullivan is moving in. He and Miriam are going to be married."

"So that's how you got rid of him!" Rosa Lee seemed highly amused. "When a man takes it into his head he wants to get married, there's just no way of stopping him."

"Mr. Sullivan is capable of holding his own." Agnes meant that, but her hearer remained unconvinced.

"I'm sure I hope so," said Rosa Lee Montgomery. "But how soon will Miss Miriam find out that a married man

298

wants something for dinner besides raw cauliflower, with maybe a raw carrot for dessert?"

"Tell me more about this friend of yours," suggested Agnes. "Is she married or single?"

"She's between husbands. Stephens just left her. She needs a job to tide her over till she can hook somebody else."

"Some wise man once described a second marriage as 'the triumph of hope over experience.'"

Rosa Lee chuckled. "That man never knew Sally Belle. Stephens was her third husband, and she's still hopeful."

"She's a glutton for punishment."

"She likes being married for a while, anyhow. Maybe it isn't such a bad idea. When are you going to give Dora Dean a man to cook for, Miss Agnes?"

"She has more than one, off and on."

"Oh, company, sure! But I mean, a man to get breakfast for."

"I don't want to steal Miriam's thunder. Besides, I'm very well off as I am."

"Very well could always be better," Rosa Lee insisted. But then she came down to earth and promised to have Sally Belle call Miss Miriam.

Sally Belle Stephens was actually in residence when Agnes went over to Antioch to pack. At their parting, Tom Jones had said, "I'll miss you. But that tearing up stakes is a step in the right direction." Dr. Sheridan confined himself to, "I'll miss you."

Sally Belle was fortyish in age and in size, a deep walnut in color. Before Miriam, she maintained a consistent reserve. But when she was alone with Agnes she chattered by the hour.

"That Rosa Lee, ain't no man good enough for *her*,"

299

she confided. "She leads 'em on till they loses their fool heads. Then she says, 'I'm so sorry,' and waits for the next one."

"She's fickle," agreed Agnes. "But haven't you ever changed your mind about a man, Sally Belle?"

"Not that fast, Miss Agnes. I stayed married to my second husband for eleven years."

"And then?" Agnes encouraged.

"Then all at once I sort of lost my taste for that bum."

"That was after you met Stephens, wasn't it?"

Sally Belle chuckled. "How you guess that, Miss Agnes? Served me right when Stephens lost his taste for me. Oh, well, there's as good fish in the sea as ever came out of it."

That was a consoling belief. If Agnes could not quite share it, that was simply her hard luck.

She decided to leave most of the furniture for Miriam. She packed a lot of books, gave away or discarded others. Her wedding china she would take with her, of course. Her wedding silver. Photographs and keepsakes. All her clothes. There was a finality here which was almost gruesome.

Miriam was finally driven to remonstrate with her. "But Agnes, this was your home for years."

"*Was*," said Agnes grimly, and changed the subject.

On other subjects, however, she was more communicative. Getting Sully and Miriam together one evening, she went into the subject of their marriage plans.

"I'll give you as big a wedding as you want here in Antioch," she said. "Or you can come over to Marshfield for a slightly smaller ceremony. In either case, I'll be 'the mother of the bride,' in *those* clothes. Why is the old lady

300

always supposed to make herself look as frumpish as possible?"

"That's why," said Sully. "She generally isn't old at all. Especially in the case of these very young brides, the mother is a woman in the prime of life. If she were allowed to look her best, she would steal the show."

"Agnes would do that anyhow," said Miriam generously. "But I don't think I want a big wedding. A lot of married women chasing down the aisle ahead of me, and poor Sully turning a delicate shade of green."

"And dying to run his finger around inside his collar, and trying to remember that he's here of his own choice."

Then, almost under his breath, he added, "More or less." Agnes affected not to hear him.

"Marshfield would be second choice," she went on. "But though you could have a simple ceremony there, that church or the Hammond house wouldn't mean too much to either of you."

Sully grinned. "Go ahead and spring it," he advised.

"Spring what?" asked Agnes innocently. Too innocently, in fact.

"Whatever you are leading up to."

Miriam laughed. But she too looked eager for Agnes to get to the point.

"What I think would be really sweet," said Mrs. Wainwright, "is for the two of you to slip away to New York City and be married in the Little Church Around the Corner."

Miriam drew a sharp audible breath. "I had thought of that myself, Agnes. But I was afraid of hurting your feelings."

Miriam was afraid of hurting Agnes's feelings. Miriam!

It had been a most successful visit. Yet Agnes returned

301

to Marshfield in a mood of deep depression. She tried in vain to argue herself out of it. Reasoning would not lure back the green-clad sprite who had so basely deserted her.

Tom Jones rallied her on her low spirits; but there was a certain sharpness in his tone. "It may be hard for you to settle down to one man; but you're getting much the better of the two."

"I haven't settled down to anyone—yet," said Agnes defiantly.

"How long are you going to keep me waiting? Just until after the wedding announcements are out, I suppose. 'Mrs. Jerome Wainwright announces the marriage of her daughter Miriam . . .' is slightly more impressive than 'Mr. and Mrs. Thomas Henry Jones announce . . .'"

Agnes shuddered in mock horror. "What a comedown that would be!"

"*Will* be. Yet once you get used to the first shock, you'll find you like being Mrs. Jones."

"You could go to court and have your name changed; but I suppose for business reasons you'd rather not."

"There are other than business reasons for such a change. I'm attached to the name; I've had it for some time. I expect to be known in Marshfield as Agnes Wainwright's husband; but in my own bailiwick I prefer to remain Tom Jones."

"Tom Jones, bachelor."

"Only until you name the day."

"I'll give you my answer in October," she said.

He grinned and put out his arms. Agnes felt an impulse to go into them; the warmth and intimacy might do a lot for her. But although she was only too well aware of the direction in which she was drifting, she mustn't let him assume

302

the status of an accepted lover. Not yet awhile, at least. Not yet, if ever.

Two days later, Dr. Sheridan paid her a visit. It was the first time he had seen her since her return from Antioch. Wishing to give him the news about Miriam, Agnes opened with, "Do you catch the odor of orange blossoms?"

He looked blank for an instant. When she went on to explain, he nodded in relief. "I'm glad they're all set. There for an instant I was afraid you meant yourself."

Agnes flushed guiltily, and hesitated before she disclaimed, "Nothing like that. I know when I'm well off."

"I hope so. Don't you go accepting the first man who proposes to you."

"I did just that," said Agnes sharply. "I've never been sorry."

He smiled. "If you hadn't accepted Mr. Wainwright, I wouldn't be here today. I was speaking of something else."

Agnes shrugged. She simply did not relish his attempt to do her thinking for her.

Dr. Sheridan misunderstood her silence, and proceeded to a second and worse blunder. "I can appreciate how you feel. I once knew happiness myself. Nothing has been the same since Norma left me. My case is worse than yours, however. I've never told you this; maybe I shouldn't mention it now. But it isn't just loneliness that ails me; it's also a sense of guilt."

It was coming now, an explanation of the shadow which always overhung him. It must be that he had never been really happy in his married life, for happiness does not die, though the beloved may do so.

"Don't stop now," she said softly.

He acted as if he hadn't heard her. "She was all alone when

303

she died. I had gone out on a case. The maid had been sent on an errand. When she came back, she found Norma slumped in her chair. At first, she supposed her mistress had fallen asleep. She was becoming uneasy, however, when I returned. She met me at the door. I was beside Norma in three or four strides. But by that time it was too late."

"That was a horrid shock," Agnes sympathized. "You had had no warning?"

"Warning enough, if I had only looked at it that way. I'd left not only with her permission but at her urging. She had laughed at my reluctance. She did indeed appear to be only slightly indisposed; and she was used to being a doctor's wife. But I continue to feel that I should have known I was needed right there at home. Something should have told me!"

Agnes's sympathy began to curdle. A little tartly she inquired, "Would your lovely Norma approve of your acting this way?"

"She would realize that I haven't forgotten."

"Nobody is asking you to forget. But moping won't bring her back."

The instant the words were out, she would have given anything to recall them. She began to stammer an apology, which only made things worse. Dr. Sheridan's lips set with a grimness of which she would not have supposed him capable. He rose slowly from his chair.

"I'm sorry to have bored you," he said quietly and distinctly. "I can assure you it will not happen again soon."

"Please don't misunderstand," begged Agnes. It sounded like a line out of a bad movie; but in her distress she kept repeating it.

This was like a nightmare from which she could not

304

waken. She had given up all hope of fairy-tale happiness; or rather, it had given her up. That was what had been wreaking havoc with her lately. But at least she could have remained friends with him.

Even this minor happiness she had now forfeited. In miserable silence, she saw him out. Her wretchedness was all her own doing; there was very little consolation in that.

That night, Agnes lay awake hour after restless hour. Toward dawn, she dozed fitfully, conscious even in her sleep that something was badly amiss. In full daylight, she wakened to a sense of overwhelming calamity. At first she could not remember what was the evil thing which had happened to her. Recollection returned all too soon.

There for a few minutes she wished that she could die. Just close her eyes and forget, and keep on forgetting. But there was no such easy way out. The day had to be faced, and got through somehow. Agnes had got along very nicely before she ever met Hugh Sheridan.

The devil of it was that she had met him. She could not well avoid seeing him sometimes, especially at church; not so long as she remained in Marshfield. Even that would be better than nothing. Or if it should in the end prove too much for her—well, Marshfield was not the world, and Sully had already showed her how she could make a paying investment out of the Hammond mansion if she decided that she no longer cared to live there.

Dora Dean, noticing Mrs. Wainwright's dejection, diagnosed "spring fever" and went on to relate, "My grandmother used to dose us with sulphur and molasses at this time of year. Think you'd like to try some?"

Tom Jones suggested a shopping trip to New York. "New clothes do cheer a woman up. You can buy nice things right

305

here in Marshfield; but that isn't the same, somehow. What you need is to go on a real spending spree."

That idea, too, Agnes turned down. What she needed couldn't be poured out of a bottle or bought over a counter. It had to come as a free gift, when it came at all. It just wasn't for Mrs. Wainwright.

She had stayed away from church that morning; then when it was too late, she wished that she had gone. It wouldn't do her any good to duck Dr. Sheridan. Had he by any chance stayed away from church in order to duck her? Agnes managed a rueful grin at the idea. But she didn't take any too much stock in it. After all, he was the offended party.

Monday actually was Blue Monday that week, and Tuesday little if any better. Then on Wednesday, Agnes suddenly came to her senses. She had accused Dr. Sheridan of moping, just as if she had never heard of the traditional pot and kettle. Who was moping now?

Agnes went out into the garden and began to stroll around. She drank in deep breaths of the sweet-smelling air. Her lungs felt free and clean. The vapors vanished from her brain. Under her breath she began to hum "Count Your Blessings."

What on earth had she been crabbing about? For crabbing she certainly had been. Concentrating on what she didn't have. Making herself miserable. Never stopping to think of those poor souls who had so much less than she did.

Worst of all, not thinking about her choirboys. The school year would end very soon now. She could help them make their vacation plans.

Which would include, Agnes hoped, a great many visits here. What could be a nicer way of spending the summer

306

than to maintain open house for little boys? It was a rather large order, maybe. But since when had Agnes Costen Wainwright confined herself to small orders?

Agnes, turning toward the house, saw Dora Dean standing in the doorway. She smiled and beckoned. Dora, looking very much relieved, hastened to join her mistress in the garden.

"Spring fever wears off, doesn't it?" Agnes said. "Those nasty concoctions may or may not help. I wouldn't know. Yet even if I were willing to swallow sulphur and molasses, where would you buy sulphur nowadays? Molasses, maybe; but *sulphur?*"

"I never could see that the stuff did me any good," Dora confessed. "But I loved my grandmother."

Agnes nodded. "We'll dispense with those obnoxious remedies, I think, and get on to something important. Since little boys will be around here a good deal of the summer, don't you think we should be prepared to give them a good time?"

"If we don't make them happy, Mrs. Wainwright, boys can turn into powerful pests."

"I suspect as much, Dora. We always have plenty to eat on hand; that doesn't worry me. With lemonade and your homemade cookies on hand, we have a fine start. We can keep some ice cream, too, can't we?"

"Looks that way to me, Mrs Wainwright. It's a big place."

"A big place, and hospitable. A place for people to be happy in."

"That's the way it has been," Dora agreed. "No reason to change now, is there?"

"No reason at all. Now I'm going back in the house for a time. The house! Your home. Your home and mine, Dora."

307

She was scarcely back in the house, and had not yet had time or opportunity to wonder which book she was going to read that night, when her telephone rang and that well-remembered, that much-longed-for voice came over the wire. Agnes could scarcely believe her ears when Dr. Sheridan led off by saying, "Harsh words are a drastic remedy, but they are sometimes needed."

Not knowing what to say, Agnes said nothing. Dr. Sheridan went on, "You accused me of 'moping,' and I was highly offended. But that was exactly what I was doing. In my regret for a past mistake, I was going on to a whole series of bigger and better mistakes."

"Oh, I wouldn't say that!" protested Agnes. But he had already said it; and the words rang in her ears like heavenly music.

"After I was accused of moping, I went home and moped some more, just to show how stupid a man could get. But I finally came to my senses, I hope not too late. Now . . ." He hesitated.

"Now you've eaten humble pie long enough," Agnes assured him. "It won't do as a steady diet."

"Thank you for those kind words. I'll do my best to deserve them." She could fairly hear his smile.

"I know enough to let bygones be bygones. At least I hope I do."

"Then let's look forward, shall we? Will you take pity on a lonely man, and let me come over now and ask you an important question?"

"An important question?" This was the same record that Sully had played. But oh, what a difference it made who did the playing! She hadn't wanted Sully to put his foot in his mouth. But that the present speaker could possibly mean

308

what he appeared to mean was just too much for Agnes to take in this suddenly.

"Important to me, highly. That question which in Mrs. Hammond's youth a man didn't ask; he 'popped.' "

"If he hadn't popped it— But that's a fruitless speculation, isn't it, Dr. Sheridan?"

"The name is Hugh. I used to think that I didn't like it any too well. But when you pronounce my given name, I know that I am going to love it."

"Thank you, Hugh. The name here is Agnes."

His voice took on a lilt of which she would not have supposed it capable. "In a few minutes then, Agnes?"

"Yes, Hugh. I'll try not to keep you waiting."

She was still holding the handset when Dr. Sheridan hung up. Dr. Sheridan? Hugh! Her Hugh! Her head was in a whirl. She should spare a thought for—strange, but for a moment here she could scarcely recall his name. That other friend of hers. It was a commoner name than Hugh. His name was—yes, it was Tom.

Agnes would call him up and talk to him tomorrow. Generally, she waited for him to call her. This time she owed him, not of course an apology, but an explanation.

She suddenly realized that anybody who tried to telephone her would simply get the busy signal. Agnes banged the handset back in place and rushed upstairs.

She was no longer tired. She was no longer looking forward with mingled hope and dread to her thirty-fourth birthday. She was not Mrs. Wainwright expecting Dr. Sheridan. She was an eager woman awaiting the arrival of her lover.

Her first, her only real lover. He was coming. He was on

309

his way. He was almost here. If she hadn't come in from the garden exactly when she did—

If and if and if! Agnes turned and ran back down a few stairs to call to an attentive if somewhat startled Dora, "Should the doorbell ring before I come down, don't be in any hurry to answer it, please."

"I'm not in any hurry, Mrs. Wainwright," Dora assured her. "I never have been."

But she tidied an already tidy hall and front parlor, and began to turn on lights and then to turn them off. The ring at the doorbell would be preceded by a firm masculine tread on the front porch. It was too bad Mrs. Hammond couldn't have lived to see all this.

Maybe she knew about it anyhow. Nobody could prove she didn't. On the other hand, nobody could prove she did.

Dora was in a pensive mood, almost devotional. It was a great relief when Mrs. Wainwright's voice rang out, "It's all right now. I'm coming down. I won't need you any more just now, thank you."

She came. Her step on the stairs was like a girl's; and her faithful follower could fairly hear the singing at Agnes's heart.

This book has been read
by:-
Barbara Zahn --- October 1964
Barbara Zahn --- August 1967
Barbara Zahn _ __ October 1969
Doris Dietmeier -- Dec. 1971
Mary Dietmeier -. Aug. 1972